TICKET
TO
PARADISE

TICKET TO PARADISE

A NOVEL

BY

JOSEPH J. BRADLEY

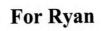

For Ryan

Acknowledgments

I offer my sincere thanks and gratitude to Miriam Gonzalez. I would also like to thank, Tom Percoski and Anthony Bradley, for their valuable input on the content of my story. Huge thanks to Yvonne, Ryan, Taylor, and Sarah for all their unconditional love and support. Finally, I want to thank my three wonderful sisters, Lynn, Kathy and Kim, for continuing to encourage my efforts.

Also by Joseph J. Bradley

Bottle Park
The Alpha
Lions and Men
The Lyme Conspiracy

josephjbradley.com
thelymeconspiracy.net

Before you embark on a journey of revenge, dig two graves.

-Confucious

1

A powerful storm swept in from the north, like an unwelcome stranger in the night. Liquid darts pounded the automobiles that were parked outside Artie's Bowling Alley.

Unable to find a sail, the howling wind blew against a neon sign, causing it to sway back and forth. The letter R was blinking on and off and was nearing the end of its first life. Brilliant flashes of light illuminated the sky and the rolling thunder rumbled with the clouds.

Inside, a similar crashing sound filled the room – the sound of a sixteen-pound bowling ball colliding into ten pins, set in perfect order. The musty, stagnant air carried the stench of stale cigarettes, old shoes, and french-fries.

Due to inclement weather, the bowling alley was very busy for a Tuesday night, in South Walton, Rhode Island. The streets were flooded with the recent thawing of Mother Nature's final winter's gift, giving way to an early spring rain.

Many customers felt temporary relief slipping out of their damp footwear and replacing them with dry bowling shoes.

Nick sat snarling, as his younger brother, Chris, performed a short victory dance, after getting his second strike in a row.

"You must have gone to church this morning, you lucky bastard." Nick said, prior to pouring down half of a beer.

"Skill my brother, it's all about skill," Chris boasted.

"Skill my ass, let's get another beer."

"You're buying, right?" Chris asked.

"I ain't buying you shit. You make all the money. I'm just a slob, laborer."

"Quit crying poorhouse to me. You have enough money to put that shit up your nose, but you can't buy your brother a beer, especially after I just dusted you off the lane."

"That's more reason I'm not buying." Nick defiantly responded, while stuffing his bowling shoes into his leather carrying case.

They walked over to the bar and took a seat. Three older guys that appeared to be in their late forties and early fifties were already sitting, as they pulled up two stools. Tommy, the bartender, came right over wearing a smile, after he saw Chris take a seat. Tommy was a life-long bartender. He had tended bar in some of the worst dives in Rhode Island, and his wrinkled face and gray hair confirmed it.

"Hey, Chris," Tommy extended his hand and shook it longer than Chris was comfortable with. "How's it going?"

"Good, Tommy. How about you?"

"Same old shit, here." Tommy didn't acknowledge Nick. He had called the cops on Nick on a few separate occasions in the past, and he had a scar to prove it.

"Are you going to shoot the shit all night, or do your fucking job? Give me a bud," Nick demanded.

"Take it easy, Nick." Chris scorned. "I'll have a bud too, make it a light," Chris asked.

Tommy shuffled away, without glancing back, mumbling a curse under his breath.

"What's with you, anyway?" Chris asked.

"I don't like that prick." He quickly pointed in Tommy's direction, as if he just threw a dart.

"Is there anyone that you do like?"

"Yeah, I like you, bro." Nick moved closer grabbing Chris in an attempt to plant a kiss on his cheek.

"Get the hell away from me," he pushed his Nick away.

Tommy carried two beers over and they each paid for their own drinks.

"So, Chris, how's the electronics business these days?" Tommy asked, while keeping a safe distance from Nick.

"It's good Tommy, thanks. I spend more time putting out fires and less time troubleshooting and refurbishing these days."

"Yeah, I hear you got promoted -supervisor now, right?"

Chris rolled back his shoulders a notch. "Yes, I am."

"Congratulations kid, let me buy you a beer." His eyes shot at Nick and he moved away to get the beer.

"Thanks, Tommy."

The guy sitting next to Nick was in his late forties and overweight with balding hair, wearing a red and white sweat suit that was a bit too tight around the waist and barely reaching his ankles. He reached over picking up an ashtray situated near Nick.

"Hey, what are you, blind? I was using that ashtray." Nick roared.

"Sorry pal, I didn't read your name on it." He came back with a sarcastic grin across his face.

Nick reached over and snatched up the plastic ashtray. "Well, maybe that's because you didn't look close enough, dipshit." Nick said, as he shoved the ashtray into the guy's face, twisting it side to side.

With cancelled butts and ash covering part of his face and jacket, the bald guy retaliated by throwing a right-hand punch at Nick. Before Chris could get in between them, Nick blocked the punch, grabbed the guy by his jacket lapels and head butted him, smashing the top of his forehead into the bridge of the guy's nose. Blood immediately began to flow and once again, Tommy headed for the phone to dial 911. Nick's victim fell to his knees, pulling his hands up to his face in an attempt to stop the blood from pouring out. The injured man's two friends went after Nick, and Chris jumped in between them.

"I called the cops!" Tommy shouted. "You get the hell out of here." His hands were shaking as he yelled across the bar at Nick, pointing toward the door.

Chris was using all his weight to hold Nick back. "Come on Nick, let's go," he demanded.

"I'll break all your fucking noses," were Nick's last words, prior to being ushered out by his brother.

They dashed through the downpour to Chris' truck. When they made it to the cab, they were both soaked to the skin.

"God damn rain, I'm sick of it." Nick said, reaching into the glove compartment, in search of napkins.

"You're absolutely crazy." Chris said.

"Screw that old bastard. You heard him give me shit. Now he has to have his beak set straight."

"You started it, you asshole," Chris barked, before turning the ignition key.

"What, are you siding with him?"

Chris was heating up much faster than his car engine.

"Yeah, I am, you were wrong, man."

"Hell with you! You ain't no brother of mine."

"Yeah, okay Nick. You have a serious drinking problem."

"You're right. My problem is I don't have a drink. Let's go to Sam's for a few more."

"You're crazy. I'm going home."

The rain began to lighten up, as they drove through town.

"Stop at the store over here, I need some cigarettes," Nick said.

They both went into the store, shaking off the rain as they walked in. Nick got in line and Chris walked toward the cooler for a bottle of water. He looked for a brand with a label that best resembled a mountain spring, and then got in line behind his brother.

"Look, the lottery is over eight million." Chris said.

"It's a big scam," Nick blurted out, loud enough to turn a couple of heads in line.

Embarrassed, Chris lowered his voice hoping his brother would follow suit. "Yeah, you're probably right, but I'm buying a ticket anyway."

Nick ordered his cigarettes and handed fifty cents to Chris. "Put me in. Go for the lump sum payment."

Chris bought a quick-pick ticket and paid for his water. He put the ticket in his wallet without looking at it and followed Nick back to the truck.

"The cops are going to be looking for you," Chris said, pulling up in front of Nick's apartment.

He shrugged his shoulders and turned his palms up facing the sky. "You think I give a shit?"

Chris hesitated for a few seconds, studying his sibling. "No, no I don't."

"See ya later." Nick said. He got out and slammed the truck door shut. Chris sat and watched his brother walk into the building. He wondered why Nick had such a huge chip on his shoulder and when it first began. He loved his older brother, but didn't like him very much. The memories of their childhood together, reinforced his love for Nick whenever he did something mean or stupid. When he looked into Nick's eyes, he still saw an eleven-year-old boy with a fishing pole, teaching him how to cast a line. He remembered a time in the distant past that he admired his older brother, but the years had been cruel and turned his admiration into pity.

He turned up the radio to hear his favorite band playing a song he liked, *Steely Dan's, "Home At Last"*. He put his truck into gear and accelerated up the wet, motionless street.

2

Gennaro's meat market had been in business for twenty-four years. Nick and Chris's father opened his first store when Nick was seven years old, and his brother Chris was four. Nicholas Gennaro was a hardworking man who emigrated from Southern Italy just prior to reaching his seventh birthday. Nicholas was well respected in town. He had a sincere and kind way about him and it was well reflected onto his customers. He loved all his children, but as time passed and his children grew older, he regretted naming his eldest son after himself. He thanked God every day for his son Chris and his two daughters, Ashley and Marybeth. The aggravation his son Nick caused was barely leveraged by the joy his other three children gave him.

Although well connected, Nicholas kept himself a comfortable distance away from his friends in the La Costa Nostra. His lifelong friend, Franco Baccio, had reminded him on many occasions how he could have been a 'made' man in the Patriarca family, had he made a commitment to them in years passed. Nicholas and Franco had traveled over on the boat together, but both of them had very different ideas on what they wanted to do with their lives in America. The two immigrants started out running numbers for one of the local wise guys. Nicholas ultimately became a bookie taking bets out of his store, but he never wanted to participate in a blood and fire ceremony in the back room of the Italian Social Club. Franco, on the other hand, moved up the ranks as an enforcer, collecting money the hard way from people who didn't have the sense or cash to pay their debts on time.

It wasn't until Franco committed his first murder, that he was considered by the family to be worthy enough to become a *made* member. Several years later, he was promoted to Captain. The dilemma Franco had faced was the guy he was ordered to whack, was one of his friends that allegedly had been stealing money from the family. He was told his friend, Pete, was skimming off the top for nearly a year before it caught up to him.

Pete didn't realize the family knew about his disloyalty until the very second before he took two bullets through the brain. Pete knew the many rules one had to obey when connected to the mob, and one being: You don't steal money from them.

The execution of his friend, Pete, was the hardest thing Franco had ever done, and he thought about it, often. Apologizing before pulling the trigger wasn't enough absolution for him; he didn't think anything could be. He figured he had to live with his past, and he attempted to justify his actions by enjoying the good life. He bought a big house, drove a Mercedes Benz, and drank the finest scotch and wine money could buy.

Nicholas Gennaro, alias (Nicky the Butcher) as he was called by his acquaintances in the Patriarca family, sat in a small office in the rear of his store. Monday morning was always a busy time for him. He had to figure out the bets played from the weekend games. Usually, he came out on top, and that was going to be his retirement fund. Monday was also his biggest meat delivery day and he would spend a good part of the afternoon swinging a cleaver. The bell on the door sounded out, as it did almost every Monday at the same time.

"Hey dad, how are you, this morning?" Ashley asked.

"Good, how's my baby girl?" A smile formed on his face.

"I'm so tired." She handed him a coffee and leaned over to kiss him on the cheek.

"Tired, you should know what tired is. Wait until you're my age." Nicholas said.

"Kurt took me to the concert last night in Providence. It was so wild."

"What concert?" he asked without looking up. He was figuring out his weekend winnings.

"Skinny Willie and the losers. They were awesome."

"Sounds inspirational." He said, looking up at her with a hint of sarcasm.

"Dad, they're good."

"If Skinny's last name was Sinatra, I might believe you. You should be careful going to these shows. Those places can be fire traps."

"I know Dad." She rolled her eyes. "I'm careful."

"Alright, I worry about you." He patted the back of her hand. "Thanks for the coffee, Princess."

"You're welcome, Daddy. I have to go. I don't want to be late for class." She kissed him again.

He watched her walk out, thinking how lucky he was to have such a good daughter.

Ashley was his youngest child and she was preparing to graduate from high school. His older daughter, Marybeth, was the third youngest of the four. After having Marybeth, he and his wife Maria agreed they wouldn't have any more children. Ashley came along, as an unexpected bonus seven years later.

Marybeth had given birth to their first grandchild, Angelo, when she was twenty-one. She was a single mother and found it difficult taking care of an infant. Even with the help of her parents, she found it very overwhelming. Marybeth became pregnant out of wedlock and she regretted it, every day. She loved her son, but often felt that her youth had been stolen from her before she had a chance to enjoy it.

Angelo's father, Walker Thomas, had assured Marybeth, how much he loved her and that he wanted to spend his life with her. He told her how much he wanted to have a family and make a beautiful home. "We are soul mates," he used to say in a convincing tone.

However, not long after her belly began to grow, Walker started going out drinking with the boys, coming home late, stinking of stale booze and cheap perfume. The arguments had gotten worse, and one night he blackened her eye with a straight right punch.

Unknown to Marybeth, Walker had grown up in an environment accustomed to violent behavior. His father Spencer was serving hard time in a Connecticut prison for armed robbery. When Nicholas saw his daughter with a shiner under her left eye, he did all he could to contain the rage that was building up, inside. She begged him not to hurt Walker, and he calmed her down, reassuring her he wouldn't do anything to cause him harm. The next day after her brother, Nick, found out about the abuse, he went to the three-family house they lived in and waited for his sister to leave, and then, he beat Walker senseless right on his front porch with a steel pipe.

As Walker laid in a hospital bed, with a broken arm and three cracked ribs, Nicholas paid him a visit.

"I promised my daughter I wouldn't do any harm to you for beating her." Nicholas said, standing over his hospital bed. "I kept my word. I didn't know my son was going to do this."

"Mr. Gennaro, I didn't mean to hit her."

"Shut up, and listen to me." Nicholas said through gritting teeth. If you ever raise your hand against my daughter again, I will cut it off. Do I make myself clear?"

"Yes sir." Walker's good arm was trembling.

"Good." Nicholas said and turned to leave. "One more thing," he said as he turned around. "You stay home and take care of your family. Find a job."

"Yes sir, I will," Walker said in a speedy and shaky manner.

Nicholas walked out, hoping he had gotten the message.

Four months passed by, and Marybeth was getting closer to her due date. Not long after Walker had his cast removed, he started hitting the bars, picking up lounge lizards, and having unprotected sex with anyone who would have him. Nicholas knew what was going on, but kept his cool. He didn't want to upset his daughter by interfering, because she was in her third trimester.

It was a Saturday morning when Maria called Nicholas at the store; she was crying. She told him that Walker had come home drunk the night before and beat Marybeth, sending her to the hospital with a broken nose and complications from being knocked down the stairs. She informed him the baby was going to be fine.

Nicholas figured one day this may happen, however, he wished it wouldn't. The anger he felt was beyond measure.

***

Franco was losing badly in a poker game, when he received a call. Ordinarily, he would ignore calls, but he thought he could use a break, that may in fact change his luck.

"Franco, it's me."

"Nicky, what's up?" He stood silently, listening for over a minute. "I'll be there in ten minutes," Franco said, before hanging up. He got up and walked out, leaving his money on the table. He didn't need to worry. Every cent would be there, when he returned.

Nicholas was waiting in his store, when Franco arrived. "You okay?"

Franco asked, while entering through the back door. Nicholas was sitting behind his desk.

"I warned the son of a bitch. He put my Marybeth in the hospital. She's eight months pregnant."

"What do you want me to do?" Franco asked.

"Get another guy and bring him here. Come in the back, quietly. I don't want Marybeth to find out so, don't let anyone see you. You'll probably catch him coming out of Ricky's strip joint, Fantasy's."

"Alright, I'll be back," Franco said, with confidence.

Nicholas looked at his watch when he heard the car pull up behind his store; it was 12:52 AM. Franco and Dennis, one of his soldiers, brought Walker in through the back door with his feet barely touching the ground. His wrists, mouth, and eyes were secured with duct tape.

"Bring him back here," Nicholas commanded, pointing to a large, wooden butcher table. The small room was clean, but there were still small traces of blood from the animals that had been carved into edible size filets and ribs.

"Take the tape off his eyes. Undo his hands, but leave the tape on his mouth." Nicholas requested.

Dennis did as he asked. The fear Walker was experiencing was not only evident from the look in his eyes, but also, from the wet spot forming in the crotch of his pants.

"Hold his right hand down on the block," Nicholas ordered.

It took both men to hold Walker down. He began thrashing, attempting to pull his hand off the block. His eyes nearly bulged out of their sockets, as he watched Nicholas pick up a shiny meat cleaver from under the table. Franco gave him two quick uppercuts to the stomach, and he calmed down, struggling to take in air that couldn't be found.

"I warned you not to raise your hand to my daughter. You didn't hear me, did you? Who do you think you're fucking with, huh? This is my little girl, my family. You could have had a good life, you fool."

Nicky the Butcher raised his cleaver high over his head and came down with one swift, decisive blow. The blade landed exactly where he intended. With many years' experience, and a razor sharp cleaver, he only had to swing once. The tape muffled Walker's screams, but there was no doubt in anyone's mind that he was in extreme pain. His eyes rolled back into his head displaying the white part, like a shark, while biting into its prey. Dennis was thinking how glad he was that he wasn't dating Marybeth. Walker fell to the floor with his bloody hand still on the block, twitching. Nicholas threw a towel down at Walker, hitting him in the face.

"Wrap up your arm. You're getting blood all over my floor." Nicholas demanded, totally void of any empathy.

Walker did as he was told, knowing it was in his best interest because he was bleeding out.

"What do we do with this piece of shit now?" Franco asked.

Nicholas stood looking down in silence as Walker laid in a fetal position weeping, and for a moment, he felt a sense of power – like an executioner passing sentence. "I don't want to ever see this piece of shit, again. He is to disappear." Nicholas said in a stone -cold tone.

They hoisted Walker onto his feet and shuffled him out the back door. Refusing to walk on his own, they carried him out. As Franco and Dennis brought him out the back door and threw him into the trunk of the car, Walker was shaking his head from side-to-side pleading for his life in silence. Walker Thomas was never seen again.

3

The market was busy with customers waiting in line to place their order at the meat and deli counter. Many were browsing the already prepared pasta dishes and homemade casseroles. It was Wednesday and Chris had just gotten out of work. He was happy to be outside. The sun was shining and Main Street was crawling with people. Most had put away their winter coats and were walking about less constricted.

"Hey, Pop," Chris called out, as he entered the store.

Nicholas looked up from the register. "Christopher, what's up?"

"I'm just stopping by to say hello." His smile brightened the room. Nicholas had made it a point to get braces for Chris when he became a teen. His teeth were pointing in many different directions and he didn't want his son's mouth to look like a rake, he used to tell his wife, Maria. His investment paid off because Chris had perfectly straight teeth and white as freshly fallen snow. They glowed even brighter next to his straight, dark brown hair that tickled his collar, and matching walnut eyes.

"Kevin, can you take the register for a few minutes?" Nicholas asked one of his helpers, who was in the back room dicing onions. He came around the counter and kissed Chris on the cheek. "Come into my office for a minute," he said to his son. Nicholas closed the door behind them. "What happened at the bowling alley the other day?"

"You heard about that?" Chris was surprised he heard the news so fast.

"Not much happens around here that I don't hear about, especially, when it involves Nick."

"Nick got into a scrape with some guy at the bar. That's all." He turned his eyes away playing it down. His father knew better.

"Well, I heard Nick beat the shit out of an older guy, for no reason."

"Yeah, that about sums it up, Pop."

"That kid won't be happy until he ends up in jail or dead," Nicholas said, shaking his head clearly disappointed.

"I know, Pop. I don't know what his problem is."

"I'll tell you what his problem is. He doesn't care about anything or anyone except himself. He is a selfish, miserable kid. I've washed my hands of him."

"Let me have a talk with him. Maybe he'll listen to me, Chris offered."

"Alright, but don't get too close to him. He's trouble, that kid."

"Okay, Pop."

"Come here; give your old man a kiss." Nicholas reached out and embraced his son, then kissed him on both cheeks.

"Thank God for you. At least I have one good son."

"Love you, Pop."

"I love you, Christopher."

"I'll see you in a couple days, alright?" He waved with one hand and reached for the door with the other. His father waved back, and stood watching Chris with pride, as he carefully closed the door and left.

Chris stood an inch taller than his father, yet the pounds hadn't found their way to his lean body. He had a medium build, although his parents thought him to be skinny. He had been a star soccer player in high school and after graduation he joined a gym, where he worked out on a regular basis.

He walked out, took in a deep breath of cool air, and made his way up the busy street, blending in, and eventually fading into the crowd.

***

Two days later, Nick sat in Shaky's, pushing down shots of Jack Daniels with Budweiser draught beers. Like most Friday afternoons, he sat alone, after a hard day of laboring on a new building construction site. Shaky's pub was his watering hole of choice. Most of the regular customers knew Shaky's to be one of the very few local bars that Nick wasn't banned from entering. The owner, Shaky, didn't like cops, and neither did Nick.

So, that was one thing they both had in common. This alone, was reason enough for Nick to drop half his paycheck there every week. Shaky had earned his prestigious nickname when he was a young hood working the streets of Providence. He was a person not to be trusted by anyone. When he was fifteen years old, he lifted the gift basket at his older sister's wedding reception. Although he denied it until he was blue in the face, he couldn't explain where he got the money to buy his new wardrobe, and fancy pool cue. It was in Smitty's pool hall that he was awarded the name Shaky, by a pool shark that ultimately took half the money he had stolen, in a game of straight billiards.

"Nick, the phone is for you." Walter the bartender sounded out.

Nick got up and walked to the pay phone by the restrooms.

"Yeah, who's this?" Nick inquired.

"It's me, Chris." He cupped the pay phone and pulled it in close to his chest. The pay phone was situated near the pool table where a few guys were playing eight ball. The Buck and Bull tavern had many nosy customers and he couldn't be too careful. "You're not going to believe this, man. Are you sitting down?

"What, what is it?"

"We hit the number." Chris's tone was firm and excited and he was laughing like a child.

"What number. What the hell are you talking about?" Nick asked.

"The lottery!" he said in a rough whisper. "We hit the Lotto for nine million bucks." Chris could barely contain himself over the phone.

"Get the hell outta here," Nick said in disbelief.

He took a quick glance around the bar, lowering his voice. "I'm serious, Nick. We hit the lotto. I checked the number a hundred times. We won, man."

Nick tightened his grip on the phone. "You better not be screwing with me, Chris."

"Nick, the ticket we bought last Tuesday is the winning ticket. It was drawn last night."

"Holy shit, Chris!" Nick's heart started pounding. "You better not be fucking with me."

"I'm not. We are millionaires, man."

"Have you told anyone about this?"

"No."

"Are you sure? Nobody?"

"Yes, I'm sure. You're the first person I called."

"Okay, listen. Don't breathe a word about this to anyone. You understand?"

"Yeah."

"Take the ticket and seal it in a plastic baggie and meet me at your boat."

"Alright, I'll meet you there in an hour."

"Remember, don't tell anyone."

"You got it." Chris hesitated, "Nick?"

"Yeah," Nick responded.

"Our ship has finally come in," Chris said.

"Yeah, finally," Nick replied.

Nick went back to the bar and sat down. "Walter, give me another shot and set up the bar, drinks for all these clowns." Sitting at the bar, Nick ignored how his hand stuck to it, when he rested it down. He didn't think about all the drunks and losers surrounding him, praising him for buying them one more nail that would ultimately seal many of their coffins. His mind drifted, as he began to fantasize. He had done this many times before, but it was always a distant dream, untouchable. Today was different. It was real, and within reach.

The sun and the temperature were both descending, at an even pace. The marina was nearly deserted, as Chris climbed aboard his twenty-six foot boat. He had purchased the used boat three years earlier for eighteen thousand dollars, and he loved every minute he spent aboard. It was an ivory-white cuddy that slept four people. He sat sipping a beer, remembering the many times he had fought with blues and stripers. Now, his thoughts quickly shifted to the money. He wasn't aware that a smile had found his face as he drifted away. *First I'll give my father, mother, and two sisters, three hundred thousand each. Well, maybe, two hundred thousand; Uncle Sam will take a big chunk. I'll quit my job and open up a small fishing and bait supply store near the water. I might even buy a bigger boat and I can work part time at the shop. I can work in the mornings, cut out early and go fishing until sunset. In the winter, I'll live down south, maybe Florida.* Chris fantasized about watching a marlin breach from out of the open sea, as he battled to reel it in. He thought he might even do volunteer work somewhere. It would make him feel good to give something back to the community and help people in need. The last thing he thought about was a family. He saw himself with a beautiful wife and two children on a perfect autumn day, rolling around in a pile of leaves in the front yard of their big white house. He pictured himself totally happy with his family and his new life.

***

Ricky Kane cursed to himself, while he polished the stern of a boat that belonged to a local real estate tycoon. He knelt in an awkward position that caused his lower back to cramp up. *Twelve bucks an hour, he thought to himself. That cheap bastard makes that much a minute.*

Ricky was middle aged, but looked ten years older. His back had rounded more and more as the years passed by. Growing up, he was the best athlete in the neighborhood, and most likely the state. He could play any sport and do it well. Although, he stood five foot eight, he would outplay anyone who dribbled a ball on his court. He was fast, and not only could he successfully lay up the ball against guys over six feet tall, he barely missed a shot from outside the key. It didn't matter to Ricky what the game was, he excelled at it. Baseball, football, street hockey, he was a natural-born athlete.

Unfortunately, when he reached his late teens, he began to replace picking up the ball with a drink. It wasn't long after the partying began, that he found his true talent. He used to recite to his bar room buddies, "I could have been a contender," as he swallowed down another shot of cheap whiskey. The sad part was that he was right. Anyone who had seen Ricky play, would have to toast with him in agreement.

Ricky stayed back two times before attending the eighth grade, and he barely managed to finish high school. Finally the system pushed him through to his senior year. He was a hindrance to the other students and spent his day interrupting the class and getting into fights. The school wanted Ricky out, and his teachers had been notified. He graduated from high school at a ninth grade level, at best.

Every day was a struggle crawling out of bed and making an effort to get to work. With a hangover and a few coins in his pocket, he would usually arrive late to the car wash or the construction site, and now, the boat docks. Ricky never cared to get a license and drive an automobile. If he couldn't bum a ride, he would take the bus or walk to wherever he needed to go. He didn't venture far from his mother's house, where he lived his entire life. After his father died of a heart attack, in a local pub, it was just Ricky and his mother. Rose, was a good Christian woman who was heart-broken watching her beautiful boy slowly destroy himself, year after year. Countless times, she had thrown him out of the house, but always took him back. If she didn't, it would probably be a death sentence. He would most likely freeze to death or end up dead from a knife wound.

It would be getting dark soon, so Ricky decided to call it a day. He sealed his can of wax and secured his tools into a canvas bag and started off the dock. As he approached the marina complex, he ducked into a doorway to avoid the wind as he lit a cigarette. He took a long, hard drag and blew it out. As the smoke cleared, he watched a guy hurrying off the central dock, making his way toward the parking lot. The guy looked familiar so he took a few steps closer. *Nick Gennaro, where is he going in such a hurry?* Nick had given Ricky a severe beating a few years back outside a neighborhood bar, so he avoided him at all costs.

Ricky stood puffing on his cigarette observing Nick, as he quickly shuffled off the dock. He appeared nervous as he kept taking quick glances to his flanks, as if someone were going to attack. Ricky watched until Nick got into his car and drove away.

Nick turned down the radio, as his tires pushed sand a foot into the air, as he accelerated. He didn't want any distractions, because he had to think clearly. He drove up Ocean Bay Drive and took a left onto Sea Cliff Way. He pulled over to the side of the road and took out a plastic bag from his pocket - inside, was the lottery ticket. He picked up a newspaper from the passenger seat and held the bag next to the paper and began to compare numbers, 3, 4, 6, 17, 28, 30. His heart began to beat faster and he was growing warm. His mouth was getting dryer as he read it over and over again. "Yes," he yelled out. "Yes. I'm fucking rich. I am really rich!" He slid the ticket back into the plastic bag and sealed it tight and put it back in his pocket. Shifting the car into gear, he drove off a wealthy man.

4

The gulls were hollering, as if they were kicking off the day with another wild party. The blinding glare of the sun reflecting off the water disrupted Andy Radcliff and his son Ryan's view, as they carefully negotiated their boat away from the docks. The night wind had laid to rest, setting the stage for a calm morning. A fisherman's dream day, Andy thought.

"Here you go," Andy handed his son a pair of sunglasses. "You may want to clean the bait off them, first." Ryan smiled and began wiping the lenses with his shirttail. He was ten years old, and his father was his whole world. Ryan had been looking forward to an entire day alone with his Dad – just the two of them and the sea. All he really wanted was his father's attention and like most ten-year-old boys, he wanted to be heard.

"Take the wheel for a minute, while I see what's inside my shoe, poking me in the foot," Andy requested. As he took off his shoe and began shaking it up-side-down, he saw something floating in the water. He rested his hand on his forehead acting as a visor to get a better look, but the sun distorted his view.

"What the hell is that?" Andy asked. "It looks like a manikin. Who would put that in the water?"

He quickly put his shoe back on without tying it. "Give me the wheel," he said. As Andy moved his boat closer, he realized it wasn't a manikin. "Holy Jesus!" he gasped.

"Dad what is it? It looks like a dead guy."

"Yeah, it looks that way, Son." Andy pulled Ryan into his chest, holding him close, shielding his view to protect him.

***

Samuel Carra and Donald Burke stood on the edge of the dock, watching as the rescue vessel sailed closer.

"What a way to start the weekend," Donny said.

"I hope they remembered to drop an anchor," Sam followed, while adjusting his sunglasses. "Remember a couple years ago, when we pulled the old lady from the drink. They forgot to set a buoy and mark the spot where she was found floating. What a pain in the ass that was."

Donny slightly nodded his head, thinking back. "I remember. She was the lady who got bombed, whacked her head on the dock, and plunged into the water. She had big bucks, too. Remember the palace she owned on the water? What a shame." Donny stopped talking, and looked at his watch hoping he would get out of work in time to work on his book. "People like us work our asses off our whole life with the dream of living in a house like that, and someone who realized that dream, threw it all away by hitting herself over the head with a vodka bottle."

"I guess some people lose appreciation for what they have. They become complacent and take it all for granted," Sam said.

"When I get there, I promise you, I won't," Donny assured him.

"When *you* get there? You're not going to get there working for the state," Sam said while grinning.

"This is your bag, not mine. To me, this is just one short step in a long journey I am destined to take," Donny replied.

"Well, good luck. I'm not complaining. I put two great kids through college on this job and I have a nice home and a wonderful wife. Now, if I could only straighten out my slice, I'd be a happy man."

Donny gave Sam a soft punch on the shoulder. "You've done well for yourself. I just can't see myself pulling bodies out of the water for thirty years."

"It goes by faster than you think. Twenty-seven years. Where have they gone?" Sam gazed out at the sun bouncing off the water. He thought about his rookie days in uniform. He was young and his energy and strength poured out of him like an EF5 tornado. Sam was going to change the world, or at least a small part of it. He joined the Rhode Island State Police right out of the Marines. He wished that he had attended college, but never made the effort. In those days, most troopers didn't go to college. The ranks were lined mostly with veterans all standing six feet tall or better, and in good physical condition.

Sam was married young, and soon after their wedding day, his wife, Susan, had decided on a family. Sam wasn't opposed, but he would have liked to have had more input on when to start and where to raise them. Sam was so content being a trooper that he just went along with whatever Susan was planning. He wasn't one to argue. Sam figured as long as his wife was happy, his home life would be free of conflict and turmoil.

The young officer started out working the dogwatch shift, as all troopers did, with the exception of those who had strong political connections. After five years, he moved to the day shift, where he worked in uniform for another six years before making detective. Sam was well liked and respected by his peers, and generally anyone that took the time to know him. Sam was one that thought things through before speaking, and that helped him move up through the ranks faster than most. He was proud of his Italian heritage, and he wasn't afraid to show it. Growing up in the Italian section of Providence, he was the son of a tailor that owned a small shop downtown. His mother would pick him up from school and take him to the shop to help out. Sam would do his homework in the back room, and when he was finished, he would work with his father, while his mother sat behind the sewing machine. It was a Saturday afternoon in the spring of 1964. Sam was dusting off suit racks when two local wise guys entered the shop. Both men were dressed in fine suits. Sam knew this, because on many occasions, his father had shown him the difference between quality suits and cheap ones. Sam figured the taller of the two men was the leader, because he was doing all the talking. The other guy just stood listening and shaking his head up and down like a puppet on a string. He had a toothpick wedged between his teeth and a fat nose with little holes in it. Sam thought it looked like someone had been chewing on it. The tall guy was irate and talking with his right fist clenched, holding it in the air, like a cocky prize fighter. He was slim and stood over six feet tall and wore a wide-brim hat, concealing black hair greased back with Brylcream. He was handsome, but his dark eyes hid a past filled with hate for his abusive father.

"Sammy, go in the back and sweep the floor," his father ordered.

"Okay Pop." Sam hurried out of the room, turned the corner and stood listening.

"Where the hell is my money?" The tall man asked.

"I told you I don't have it. I can barely afford to feed my family."

"I don't want to hear a song and dance about your stinking family. I have a family, and you're taking food off our table."

"I'm just a tailor. I don't make a lot of money. I'll repair your suits, at no charge."

"Listen to me, you dirty deadbeat. This is the third time I've come by here and you still have nothing for me but a promise to fix my suits. I run this block, and if you want to do business here, you pay like everybody else."

His voice was getting louder and Sam was getting scared for his father. With his sense of security being compromised, he was feeling anxious and he started to become nauseous. He peaked his head around the corner and watched as the tall man punched his father in the stomach, causing him to buckle to the floor. Sam was afraid, and could barely move, he stood watching helplessly as the man he loved and admired was being humiliated and beaten. It was the worst feeling he had ever experienced.

"Just like baseball. You know baseball, right? Three strikes and you're out. Anthony, grab this peasant's other arm. Let's take him to the sewing machine and sew a reminder to his ear."

"No, don't!" Sam ran out from around the corner and bolted to the tall man, pulling on his arm.

"Don't hurt my Pop, please!"

"Well look at this brave little shit." He grabbed Sam by the throat. "You can watch and learn a lesson for when you grow up to become a peasant like your father."

As the two men began pulling Sam and his father toward the back room, the commotion was silenced by a voice. To Sam it was the voice of an angel.

"Good afternoon boys."

Just then, at that very moment in time, beat patrolman, Shawn McFarlin appeared and observed what was happening in the shop. McFarlin was a tough Irish cop who didn't much care for Italians. However, he liked Sam's father. He was always pleasant to him, offering him to step in from the cold and have coffee. He showed respect for the badge and that was a gesture seldom seen in Providence, but always welcomed.

"What's going on here?" Both men immediately let go of the tailor and his son.

"Nothing, just having a talk," replied the tall man.

"A talk, I like to talk. Why don't we all have a talk, then?" He demanded, with an Irish brogue.

"Maybe another time, we have to be going," the wise guy said. He motioned to the short guy and started toward the door.

"Not so fast, Vince," McFarlin sounded out, using his night stick as an extension of his arm, blocking the mobster's way. I heard what was going on here and I'm very surprised that a gentleman like you would conduct himself in such a manner, especially in front of a young boy.

"We just had a little disagreement, that's all."

Sam began to calm and his shaking was subsiding. His father stood erect, now sticking his chest out.

"I think the disagreement is between me and both of you, now," McFarlin said. Then in one quick motion, he stepped to his right, pivoting his hips counter-clockwise; he whipped his club in a sideways direction, delivering a massive blow to Vince's left leg, six inches above the knee. The force was so powerful making a loud crack that was music to Sam's ears. The wise guy let out a howl that raised the hair on his friend's neck. As Vince fell to his knees, McFarlin did a reverse jabbing motion with the end of his baton that caught the short wise guy directly in the bread basket, causing him to keel over, gasping for air. He turned to Vince who was still on the ground, now raising his hand up in defeat. Just then, McFarlin swung his baton, cracking Vince on the back of his hand with one single vicious blow, shattering five bones in his left hand. Once again, Vince screamed out in pain; this time the pitch was a note higher.

"Now gentlemen," both men were still lying on the floor. "Let me make myself very clear. I am going to come in this shop at least twice a day. If I hear from anyone, Mr. Carra, a customer, or even a leprechaun, that you or anyone affiliated with your kind bother these people or their family again, I promise you I will find you and put a bullet through your brain. Do we have an understanding today, gentlemen?"

"Yes", Vince mumbled.

"I didn't hear you so clearly," McFarlin said, raising his baton a few inches higher.

"Yes sir!" Vince called out.

"Good. Then you gentlemen will be on your way."

The short guy helped Vince up onto his feet. Not making eye contact with anyone, they limped out into the unforgiving street.

Sam never forgot that day. It was a turning point in his life. It was that very day he realized who really had the power. That was the day Sam knew what he wanted to do with his life. He was going to be a police officer.

As the vessel moved toward the dock, a dive team trooper in the boat threw the line out to another trooper in uniform that was standing on the dock near the two homicide detectives. After tying down the boat, they all watched as the body was hoisted onto an awaiting stretcher.

"Did you guys mark the spot?" Donny asked.

"Yes we did," replied one of the divers. "We're going back to take a look under the water. With any luck, we'll find the weapon that was used to bash this poor kid's brains in."

"We should be so lucky," Donny said.

"Any identification found on this guy?" Sam asked.

"Yeah, he had a wallet in his back pocket. Here's his license."

Sam took the license, looked at it briefly, and then gazed out toward the water. Once again, he studied the document.

"What is it Sam. Do you know this guy?" Donny asked.

"I know his father."

"Let me see that." Donny took the ID. "Christopher Vito Gennaro, age twenty-seven. How do you know his father?"

"He has a meat market in South Walton. He isn't going to take this lightly. He's a real family man, in more ways than one." He snapped his index finger against the license.

"Are you saying he's connected?" Donny asked.

"Let's just say, he has many friends in the Italian community. Let's head down to the morgue and meet the coroner."

On the way to the morgue, they stopped for a cup of coffee to kill some time. It would take a while for the body to be brought down to the examination room and be prepared for the initial exam. They sat in a booth drinking hot coffee and Donny was chewing on a bagel.

"So, what do you think, mob hit?" Donny asked.

"No. If that were the case, we wouldn't have found a body. Besides, I doubt he was that close to the action."

"Then why would someone take that kid's life? Maybe it's a drug deal gone bad."

"It's possible. I can't speculate until we see all the evidence and find out who this guy was," Sam replied, while adding more sugar to his coffee.

"Yeah, let's wait and see what turns up. The dive team photographer is dropping off the crime scene photos this afternoon, right?"

"Yeah, I doubt the pictures will reveal any evidence. He was floating for a while. He could have been killed anywhere and dropped a mile away from where they found him. We need to make sure we get the report from the responding officer as soon as possible," Sam suggested.

"Imagine taking your kid out fishing and instead of spotting a striper in the water, you find a body floating face down. That kid will never look at salt-water fishing the same."

"Neither will Christopher Gennaro," Sam said, resting his cup down.

Donny entered the morgue, and it was no more comforting than his first time eight years ago. He could never get used to the sight of dead bodies lying on slabs, carved open like a Thanksgiving turkey. The lingering smell seemed to stay with him, until he was able to remove his clothing and take a hot shower when he got home. Standing six-feet-two inches and weighing two hundred and thirty-two pounds wasn't any consolation.

Deep inside, Donny carried a painful memory that had ripped his heart apart. Often, he would wake up in the middle of the night shaking and drenched with sweat. When he was seventeen years old, his only sibling was killed in an automobile accident. His younger brother, Craig, was taken from him, after being struck by a UPS truck. The sight of his seven-year-old brother stretched out in a box had been a constant reminder of how unfair life can be. Donny loved his brother, so much, that words couldn't explain how devastated he was the day they lowered the miniature casket into the earth. It was on a Sunday that Donny completely lost his faith in God, and he hadn't regained it since. He never spoke of it to anyone, not even his partner, Sam.

"Hello Doc," Sam called out as they entered the examination room. "Where's Scope?"

"I have really grown to despise being on call," Doctor Livingstone said in a near whisper. "He called out sick." Livingstone was standing over a corpse with a hand-held recorder and latex gloves tightly snug to his hands.

Sam moved in for a closer look at the corpse. "Is this our guy, Gennaro?"

"This is him. What a shame, losing his life at such a young age, handsome kid, too."

"What have you got?" Sam asked.

"He's been dead less than twenty-four hours. He was killed and then dumped into the water.

"Cause of death?" Sam asked.

"Blunt force trauma to the parietal and the occipital lobe. It looks like he was struck with a very heavy instrument to the parietal lobe first. This area of the brain is responsible for our bodily sensations, our five senses. Then two more blows to the occipital lobe, which allows us to speak, hear and read. Most likely, he was struck from behind by surprise, and then as he fell forward, he was struck two more times. All three blows fractured his skull."

"Poor bastard didn't even see it coming. Didn't even have a chance to defend himself," Donny said.

"Are you planning to do the nine yards today," Sam asked.

"Yup, the whole nine – later this afternoon."

Sam turned away, he had seen enough. "Let me know what you come up with."

"No problem," Livingston said, peeling off his gloves.

"Well, let's go notify the boss and get the information for family notification," Sam suggested.

"Yes, my favorite part of the job, notifying the family that a loved one has been murdered."

"You say that every time, you know?"

"I hate it just as much, every time," Donny responded.

Sam held the door open as Donny passed through. "I know, so do I."

5

Just before dinner on Saturday the detectives pulled up in front of Mr. and Mrs. Nicholas Gennaro's house in South Walton. The sun was still shining bright and the air was fresh and clean. It had been a perfect day. A couple of kids were playing kick ball in the street. Donny sat behind the wheel watching as the boy kicked the ball and ran to the base. A little girl that appeared to be his sister ran after it, moving a bit slower than the older boy.

"You alright?" Sam asked.

"Yeah, I'd much rather be golfing."

"Me too. I'll handle this one, I know the father. Besides, they're Italian."

Donny's face seemed to lose a few wrinkles. "Sounds good to me, thanks."

Both men felt uneasy as they made their way up the front walkway. Donny felt increasingly nauseous with every step closer to the front door. Sam rang the doorbell and they stood waiting. Donny turned and watched the kids playing in the street. They were running and laughing and just doing what happy kids do. He thought about the times he used to play with his brother. It seemed like yesterday — how he missed those days. The door opened and Mrs. Gennaro stood looking at the two detectives. Once she saw the expression on Donny's face, her heart began to beat faster.

Sam could see the worry her face adopted. "Mrs. Gennaro?"

"Yes."

"I'm detective Carra and this is detective Burke. We're with the Rhode Island State Police."

"How can I help you?"

"May we come in, Mrs. Gennaro?"

She hesitated at first as if she wanted to slam the door, shutting out the pending anguish." Yes, please come in." She pushed the door open wider, wondering what her son Nick did this time.

They entered the house and she escorted them to the living room. The house was well kept and moderately decorated.

"Please tell me what the matter is?" She impatiently asked.

They all sat down. "Is your husband home?" Sam asked.

"No, he's at the market, working."

Sam took out Chris's license and handed it to her. "Is this your son, Mrs. Gennaro?"

"Yes." Her lips began to tremble and her palms grew moist. "That's my Christopher. Is he alright?" She was praying in her head. *Please God let him be alright. Please God.*

"We found a body near the Sunset Marina, Mrs. Gennaro. I'm sorry, but he had your son's ID in his wallet."

"No, God!" She cried out. "Not my boy, not Christopher. It can't be."

Once again, Donny had to work hard at holding back tears of his own. He could see the pain in her eyes to the point where he could almost feel it. Sam was stronger than Donny, although he contained a strong sense of compassion. His mouth was getting dryer, as he continued.

"Mrs. Gennaro, I would like to have your husband come with us to the morgue to identify the body. Can you call him?"

She began sobbing uncontrollably. She went to the phone and began to dial, but her hands were too shaky, so Donny took the phone and she cited the numbers as he dialed.

Nicholas answered the phone. "Gennaro's."

"Nicholas." Her voice was broken and she sounded hysterical. He knew right away something was terribly wrong.

"Maria, what is it. What's wrong?" Nicholas asked.

She tried to tell him, but her voice was unclear. All he could make out was the word detectives. Sam reached out and Maria handed him the phone.

"Mr. Gennaro."

"Yes."

"This is detective Carra with the Rhode Island State Police. We need you to please come home right away so we can discuss an urgent matter with you."

"Son of a bitch. What did Nick do this time?"

"Mr. Gennaro, please, we can't discuss this over the phone. Can you please come home, now?"

"Okay, I'm leaving now. I'll be there in ten minutes." Nicholas hung up.

The three of them were sitting in the living room when Nicholas arrived. Maria was sobbing as she got up to greet her husband. She took two steps and fell down. Her legs were too weak to hold her up. Nicholas knew something very bad had happened. He helped his wife back into the chair. Sam reached out to shake hands. It was left stretched out without contact.

"What is it, tell me now." Nicholas demanded.

"We found a body in the water this morning. We think it may be your son and he was murdered."

"Oh no! I knew this would happen. I told him he would end up dead or in jail."

"Nicholas," Maria called out. Her voice was unstable. He knelt down next to her. "It's Christopher."

He wasn't sure he heard right. "Christopher? It can't be. He's a good boy. He never hurt anybody." Nicholas sat down on the floor next to his wife's chair. He sat in disbelief. "Are you sure it's Christopher?"

"We found his license in the victim's back pocket. We would like you to come with us to the morgue to be sure."

His face had changed to a pale white. "Alright, let me call my daughter and have her come over to stay with my wife." Appearing lost, he searched for the phone.

The ride to the morgue was traveled without conversation. It was the longest ride Nicholas had ever taken. He prayed over and over hoping they were mistaken. He even bargained with God in his head, that he could take Nick, but not Christopher.

They entered the viewing room and Sam walked in just behind Nicholas, placing his hand on his shoulder. Donny stood back watching from the entrance. The broken man walked in, as if he had undergone a lobotomy operation earlier that day. Sam pulled the white sheet down that covered the corpse, exposing the face. Nicholas looked down at his son lying dead on the table. He showed no emotion as he reached out and placed his hand on Christopher's cheek. To Nicholas, he was still a young boy. The many wonderful years he had with his son flashed through his mind in an instant. Christopher was his pride and joy; he was good, pure, and innocent. He loved his son more than anyone could ever know. A single tear rolled down his cheek, resting on his chin before dropping to the floor.

"It's my boy." He gasped. "It's Christopher."

He leaned over and kissed his son on the forehead and then turned and walked out leaving his heart behind.

6

Sunday morning was coming to a close, as Nick entered his neighborhood store. His head was pounding from a hard night of drinking and snorting cocaine. His mother had called the night before and left a message regarding Christopher. He didn't want to deal with it right then, so he didn't call back. All he wanted to do was get numb and enjoy as many lap dances as he could afford. He had withdrawn most of his savings and drove into Providence, where he blended into a strip bar hoping nobody would recognize him. The Crystal Palace was dark and he had only been there on one occasion several years ago, so he felt comfortable knowing he probably wouldn't run into anyone he knew. That's where he spent the night.

Nick stood in line waiting to buy cigarettes and aspirin. He glanced down to the many stacks of newspapers piled on the floor. He reached down, picked one up, quickly folded it in half and made his way to the counter. The murder of Christopher Gennaro was being covered all over the television, radio and on the front page of all local newspapers.

Once he arrived back to his apartment, Nick popped open a beer and swallowed down several pills, directly from the bottle he just purchased. He opened the paper and began reading. Without finishing the entire story, he squeezed the paper with all his might and threw it against the wall. He spread a line out on the table, rolled up a dollar bill and began snorting. When he finished, he put the bill in his pocket and guzzled down his beer. His mind was on the winning ticket *now*. He opened another beer and sat down to his thoughts. The lottery commission in Cranston wouldn't open until eight, Monday morning, so he would have to wait until then. He decided to remain anonymous and would call his lawyer and attempt to convince him to represent Nick at the commission.

Mark Azanaro had represented Nick many times in the past for drug and assault and battery charges. On the last occasion, Nick choked him outside the courthouse, refusing to pay his bill. Nick knew it would take much convincing, but money has a way of changing a person's mind, he thought.

With the remaining two hundred dollars Nick had in the bank, he decided to buy a new suit for the funeral. The wake was to take place Monday at Zamboni's funeral home and Chris would be buried on Tuesday. Although, he was itching to get his hands around the money, Nick decided it could wait until Tuesday after the burial.

Before showering, he drank down four more beers. It was just enough to take the edge off, before he drove to his parents' house to see his family.

"Where the hell have you been?" Marybeth jumped down Nick's throat as he entered the foyer.

"I was out. What's it to you?"

"Your brother was found murdered over twenty-four hours ago and you are nowhere to be found. Have you had your head up your ass? It's all over the fucking news, Nick!"

"I was out of town and just found out this morning, so shut the hell up."

"Pop is pissed and I don't blame him."

One eyebrow took a stand. "Yeah, he'll get over it."

Nick entered the family room where the whole family was situated along with the parish priest and their Uncle Johnny, Nicholas' brother.

"Where have you been?" his father asked. "Your mother is a wreck and you are nowhere to be found. She called you yesterday. What's the matter with you?"

"I was out of town and just found out this morning."

"Out of town, where out of town?" Nicholas asked.

"I was in Providence, alright?"

"Okay, let up on Nick now." Johnny said as he embraced his nephew, kissing him on the cheek.

Uncle Johnny had always been close to Nick. Ever since Nick was a young boy, Johnny took to him. He liked that Nick was tough and defiant; it reminded him of himself. Johnny was an ironworker who had more than his share of trouble throughout his life. When he was thirty-four, he was arrested for armed robbery, and after a long trial, he was convicted and sentenced to eight years in prison. He was released early for good behavior, just after completing his fifth year.

Johnny, along with two other guys, robbed a bank in Woonsocket, Rhode Island on a cold winter day. Johnny was the mastermind of the heist, and he had a solid plan, that almost worked. He devised a plan, assembled a team, and put the entire robbery into action, step by step. Johnny spent days staking out the bank, watching bank employees and their customers for hours. He watched how often the beat cops drove by, and what time the armored car stopped to pick up the large bags filled with money. Johnny patiently waited for the right day to make his move, and that came on a Tuesday, during a blizzard that dropped over two feet of snow on the town. He knew the cruisers wouldn't be able to maneuver around quickly in the storm, and nearly all vehicles on the road would be moving like snails.

They waited just prior to the cash pick up from the armored car company, in order to maximize their stake, and then they hit the bank and drove off in a Ford Bronco, with chains wrapped around the tires. As the three men took off down the white street, they were hooting and hollering. They had successfully stolen three hundred and sixty thousand dollars. Their vehicle was ripping through the snow, passing several motor vehicles abandoned on the side of the road stuck in the deep snow.

It was a perfect plan. Johnny and Mike wore ski masks during the robbery, while Leon waited outside in the get-away vehicle. The Bronco was stolen from long-term parking at the airport, so Johnny figured he had all the bases covered. He was right except for the one thing that unfolds most robberies that are committed by more than one person. Leon had a big mouth and bragged to someone that he had robbed the bank.

Two weeks later, they were picked up after Leon sang like a bird in order to avoid a long prison sentence. Johnny and Mike were convicted and sentenced to prison, and Leon walked away with five years' probation. Less than a year after Johnny was released, Leon disappeared, and was never seen or heard from again.

"Ma, how are you doing?" Nick sat down next to his mother.

"My poor baby, someone killed my baby. Why would anyone want to hurt Christopher?"

"That's what I want to know." Nick said, as he held his mother.

Nick turned his head glancing at his father. Their eyes met for a brief moment, and Nicholas contemplated how his own son had become a stranger to him. He had a bad feeling that somehow, Nick had something to do with Chris's death. He wasn't sure how or why, but his heart told him Nick was connected to this tragedy in some way.

"What are the cops saying?" Nick got up and walked over to where his father was standing by the fireplace.

"His father appeared to be medicated, but he wasn't. He stood hunched over, looking shorter than normal, Nick thought. Seeming like a beaten man, with no hope, no soul.

"Nothing yet," he managed to say.

"I'll find out who did this and I swear I'll kill them with my bare hands. I swear I will!" Nick testified, clenching his fists.

Ashley and Marybeth just sat watching, as Nick once again lost control. They had fully expected this reaction from him. They both despised Nick. He was one side of a coin balanced by Chris who was on the other – the side that shined.

The room evolved into a silent void with everyone occupying their own space, trapped in their own thoughts and the memory of their son, brother and friend. Chris was the one that kept the family whole, the one that always offered light. Now that the light was burned out, how would they make their way through the dark? How would they survive as a family?

The day turned into night and the next day came with little sleep. The whole family stood in a receiving line waiting for the doors to open; the line outside stretched nearly two blocks. Most were friends of Nicholas and Maria, some were friends of Chris and his two sisters – none were friends of Nick. The doors opened and people began filing in. Most of them muttered the same words, as they greeted the grieving family members: "I'm sorry" or "My condolences." Ashley heard one of her mother's friends mutter, "He looks so good." She wanted to slap her. *How can a dead person look good?*

The coffin sat fifteen feet directly in front of the line and the family stood staring at Chris's body laid out on display. Nick was already half drunk and was glancing at his watch every ten minutes or so, and it hadn't gone unnoticed by his father. After a half hour, Nick walked out and went to the men's room where he fell to his knees hovering over the toilet, vomiting. When he finished, he got up and made his way to the sink. He rinsed out his mouth with cold water and looked up into the mirror. His eyes were filling with water and his hands were shaking. He cupped water into his hands and brought them to his face several times, washing away the tears. He dried himself off with a paper towel and threw it on the floor as he was half way out the door. Everyone watched Nick as he took his place back in line next to his mother, who was now sitting.

The day seemed to drag on forever and they all wanted it to end. They didn't want to look at Chris's dead body any longer; they just wanted to remember him as he was. Everyone except Nicholas, he didn't want to leave his son. He knew it would be the last time he would ever see Chris again, and he couldn't bear that thought.

When the service ended, Nicholas refused to leave with the rest of the family. He sat next to his son's coffin, until they closed the funeral home – then he broke down. It hit him like a cement truck as the pain and sense of loss settled in.

The funeral home director could see the agony in Nicholas's eyes. He helped him onto his feet and Nicholas did something he had never done in his entire life. He wept in the arms of a stranger.

When Nicholas walked out of the funeral parlor, he was a different man. Pain and despair had invaded his inner being. He was totally lost in despair.

***

It was dead calm. Except for the wind and rain, there were few sounds to be heard. Sam and Donny stood watching from a distance as people were gathering around the burial site.

"There isn't anything worse than this." Sam said, looking straight ahead.

Donny thought about the day he buried his baby brother. "I don't have kids, but I can only imagine how hard this would be." Donny replied.

"Our children are supposed to bury us. This isn't natural. I would die ten painful deaths to avoid burying one of my kids."

Donny inspected Sam, believing what he said to be true.

"When should we start interviewing the family?" Donny asked.

"Tomorrow, I don't want this running cold."

The two men watched in silence, both wearing black raincoats and holding black umbrellas above their heads. They were an attractive pair of detectives, yet quite different. Sam was dark and more rugged looking. He stood a few inches shorter than his partner, who was much younger with wavy light brown hair. They came from different backgrounds, but they shared a common value; they both had integrity and compassion.

As people finished settling in around the casket, and the priest was preparing to offer his prayers, the weeping grew louder. Nick stood next to Marybeth, who was standing beside Ashley.

"Did you see the news, today?" Nick overheard Marybeth as she spoke to her sister in a whisper. "Somebody hit the lotto for nine million bucks. The ticket was bought at the quick mart."

"The quick mart in South Walton?" Ashley asked.

"That's right."

"Someone is having a much better morning than us," Ashley said.

Marybeth nodded her head in agreement.

Nick wanted to reach into his coat pocket, pull out the plastic bag with the winning ticket and yell out at the top of his lungs. *"I'm rich, I won the lotto and you can all kiss my ass."*

He just stood quietly listening as the priest started the service, with his hand inside his coat pocket fingering the plastic bag between his fingers. The bag hadn't left his possession since Friday night. He wasn't taking any chances with his ticket – his ticket to paradise.

7

The yellow police tape surrounding Chris's boat snapped in the wind. Blood stains, now dry, had turned to a dark red, almost appearing black. Sam and Donny had spent a good part of Saturday afternoon on the boat going through Chris's personal effects and searching for evidence. They were unable to find anything on the boat that could have been used as the murder weapon. The crime lab team had removed blood samples, clothing fibers, hair, saliva from a glass, and traces of urine from the head. Most of the interior was dusted for prints and photographs were taken prior to anyone entering the vessel. Sam and Donny questioned everyone in the area they could find, but came up with no witnesses. They couldn't locate anyone who remembered seeing Chris, or anyone else on or near his boat the entire week leading up to the murder. They came to the conclusion that Chris was attacked on the boat sometime late Friday, and was thrown into the water, where he floated with the current until he was found by the Radcliff's, Saturday morning. Finger prints removed from the boat were mainly that of Chris's. There were several lifted that matched his brother Nick, and many unidentified prints.

It was Wednesday morning. Sam sat behind his desk in an office situated in the district attorney's office located in Providence. Donny had a smaller office, a few doors down.

"Mind if I come in?" Even after all the years they worked together Donny still respected Sam enough to knock on his door when entering his office.

"Sure, come in." Donny saw that Sam was reading a file. The office looked like a shrine with photographs of his wife and kids at birthday parties and picnics. Most of the south wall was decorated with pictures of sporting events and teams posing in their brilliant uniforms. It was evident that Sam's family was important to him and he was proud of them.

"I hate to say it, but I like the older brother on this one." Sam said, handing a file to Donny with a picture of Nick attached.

"You think he is cold enough to bash his kid brother's head in and dump him into the drink?"

"Look at his sheet. Assault and battery, assault and battery with a dangerous weapon, threat to commit a crime, sexual misconduct, disturbing the peace, drunk and disorderly, possession of a controlled substance, assault and battery, and the list goes on. This is not a model citizen. All this, and the most he has ever done is thirty days, back in ninety two."

"He certainly does have a history of violence." Donny agreed, while thumbing through his folder.

"I think it's safe to say, he is the first family member we should interview," Sam said

"Yeah, I'm with you on that. I think we should talk to him here, in our interrogation room."

"Definitely." Sam nodded in agreement.

A couple hours later, the two detectives were knocking on the apartment door of Nick Gennaro. After a few minutes, Sam wedged a calling card into the door jam and they continued on their way.

At that very moment, Nick was sitting in the back of a long, black stretch limousine drinking champagne. He sat waiting for Mark Azanaro to return from the lottery commission building at 1425 Pontiac Avenue, Cranston, Rhode Island.

Azanaro sat inside a small room outside the reception area filling out paperwork with a clerk pointing him through the state and federal tax laws. He was nearly finished, when the clerk excused himself, stating he would return with a lottery commission community liaison. Azanaro had a feeling what that meant and wasn't thrilled about it. He wasn't one that liked being in the public eye. He had represented some very shady characters during his career, and like most of them, he avoided attention. He was forty-four years old, but looked older. His black hair was starting to turn, but only above the ears. His hair was greased back and shiny and neatly kept. When reading, he needed to wear glasses and always wore gold rims to match his fourteen carat gold Geneva watch.

The door opened, and the clerk returned with a large man wearing a cheap suit and a fake smile.

"Hello Mr. Azanaro, my name is John Coffee."

"Yeah, how are you doing?" The lawyer responded.

"Fine, since your lottery winner has chosen to remain anonymous, I was hoping you would have a few words for the press and allow us to present you, on behalf of your client, a check in the amount of 8.9 million dollars. That is before any applicable taxes of course. The amount of the real check will be quite a bit less."

"Yes, I read that. They say it's a free country. Let me tell you something, it aint free, not even close. I'll do it, but let's make it quick." Coffee wasn't surprised by his attitude; after all, he is a lawyer, he thought.

Azanaro finished signing the paperwork and was escorted to a small room with a door that joined the press room. He could hear the commotion on the other side of the door.

"Are you ready?" Coffee asked, with one hand on the door knob, as if it were the start of a relay race.

"Alright, let's get this over with," Azanaro said.

He opened the door and the flashes hit Azanaro, like he was a heavyweight prize fighter in the ring. He was escorted to a podium with several microphones attached. He never expected so many reporters, and he wanted to make a run for it. Coffee and another guy came over with a check from the Rhode Island Lottery Commission that was about four feet long. The other guy, also mustering a fake smile, began speaking. Azanaro figured he was Coffee's boss. He was a handsome, well-built guy with a crew cut who could easily have passed for a state trooper.

"Attorney Azanaro, on behalf on your client, who has decided to remain anonymous, we would like to present you with a check in the amount of eight-point-nine-million-dollars, for winning the Rhode Island State Lotto Game."

He reached over extending his hand. Azanaro forced a smile as he shook hands and posed for the cameras. He knew if the money was his, he wouldn't need to force a smile at all.

"I'll open the floor for questions," Coffee's boss gestured to the press.

"Mr. Azanaro, Steve Kent with WPPR. Is your client local, and what does he do for a living?"

"Yes, my client is from the local area and he's a construction worker."

Another reporter was chosen by Coffee, who was selecting them by pointing his index finger like a kid at a penny candy counter.

"Ben Rogers, WPRI. What does your client plan to do with the money?"

"I expect he will retire and enjoy the good life."

"Attorney Azanaro, I'm Arthur Neary with WQMR. Does your client have a family, and does he plan on sharing his winnings with them?"

Azanaro hesitated for a moment, as his mind drifted to the thought of Nick's dead brother. He had a bad feeling about the whole situation and his gut told him the murder was tied to the ticket. He never mentioned his thoughts to anyone, especially Nick.

"Yes, he has family and I'm not sure what his plans are, as far as his family goes. Thank you." Azanaro started toward the door. He wanted to collect the real check and get the hell out of there. Reporters were yelling questions at him as he quickly shuffled out of the room.

It was a good thing that Azanaro cut the press conference short, because Nick was growing impatient and was just about ready to kick the shit out of the limo driver. The driver, clearly a professional pontificator, had a curiosity that would make George, the monkey, look complacently brain dead. He kept asking Nick about the winnings and what he would do with the money. It was evident that it was a poor attempt to build rapport with the intent to retain a significant tip.

"How did it go?" Nick asked, as Azanaro climbed into the back of the limo.

He situated himself and closed the door. "Let's just say I'm glad to be out of there. Here's your check." Azanaro handed the check to Nick, and then reached into his pocket and took out two cigars.

"Can you believe these damned thieves?" Nick roared.

Azanaro pushed the button that activated the divider, isolating the driver. Nick thought he missed the boat by not finding that button twenty minutes earlier.

"I know it. They took a huge chunk of the winnings."

"Those bastards leave me a lousy five million out of eight point nine."

"Well look at the bright side amigo, you are five million dollars richer than you were five minutes ago. Have a cigar. It's a Cohiba, the best cigar in the world."

"I don't smoke cigars, but I guess this is a good time to start," Nick said, lighting the cigar, as an amateur would.

"What's the plan, now?" Azanaro asked.

"I am going to party like it's my last day on earth."

"Nick, let me give you a bit of advice. With that kind of money, a man could party himself right into the grave. If you were smart, you would invest your money into a secure, yet diversified portfolio and live the easy life. Living hard will eventually take its toll."

Nick sat in silence, staring into Azanaro's eyes, before turning his head to gaze out the window. For a brief moment, Azanaro thought that maybe Nick was actually listening. Nick took a big puff from his Cuban cigar and emptied the rest of the bottle into his glass, and drank it down with one devouring gulp.

Nick rolled the divider down, capturing the attention of the driver. "Here is the plan. You are going to take my lawyer back to his office and then drive me to the bank so I can take care of business. After that, I want you to drive me to the place I used to work so I can quit. Then you can take me back to your limo office so I can get another driver. You follow?"

"I'll be happy to stay and drive for you, Mr. Gennaro."

"What did I say?" Nick was becoming agitated. "I don't want you to drive me. You have a big mouth and you look like shit. Do as I say while you still have somewhat of a tip left."

"Yes sir." The driver answered like a boot camp trainee during hell week. Nick rolled the divider back up.

When Nick arrived at the bank, the manager was waiting by the door, smiling ear to ear.

"Mr. Gennaro, how are you?"

Nick shook his hand. "I'm great, but I don't have much time, so can we get on with it?"

"Certainly, step into my office." Nick followed him to a small room to the left of the teller's booth and sat down.

"I have a check here for almost five-million bucks, which I'll deposit it into my savings account for now, until I decide how I'm going to invest. What is the interest rate?"

"Well, I would suggest depositing it into a money market instead of your savings. It will pay a higher interest rate and the money is just as accessible."

"What is the interest rate in a money market?"

"Right now we can offer three point eight percent."

"That's bullshit! I'm going to put five-million-dollars into your bank and you insult me with a low interest rate like this?" Nick was getting loud.

"Please Mr. Gennaro, calm down. How about putting the money in a CD? I can offer a better rate for you then."

"A CD, did you bump your head this morning? I need access to my money. I can't have it locked up in a CD. I'll tell you what, you give me four percent interest in your money market or I'll close my account here and put my money in another bank."

Nick got back into the limo wearing a slight grin on his face. The bank manager reluctantly agreed on four percent interest and Nick demanded twenty thousand in cash, even though the check hadn't cleared. The bank manager knew the check was good, so he agreed. As Nick walked out of the bank, the manager felt like he needed to take a shower.

Entering the construction site at work, Nick watched his co-workers marching around wearing their steel-toed boots and hard hats. None of them liked Nick very much; he was lazy and confrontational. Most of them tolerated him because they feared him. He had a reputation as being a crazy hothead and a scrapper.

Nick approached one of his peers, Ben Knots. "Hey, big Ben, where's that asshole, Thomas?"

"Nick, how are you doing? Hey, sorry about your brother, man."

"Yeah, I'm going to tell Thomas to stick this job up his ass."

"What, you're quitting the job?"

"That's right. I just hit the lotto for nine million bucks." Nick pulled out a wad of hundred dollar bills and peeled one off. "Where is he?"

"He's in the trailer."

"Lunch is on me." Nick said as he flung the bill into the air and walked away. Knots scooped the bill off the ground in record time.

In the past four years, there had been many times that Nick had dreamt about walking into his boss's office and quitting. Nick hated his boss from the first day he signed on, and he knew the feeling was mutual. Now, it was a reality, and with each step closer to the trailer, his adrenalin was increasing. He walked up the steps and opened the door to the trailer and walked in.

Thomas' secretary was typing away, as he entered. "Hello Nick," she said.

Nick didn't trust or like her either. He closed the door harder than he normally would and it caught her attention. "Do you know what day this is?" He asked bearing a smile seldom seen.

She glanced up for a brief moment, and answered after she looked back down at her calendar. "No, what day is that?"

He tapped his index finger on her desk and focused directly on her. "This is the happiest day of my life. This is the day I can tell you, and that asshole Thomas, to stick this job up your tight asses."

Her face changed to a dark pink with an uncomfortable feeling of fear and embarrassment settling in. Nick opened the door to Thomas's office and walked in. He was sitting behind his desk and appeared alarmed and annoyed that Nick hadn't been announced and didn't knock on the door.

"Gennaro, what the hell are you doing barging in here without knocking?"

Nick pointed his finger at him with complete disregard. "Shut the fuck up, dick head!" he shouted.

Thomas stood up. "What? Who do you think you're talking to?" His legs seemed a bit weaker.

"An asshole, that's who I'm talking to, I've been taking your shit for four years, but not anymore. You can stick this job up your fat ass. I quit!" Small projectiles of saliva shot out spraying the desk.

"No, you're fired. Now get the hell out of my office, you piece of shit." Thomas said, pointing toward the door.

"Who the hell are you calling a piece of shit? You better watch how you talk to me, or I just might buy this company and fire your ass. You'll be standing in the soup line begging for food." Nick took out a thick stack of one hundred dollar bills and started waving them in the air like a flag. "I just hit the lotto for nine million bucks. Have fun working your fat ass off for the next twenty years. I'll toast to you while I'm sunbathing on my yacht."

Thomas looked at the money, not knowing whether to believe him or not. "I said, get the hell out of here, now!"

"You don't give me orders anymore you fat loser!"

They were both yelling at the top of their lungs and the secretary was standing outside the door listening, and slightly trembling; preparing to call the police.

"What, are you deaf?" Thomas came around from behind his desk grabbing onto Nick's arm. As soon as he put his hands on Nick, it was open season. He did a wide circle over Thomas's arm trapping it. With his other hand he grabbed Thomas by the throat forcing him back and cracking the back of his head against the wall, with a thump that shook the trailer.

The secretary finally opened the door. "Should I call the police?" She called out.

"Yes, he attacked me!" Nick responded."

The struggle continued as Nick had Thomas still pinned against the wall by the throat. With a quick strike, Thomas brought his knee up into Nick's groin. The pain was quickly overcome with rage.

"You son of a bitch!" Nick yelled. Then, with a fierce blow, Nick split Thomas' head open with a head butt, just above his right eye. As Thomas continued to try and break free, Nick released his throat and gave him two fast punches to the face, causing him to fall to the floor. Nick finished with a thunderous kick to the ribs, and then he spit in his face.

"Have a nice day, fat ass." Nick winked at the secretary as he walked past her and out the door. Thomas lay on the floor bleeding and confused over what had just occurred. His confusion turned to embarrassment, as he looked up at his secretary standing over him.

8

It was still dark out when Nicholas turned the key, opening the market door. It was unusual for him to open the store so early in the morning, but he hadn't been able to sleep since his son's body was found. His grief had set in and was converting to anger. Shortly after he opened up, he made coffee and sat down in his office, alone with his thoughts. He thought about Chris and all the good times they shared. He remembered the ball games and fishing trips. He drifted back to Chris' childhood days. He was such a beautiful boy, with a heart of gold.

Nicholas remembered the look on his son's face the day he bought him his first bicycle. It was his fourth birthday and Chris had spent the whole weekend on his new, red bike. He remembered his son's beaming face, as he rode as fast as he could without fear of falling or getting hurt. He could still hear Chris laughing with the wind blowing through his hair as he darted up the street. It seemed like yesterday.

He sat with his face in his hands not realizing that tear drops were falling onto his desk, when the doorbells chimed, indicating someone had just entered the front door to the store. Nicholas wiped his face and hands with a towel and went to see who was up so early.

Franco stood in the doorway looking at Nicholas without saying a word. Time had stopped for a brief moment as they both stood staring into each other's eyes. Franco could see the pain and sorrow Nicholas was suffering to the point where he almost felt it, himself. He walked over and put his arms around his oldest and dearest friend and kissed him on both cheeks.

"Want some coffee?" Nicholas asked.

"Sure."

Nicholas poured a cup for both of them.

"I won't ask how you're doing because I already know the answer to that question. So, what I want to know is, how I can help. What can I do?"

"I want the bastard who killed my son."

"I'll put the word out on the street and see what we can turn up. I'll attach ten grand to it," he said with a nod. "This one's on me."

"No, make it twenty large," he said. "Anyone who comes up with the name of the maggot, who killed my boy, will get twenty thousand in cash."

"Alright, twenty grand it is."

"Franco." Nicholas reached out holding onto his forearm. "I want the son of a bitch brought in to me alive. No hero bullshit. I need to find out if there is more than one person involved, and I want to make sure he is the right guy. Once I confirm who is responsible for Chris's death, then we can pay the money."

"Alright then, I'm on it. Nicholas, what have the cops got?"

"So far, they got shit. I want to find this bastard before they do. I don't want the son of a bitch playing cards and lifting weights in prison, I want him dead. I want him to suffer, do you understand?"

Franco lifted up his coffee cup. "I understand."

***

Not long after the trailer was straightened out, Sam and Donny knocked on the door and walked in.

"Hello, I'm detective Carra and this is detective Burke with the state police." Sam flashed his Badge to the secretary. She was wondering who had called them since her boss told her not to bother calling the police. *Maybe he changed his mind and called himself.*

"Yes, how may I help you?"

"Does Nick Gennaro work for this company?"

She appeared confused "Yes, well not anymore."

"What do you mean, not anymore," Donny was asking this time.

"You better talk to the boss, Mr. Thomas." She picked up the phone and pushed a button.

"Yes." His voice was more agitated than normal.

"Mr. Thomas, the police are here asking about Nick Gennaro."

He hesitated before responding, "Send them in."

She pointed to the door and they knocked before entering, which offered Thomas a sense of comfort. The detectives introduced themselves and took a seat. Donny noticed a few small pieces of a broken coffee cup on the floor. It was the "World's Greatest Golfer" cup that had been knocked over during the struggle.

"Mr. Thomas, your assistant outside said Nick Gennaro used to work for you. What happened, why has his employment here ended?" Sam asked.

"The son of a bitch quit." His face was still stinging. The Tylenol had taken effect, but not entirely.

"Mr. Thomas, does this have anything to do with the bandage above your eye and your fat lip?"

"Yes, he came in here a couple hours ago waving a wad of cash around and told me to stick the job up my ass. He was totally out of line, so I told him to get out, that's when he attacked me. I put up with his nasty attitude way too long. He is always causing problems with the other workers, and he calls in sick and comes in late more than anyone. I gave him a hundred chances and this is how I get repaid." He took out a handkerchief and began dousing his oversized lip.

"Why do you think he was waving a wad of money around?" Sam asked.

"He said he hit the lotto, and that he might buy this company, and fire me," he said. "Like he could buy this company? This kid is crazy, I tell you."

"Did he say how much he won in the lotto?" Donny asked with his pen in the ready position.

"He said nine million. A rumor is floating around that he hit the big game a couple weeks ago, but I don't believe it. I think he's full of shit."

"Do you want to press charges?" Sam asked.

"No, I just don't want that bastard coming around here again. I'll have his personal items boxed and mailed to his home address."

"Are you sure? This is pretty serious, assault and battery." Donny asked

"Yeah, I'm sure."

"Do you know where he went?" Sam asked

"No." He turned away indicating he wanted the conversation to end.

"Do you know where he hangs out, or where might we find him?" Donny asked

"I don't know. Why are you guys looking for him anyway?"

"We just need to ask him a few questions about an unrelated matter. If he contacts you, please give us a call." Sam handed him his card.

"Sure thing." He followed the detectives to the door and they walked out of the trailer, thanking his secretary on the way out.

Donny unlocked the driver side door. "This kid has an anger problem."

"Yes, he does. Do you think there is a chance he hit the lotto?"

"There was one anonymous winner from South Walton. I suppose anything is possible."

"Well, let's see if we can find out who represented this anonymous winner at the lottery commission and have a word with him," Sam suggested.

Donny turned the ignition and put the car into gear. "I saw it on the news this morning when I was at the diner. The lawyer was answering questions about his client. What was his name? I can't think of it, but it was an Italian name."

"Let's make a call to the commission and find out." Sam said.

"Do you think this has anything to do with our case?" Donny asked.

"In nearly all homicide cases, money is usually the root factor. Sometimes it's obvious and sometimes it isn't, but it's almost always the motive behind the crime. So, if our friend hit the lottery, I would say, most definitely it's connected."

"Yeah, what are the chances, one brother ends up murdered and the other wins the lottery for nine million bucks, all in the same weekend?" Donny asked.

"Yeah, what are the chances?" Sam mimicked.

Donny volunteered to make a call to the state lottery commission and he was able to retrieve the name of the lawyer and the store owner without a problem. They immediately drove to Azanaro's office where they approached him as he was preparing to leave. His office was on the third floor of an old building with an enormous brass and oak revolving door in the lobby. It was a gorgeous structure with an old elevator that was run by an operator who stood inside the elevator all day in his blue uniform, starting and stopping the elevator with a long black stick with a brass nob that was protruding from the floor.

"Mr. Azanaro?" Sam called out.

He was walking out the door to go to the bank and deposit the check he received from Nick. Azanaro didn't trust Nick and didn't rule out that he may try and stop payment on it.

"Yes." He looked at the two men and knew right away they were cops. He had dealt with the police on so many occasions that he could spot them in the dark.

"I'm detective Carra, and this is detective Burke with the state police." Donny displayed his ID.

"What can I do for you?" Azanaro asked, appearing disrupted.

"Can we talk inside your office?"

"I was just leaving. I have an appointment."

"Alright then, why don't you meet us at the District Attorney's office downtown Providence after your appointment and we can talk there," Sam said.

He tightened his jaw. "No, I can spare a few minutes. Come in." Azanaro opened his office door, showing them in. His office space was small, cluttered, and should have been declared a disaster area by the state health commission. His secretary was a middle-aged woman with bad hair, yellow teeth and reeking of stale cigarettes.

"It is our understanding that Nick Gennaro is your client and you have represented him at the lottery commission." Donny was asking as if they knew for sure Nick was the lottery winner.

"Well, who told you that?"

"Councilor, did you represent Nick Gennaro this morning at the lottery commission when you were presented a check in the amount of eight point nine million dollars?"

"Hey, I can't divulge that information. My client wishes to remain anonymous."

"Mr. Azanaro," Sam was talking now. "Are you aware that Nick Gennaro's younger brother Christopher was found beaten to death last Saturday?"

"Yes, I read about that in the paper. What a tragedy." His concern appeared less than sincere.

"Yes, it is. We are investigating his murder and it has come to our attention that Nick Gennaro had won the lotto a couple days before his brother's body was discovered. Now, what do you think the chances are that one brother hits a winning ticket for nearly nine million dollars, and the other brother is found floating face down with his head bashed in, all in the same week? Would it occur to you that they might be connected?" Sam asked.

"It's possible, but that's your issue, not mine." His cold demeanor was disturbing to Donny.

"Look, Nick is marching around town with a pocket full of hundred dollar bills bragging that he won the lotto, and that everyone can kiss his rich ass. He will never know you told us anything, and I doubt he cares. Let's be done with this, so you can make your appointment and we can find a killer."

Azanaro thought for a brief moment. He didn't like Nick and he had a strong feeling that Nick was involved in the murder. "Okay, yes, he's my client, Nick won the lottery."

"Do you know where we can find him?" Donny asked.

"No, the last time I saw him, he dropped me off here in a limo."

"Do you know which limo company?"

"No, I'm not sure. Wait, it might be *First Class* limo company. I think I saw a logo on the dashboard."

"Thanks for your help, councilor. We may be in touch, if we have any more questions."

"Hey, do me a favor, don't tell anyone I gave you his name. He is not a stable person and I don't want him coming around here bothering me."

"You have my word." Sam assured him.

Donny had previously contacted the owner of the Quick Mart and asked him to meet them at the store. Kent Bihler had owned the store for six years and had finally sold a big winning ticket. When he received a call from one of his cashiers that the winning ticket was sold at his store, he was very excited, not only because he would collect one percent of the winnings, but, it was free advertisement. Statistics have shown that many people are likely to go to a store to buy lottery tickets where a large winning ticket had been sold, and Bihler knew it.

It was approaching dinnertime and the store was busy with people stopping by on their way home from work. Bihler escorted Sam and Donny to his office in the back, where they both accepted his offer for coffee. Donny had not told Bihler what they were meeting for, because he didn't want anyone disturbing the videotape before they arrived. After an introduction, they sat in the office waiting for Bihler to return. A few minutes later, he came in with two coffees, cream and sugar.

"Detectives, what can I do for you?" Bihler assumed it had to do with two counterfeit twenty-dollar bills that had been passed there a week ago. Bihler was always willing to help the police, especially detectives. He had always wanted to be a cop, but was never able to make it happen. The closest he got was working as a security guard supervisor for a local aquarium. That had been his occupation until he received an inheritance which allowed him to buy the store.

"First, I want to congratulate you on selling the winning lotto ticket here," Sam said.

Bihler's face came to life. "Thanks, it was quite a nice surprise."

"Yes, I'm sure it was," Sam responded.

"Is that why you're here?" Bihler was confused.

"Yes, we would like to have the tape recording that captured the day the ticket was sold. Also, the lottery record indicating what time the winning ticket was purchased," Sam requested.

His smile faded. "May I ask why?"

"We are investigating a homicide, Mr. Bihler, and these items are evidence that may be helpful to our investigation. That is all I can tell you at this time."

Bihler hesitated with a puzzled look on his face before responding. "Sure, anything I can do to help."

"Also, would you provide the names and contact information of all employees that were working on that day?" Sam asked.

"That would mean, names, addresses, and phone numbers," Donny added.

"Certainly, please wait here while I get what you need."

The clock in their office read six thirteen when they arrived. The coffee had given Sam a boost. He felt it would help get him through the rest of the day. The first thing they did was pin down the exact time the winning ticket was sold.

"April 17th, at 8:46 pm," Donny said while reviewing the lottery receipts.

"Okay, let's take a look at the tape." Sam pushed the tape into the VCR and rewinded it to eight-forty. Both men sat in anticipation hoping it was Nick Gennaro, so they would be one step closer to solving the murder and closing another case.

"Right there," Sam said. "Stop the tape!"

"That looks like them," Donny said, with a hint of excitement.

"Yeah, both of them," Sam responded in a low, steady tone.

The tape was paused as the detectives sat watching. Both brothers had entered the store, with Nick entering first and Chris following. Nick was heading directly towards the cashier and his brother in the other direction, toward the cooler.

"Looks like they're in line for the cashier," Donny said.

"Resume playing the tape," Sam commanded. "Right there!" Donny pushed the button stopping the tape. Sam leaned forward. "Back it up a bit."

Donny hit the rewind button. "There it is," Donny said.

"Chris bought the ticket," Sam added, with a feeling of relief, and also a degree of disappointment.

"It looks like Nick handed him something," Donny observed. "I'll play it back."

"Stop, right there," Sam said. "Looks like he handed Chris some pocket change just before Chris bought the ticket. Keep rolling it."

Donny gladly did as he asked. This was one of the more exciting times he had recently.

"Pause it, there!" Sam said.

"There it is. Chris put the ticket in his wallet," Donny declared, as if it were an undisputed victory.

"There's his motive." Sam pointed toward the screen. "Chris had the winning ticket, yet Nick cashed it in, several days after his brother is found murdered."

"Yeah, but it looks like Nick may have pitched in for the ticket," Donny said.

"So, what does that mean, should Nick have only half killed him, or only kept half of the winnings and donated the other half to his brother's favorite charity? It doesn't matter; its murder and we have motive right here."

"You're right. What do you say we contact the cashier and have a talk with her?" Donny asked.

"It can wait until morning." It was apparent to Donny, that Sam was tired by the way he rubbed his eyes and yawned.

"What are we going to tell the family?" Donny asked.

"I wouldn't want to be his father. This will destroy him. I think we should keep this quiet for now. Anyway, let's see what the boss has to say tomorrow." Sam pushed the eject button and the VHS tape came sliding out. He pulled it out and slid it into a plastic zip lock bag and ran his fingers across the smooth surface, listening for the faint snapping sound indicating it was sealed.

Once all the evidence was secured, they walked out to the parking lot. Both cars were parked next to each other. Sam put the key in and turned it, unlocking the door. He stopped and peered over at Donny who was hovering over the roof of his car glaring back at him.

"Sam, how could anyone kill his own flesh and blood for money?"

"Money is the root of all evil, Donny."

Donny hesitated for a brief moment. "If this guy would do this to his brother, what do you think he would do to us?"

"Yeah, or someone else. We better find Nick Gennaro, fast. See you in the morning," Sam said with a wave of his hand.

"Yeah, bright and early," Donny smiled at his partner. "Hey, Sam." The older detective stopped in his tracks. "Its times like this that make me glad you're my partner."

Sam smiled back. "Me too, Donny."

They got in their cars and drove away. Both men were thinking about their accomplishment in the Gennaro case, and both were thinking of how hard this news event was going to be on the family.

9

Sam had taken the day off and Donny drove down to Sunset Marina to meet the divers. They had scheduled the State Police dive team for an underwater grid search. It was eight in the morning, and the four-man-team was on the boat preparing to begin a daylong search effort.

A large designated area surrounding the scene of the murder was blocked off with yellow crime scene tape. It was attached to Buoys surrounding Chris Gennaro's boat, in the event that the killer threw the weapon into the water after committing murder.

Donny watched, as the divers, dressed in hooded wetsuits, secured their equipment. He observed the men as they prepared for the dive in a manner that was routine in nature. They hooked duel tanks up to their BCs, checked the weight belts, and made sure their individual oxygen gages were at three thousand pounds of pressure. Once this was completed, he watched them slip on their flippers and apply the mask cleaning gel to the inside of the lenses. They had already determined in their initial briefing, which teams would search which area. The divers worked in teams of two, because the cardinal rule was to always dive with a buddy. The officers, along with their flashlights and prodding sticks, were now ready to descend into the cold, salty water of the Atlantic Ocean. Stepping off into the water one at a time, each diver held onto his mask, assuring it didn't slip off.

Donny thought to himself that he was overdue in obtaining an open water certification. He watched as the men faded out of sight, leaving behind circles of bubbles. He sat on the back of the boat, while the captain sprawled out behind the wheel, placing his hat over his face, shielding out the daylight in an attempt, to catch some sleep. Donny was hoping the divers would find the murder weapon sitting at the bottom of the ocean floor, so they could wrap up the investigation and move on. As the waves gently rocked the boat back and forth, his thoughts began to calm, and his mind began to drift back to a time in his life he would never forget.

It was nearly four in the afternoon on a beautiful autumn day in Shrewsbury, Massachusetts. It was a week after peak season and the leaves were falling at a faster pace. Donny was in the back yard with rake in hand gathering a huge pile. He and his brother, Tommy, would later roll around in it together as they had ever since Tommy was old enough to walk. It had become a tradition, and the memories had always brought them enormous joy.

His parents were in the house and Tommy was in the driveway riding his new bike. Every few minutes, Donny would peek his head around the corner of the house to make sure his brother was alright. He gave Tommy strict instructions to stay in the driveway.

Donny could hear the sound of a truck in the distance, and it was getting closer, but the house blocked his view. He continued raking, until all of a sudden, he heard the sound of screeching brakes in front of their house. The instant Donny heard the unusual sound; his entire body was overcome with a dreadful feeling. He dropped the rake and ran around to the front of the house. He looked around for his brother, but didn't see him. He began frantically yelling, "Tommy! Tommy, where are you?"

The truck stopped in front of their house, and the driver dressed in a brown uniform got out, appearing shaken and distraught. Donny ran over and heard him mumbling, "I didn't see him. He came out of nowhere. I didn't see him."

Donny's worst fear was realized when he bent over and looked under the UPS truck to find his brother and his new bike completely mangled. A pool of blood began to flow from under the truck. Donny was crying hysterically as he crawled on his belly through Tommy's blood in an effort to pull him out from under the truck. Although it was less than five minutes, to Donny, it seemed like an entire lifetime, that his little brother was underneath the truck. He tried so hard to free his unconscious brother and pull him out, but he couldn't. He was stuck, and all his efforts had failed. The frustration he felt was the worst feeling he had ever encountered. Tommy's motionless body seemed smaller than usual, almost unreal. The blood was everywhere and he felt like he was drowning in it. Donny didn't hear the piercing screams coming from his mother who was standing a few feet away. Everything seemed to be moving in slow motion. He felt as if he was going to vomit, but dismissed that, and focused on saving Tommy. The ambulance had arrived on the scene, but Donny hadn't noticed. He was lying under the truck attempting to wake his brother up and free his arm from the wheel well. Donny cried out, "Somebody, please help me! It's my little brother, please help me!" He never really knew what it felt like to be truly helpless until now, and it was ripping him apart from the inside out. His heart was pounding and his mind racing, as he cried out to his little brother, again and again.

Two emergency medical technicians convinced Donny to crawl out from under the truck. His father, who had also crawled under the truck, guided Donny out in order to make room for the two men. After a few minutes, the EMTs were finally able to get Tommy free and pulled him out. Donny and his parents watched and prayed as they performed CPR on Tommy. One of the men had Tommy's head tilted back, pinching his nose and was blowing breaths of air into his lungs. The other was kneeling over his chest, pushing down with one hand over the other. With a precise counting measure they worked as a team in an attempt to revive him.

The police were taking statements from the driver and a neighbor who had witnessed the accident. The witness stated that Tommy had ridden his bike down his driveway right into the truck's path, as it came rolling down the street.

As police helped the EMTs hoist the stretcher into the ambulance, Donny cried, as he watched them continuing to apply CPR on Tommy. His brother's color was changing to a pale white and his body was flaccid. For the exception of Donny, everyone on the scene figured the boy was dead. Donny wouldn't resign himself to that, he couldn't. This was his baby brother and he loved him more than anything in the world. He kept praying to God to spare his brother. He bargained with God. He would do anything God wanted him to do. He would trade his own life, if necessary. He completely placed all his trust into God. This was his only hope.

Thomas Burke was confirmed dead on arrival, at the hospital, by the attending physician. The news hit the Burke family like a ton of bricks and each reacted in their own individual way. Mrs. Burke fainted, when she saw the approaching doctor. The look on his face told everything. Donny's father attended to his wife while Donny busted through the emergency room door and ran down the street. He didn't stop until his legs gave out. He was in good shape from playing full court basketball, but he didn't run on a regular basis, and never would have thought he could run five miles. When he collapsed into the tree belt, he quietly wept.

The tragic death of his brother changed Donny's outlook on life forever, and had tested his faith. He no longer believed in anything, except the drug that would kill the pain that settled deep inside his core. What seemed to work best for Donny was alcohol, and that became his crutch.

Drinking his way through college was easy for Donny. There was always a party and he was always game. He hooked up with a couple of other guys who had the same thirst as he, and they stumbled through four years of keg parties and final exams.

He was in his senior year when he met Patricia. He was barely passing with a C average and she was soaring with straight As. They met in a psychology class, where the professor paired them up on a project researching serial killers' social and psychological behaviors. Patricia thought Donny was cute, but she sensed that he carried a great burden with him. Something about that attracted her and she found herself drawn to him. After graduation, they decided to move in together. She had a diploma in psychology, and Donny, in criminology. Four months later, she found a job as a school psychologist, while attending night school for a masters' degree. Donny was working as a roofer, but was taking as many tests as possible with local and state law enforcement agencies.

During their courtship, Donny's drinking had tapered off. However, after they moved in together, he began drinking on a regular basis with the guys from work.

Prior to completing graduate school, Patricia decided it was time that she moved on. She had watched Donny fall deeper into the bottle and she knew she couldn't help him. She was tired of watching him drown his life away, and no matter how hard she tried to help pull him out, he just refused to hold on.

The day Patricia moved out, Donny fell into a hole and didn't climb out until he hit bottom six months later. Patricia was his first love and he adored her immensely. Donny scraped up all the money he could muster and bought her a diamond ring in a desperate attempt to propose and win her back, but it was too late, she was already gone.

A couple months later, he showed up for work intoxicated, lost his balance on top of a three-story house and fell thirty-five feet, landing on the asphalt. Lucky for him, he landed on his head or the fall may have killed him. Donny spent three weeks in the hospital recovering from a fractured skull, collarbone, arm and wrist. He also dislocated his shoulder and suffered internal injuries. For the first four days, it was a 'touch and go' situation. He almost died, and since he didn't have a desire to live, recovering was that much more difficult.

As he lay asleep in the hospital bed, his brother Tommy came to him. He took Donny's hand and assured him he was fine and that it wasn't anyone's fault that he had died. He told Donny that it was his time to go, and that he was now in a beautiful and peaceful place. He asked Donny to let go of his anger and to keep his faith in God-and stop destroying himself. Tommy told Donny he was destined to do good things with his life. He asked him to smile and roll through the leaves, once again. Tommy kissed Donny on the cheek, waving goodbye as he faded away. Donny woke up with tears in his eyes. They were tears of joy.

10

It was pre-season, yet the streets of Newport, Rhode Island were busy with people shopping, and most restaurants were nearly full as people were enjoying lunch on a cool, sunny day.

The last time Nick was there, he could barely afford an imported beer and a decent meatloaf dinner. Now he was on top of the world. He could buy anything he wanted. It was nearly 1:00 pm and Nick was already drunk. He and his bar buddy, Paul Zollo, had been drinking since eight in the morning.

Zollo, was an iron worker by trade. His career was cut short when he was hit by a four thousand pound steel girder being lowered by a boom at a commercial construction site. The tremendous weight of the impact fractured his third and fourth vertebrae rendering him unable to continue physical labor. The accident had added a permanent limp and his frame appeared to tilt to the left when he walked. He was tall and lanky with a thin face and a pointed nose with a noticeable lump at the base. His black hair was tightly pulled against his head forming a small ponytail at the base of his skull.

With the help of a good attorney, he was deemed physically disabled and was awarded social security benefits. The amount of money Zollo was receiving from social security didn't amount to very much, but it was enough for him to survive, and continue his daily consumption of black label draught beer at the local watering holes. For extra money, he occasionally worked under the table helping a local drinking buddy with interior house painting.

Nick had chosen Zollo to bounce around with, because he knew Zollo had no other commitments and he could tolerate him, at least for a short period of time. Zollo still lived at home with his elderly father and didn't have a girlfriend or any hobbies that would interfere with his ability to go on a bender with Nick. The only surviving family member was an older brother that he hadn't seen in eight years. His brother, Ray, lived in Nevada with his wife and three children and was completely detached from Zollo and his father.

"Let's hit the Brick Alley Pub," Nick commanded as they stumbled down Thames Street. Zollo was thrilled that Nick chose him to pal around with. He was drinking top shelf and never had to reach into his pocket once. Nick had booked two rooms at the Viking hotel, and he went all out, requesting the best suite in the establishment. For Zollo, he booked the cheapest room available.

"Load up the bar, on me!" Nick shouted, so everyone could hear. "I'll have a blue label scotch and give my assistant whatever he needs." Nick smirked at Zollo who ordered a shot of Jack Daniels and a Sam Adams chaser; he raised his glass and toasted with his friend. "Here's to being one rich motherfucker," Nick barked out.

Nick squeezed Zollo by the side of his neck. "Let's hit the pisser and do a blast," They walked to the men's room and crowded into a stall. Nick pulled out a vial from his pocket and they each snorted four hits of coke. As they were filling their noses, the men's room door opened. They stood quietly listening as someone entered the bathroom. Nick put the vile back into his pocket and pushed open the stall door and they filed out. A young man about twenty-five was standing in front of the urinal doing his business. He glanced at Nick as they walked past.

"What the fuck are you looking at, are you some kind of faggot? Nick roared.

"I'm not the one coming out of the toilet with another guy," he smugly responded.

"Yeah, well you will be going in the toilet, head first." Nick threw a sucker punch hitting the guy in the jaw, knocking him to the ground, and then came the boot to his ribs. While the young man lay on the floor gasping for air, Nick kicked him once again, completely knocking the wind out of him.

"Who's the faggot now?" Nick asked as he dragged him into the stall and shoved his face into the toilet and flushing it.

"Come on Nick! Let's get out of here before you kill him," Zollo called out in a panic. He proceeded to grab Nick's arm. "Easy Nick, let's go man."

Nick kicked the man one more time before walking out. They went back to the bar and ordered another drink. A few minutes later, a commotion started near the rest rooms and they knew what that meant. Nick and Zollo watched as two guys helped walk the beaten man out of the men's room. The manager quickly went over to investigate what was happening.

"I think it's time to move on," Nick said with a huge grin across his face. They finished their drinks and headed for the door, leaving behind a disturbed establishment.

As the two drunks walked down the street, Nick never felt more alive. He loved the way he felt after beating people senseless. It gave him a sense of pride and power. Nick carried an internal anger that stemmed from his father's disappointment with him. The way his father looked at him was clearly a look of discontent and disgust. He used to watch his father with Chris and he was jealous. His father's eyes would light up when he interacted with his younger brother. As his father turned toward him the light in his eyes dimmed.

They came upon the common where a life size green statue of an organ grinder and his monkey stood erect. Nick strolled over, standing in front of it, just staring in silence. Then, he proceeded to the slap the face of the statue.

"What are you looking at bitch?" Nick shouted out. "This is my town, so take your filthy monkey and hit the road."

Zollo busted out laughing and Nick followed. People were walking by watching, yet avoiding them, as the two drunkards carried on.

"Let's go to the store. I want to buy a something nice," Nick said.

They continued down the street until they came to The Platinum House Jewelry Store. Ten minutes later, Nick walked out wearing a two-carat diamond ring.

"Not bad for ten grand, huh? Nick asked.

"It's real nice, Nick, real nice," Zollo responded wishing it were on his finger.

"All that shopping has made me thirsty, let's get a drink," Nick suggested. And they continued walking down the street in search of the next bar without a care in the world.

11

Dennis Brewster sat at the end of the bar. With eight glasses of bourbon under his belt, his head was beginning to get numb, and that was just the way he liked it. He was known to go off when he drank too much, so he sat alone at The Caprice Bar and Restaurant as he had on many occasions. Anyone who knew him avoided him when he was drunk.

The chip on his shoulder grew heavier as time passed, and he knew eventually it would sink him. The reality was he would always be a soldier, and would never have a chance at becoming a made guy. He was only half Italian, and he cursed the other half, rarely admitting he was part French and Irish. Every time he saw another soldier in the family get his stripes, it made him envious, knowing he would never get that chance, just because he wasn't a pure blood Italian.

Although Dennis was respected for his ability to crack heads, he was always just a good kid to the elite wise guys. Everyone in the family knew they could count on Dennis to get the job done, no matter what the task entailed. He had killed twice as many people as most *made* guys and he was proud of it. Standing six-foot-two and weighing two hundred and forty pounds, he wasn't afraid of too many people; but many feared him.

The front door opened, and out of the corner of his eye, Dennis saw that it was one of his runners. He walked up to Dennis like the cowardly lion approaching Oz. "Hey Dennis, how's it going?"

He emptied his glass with one large gulp. "What are you, my fucking shrink, what have you got?" Dennis would just as easily throw him a backhand, then speak to him, and Tom Shea knew it. He was smart enough to keep an arm's distance away, when Dennis was drinking.

Tom took his hands out of his pockets. It was an unconscious defense motion. "There's still no word on the street about who whacked the kid."

Dennis spun around in the stool and looked at him for the first time. "Then why the hell are you here?"

"Because there's something else: The kid has an older brother, and he's been sporting around town with a pocket full of cash."

"Get to the point!" Dennis roared.

"Word on the street is that he hit the big lotto game last week for nine million bucks and that maybe the ticket belonged to his dead brother."

"Is that right?" Dennis sat up straight thinking for a moment, before picking up a fifty off the bar and handing it to Tom. "See what else you can find out."

"Okay Dennis, thanks." Tom Shea scurried back out the way he came in, with the fifty clutched tight in his hand.

Dennis ordered a glass of water realizing he had to clear his head before he made the call to Franco. He had seen Nicky the Butcher in action the night he chopped off Walker's hand with a cleaver, and he knew how passionate Nicholas was about his family. *If what Tom heard on the street is true, how will Nicholas take the news?*

Dennis grew up without a father and had no children of his own, so, he had a hard time understanding what a father might do in such a situation. His mind wandered back to his days growing up in Boston. He was the neighborhood bully. Most of the other kids had fathers to toss a ball around with, or visit the park together. Dennis was jealous of them, and he carried an emptiness inside, a void that his mother alone couldn't fill. The emptiness sometimes turned to rage, and he sought attention by beating other kids into oblivion. His mother was a bartender in a strip club, and when things got tight, she would turn tricks to support her heroin habit. Many times, Dennis would come home to an empty apartment and refrigerator. He had no choice but to resort to stealing, and eventually, he became very good at it. He would shoplift food from the grocery store, and break into cars for change. Occasionally, he'd get lucky and lift a nice set of golf clubs that he could sell on the street. As he grew older, he moved from cars to houses, and eventually, jewelry stores.

After dropping out of school, Dennis took a job running for Jake Reaman, a local Irish mobster. He was small time, but it gave Dennis his start into a career of crime. One day his boss was found in the trunk of a stolen car with four bullets in the back of his head, Dennis realized it was time to move on. He never really liked his boss, and felt no remorse when he heard the news.

A couple weeks later, he was approached by one of Reaman's associates who told him about a job in Providence, and that is where he met Franco. After taking one look into Dennis's eyes, Franco knew he had something special – something he had only seen a few times in his life. It was the same look he saw in the eyes of his very close friend, Nicholas Gennaro.

Dennis chugged down his water and quickly went to the phone booth to call Franco. Fifteen minutes later, they met in a parking lot down the street from the bar. Franco was alone, pulling up in his new Lincoln Town Car. They both got out of their cars and walked toward each other, as they had a hundred times before.

"It better be good," Franco said, appearing somewhat irritated.

"Sorry to call you this late, but I thought you'd want to hear this right away." Dennis told him what he heard from Tom and then stopped talking.

Franco pointed his gloved finger at Dennis and spoke with conviction. "I want you to get out there and find Nick. I want you to find out the truth, and I want it done yesterday. Holy mother of God, if this is true, it will kill Nicholas. You don't breathe a word of this to anyone, understand? Break heads if you have to, but I want the truth," he said, rubbing his chin with the soft leather. "I read about the lottery win in the paper. The winner is anonymous, but the storeowner must know who won. Pay him a visit, and find Nick Gennaro."

"You got it," Dennis replied.

Franco turned and started toward his running car, then abruptly stopped and turned. "As soon as you hear something, anything, you call me."

"Okay, Franco." Dennis watched as Franco got into his car and sped off. Dennis went back to the bar to strategize his plan over several more glasses of bourbon.

The next morning came with a serious headache. The three glasses of water and four aspirins he took before passing out on his couch, did little to help the hangover–Dennis was suffering. He had a light breakfast and went to the gym where he attempted to sweat out the booze in the steam room. After leaving the gym, he made a few calls and every conversation was the same, find Nick Gennaro. He pulled up to the quick mart and popped a piece of gum into his mouth. He reached under his seat and took out his Smith & Wesson 38 revolver and tucked it in his lower back waistline. He entered the store dressed in a well-tailored Italian made suit. Dennis was a tall, rugged, yet fairly handsome man. Women were attracted to him because he had the Clint Eastwood look. People looked at him and wondered, who was he and where was he going.

"Good morning," Dennis said with a slight smile.

"Hello," the young girl behind the register responded with a smile of her own.

"Is the owner of the store around?"

"Yes, he's in the back. Who should I say is asking?"

"You can tell him Mr. Smith from the lottery commission."

"Oh!" She responded, thinking her boss would be happy to hear that. "I'll let him know." She went into the back room and less than a minute later she returned with Bihler riding her heels.

"Hello," Bihler said, extending his hand. "You're from the lottery commission?"

"Yes, I'm John Smith." He shook Bihler's hand. "Can we speak in private?"

"Certainly, please come into my office." Dennis followed him into the small office in the back.

"Please sit down," Bihler motioned toward a chair.

"I'd rather stand." Dennis stared directly into his eyes.

Bihler found himself drawn to his eyes, they seemed empty–dead. "You're not from the lottery commission, are you?"

"No. I'm going to ask you a question, and you are going to answer truthfully and to the point. Who won the big lottery game last week?"

"I can't tell you that, now please leave."

"Wrong answer," Dennis had noticed when entering the office, an old paper cutter with a large blade and a wooden handle fastened at the end. Dennis threw a right hand uppercut that penetrated Bihler's less than firm abdomen, causing him to buckle over and knocking the wind out of him. Dennis walked over, closed the office door, grabbing Bihler by the hair and dragging him to the paper cutter. Bihler resisted as Dennis tried to pull his hand to the cutter. Another blow to the stomach, and Bihler was once again submissive, making wheezing noises as he tried to find air. With one hand holding Bihler's fingers under the blade and the other holding the handle, Dennis asked him once again. "Who won the lottery?"

"It was Nick Gennaro!" He gasped the words out.

"Thank you. That wasn't so hard, was it?" Dennis released his hand. "Now tell me, was he the only winner?"

"Yes." He answered from a fetal position.

"Did he buy the ticket alone or was there someone else with him? I saw your camera, so you must know."

Bihler hesitated, until he was able to breathe normally.

"Shall we pay another visit to the paper cutter?"

"No, his brother was with him. I told the cops everything."

"Where is the tape?"

"The cops took it." Dennis glared at him with dark eyes. "I swear, they came here and took it for evidence."

"I believe you." Dennis helped him back on to his feet. "If you tell the police I was here, I'll be back, and you'll be counting your receivables with stubs. Do you understand?"

"Yes, completely." His shaky voice was proof enough.

Dennis helped straightened out Bihler's jacket and gave him two pats on the shoulder. He exited the office content, knowing he had gotten the information he sought. He walked past the girl behind the register offering a smile and a wink. He got back into his car, picked up his mobile phone, and once again dialed Franco's number.

12

Sam sat at his kitchen table staring at the yellow wallpaper with the big light green flowers. His coffee was cooling and his stomach was beyond full. His wife, Susan, sat across the table with her hair up, wearing a pink robe. As most mornings, she was absorbed in a tabloid magazine.

"Can you believe this? Jack Nicholson has dumped another one and was seen in Hawaii with Sara Goodman."

"Yeah, isn't that unusual in Hollywood?" Sam asked in a sarcastic tone.

"Say what you like, but they certainly don't lead boring lives in Hollywood."

"No, and that explains why they spend millions on therapists, because they are so content and happy with their lives."

"Well at least they don't have to worry about money, or if they will be able to take a real vacation this year," she said, before licking her finger and turning the page.

"And money is the answer to happiness, right?"

Sam's beeper started ringing and he was glad. He didn't want the conversation to continue any longer. He had the same talk with his wife several times in the past, and knew there was no point in reliving it again.

Sam read Donny's number on his device, so he went to the phone and dialed. "Good morning Donny."

"Hey Sam, Vic LaBelle from crime prevention just called, they have another rape victim."

"Damned, not another." He got up and walked out of the kitchen with his portable phone and coffee.

"I'm afraid so. I told him we would be right over."

He took a sip from his coffee "Where is she?"

"Mercy Hospital."

"Alright, I'll meet you at the office and we'll ride over together." He hung up and brought his cup to the sink, rinsed it out, and put it in the dishwasher. His wife sat reading, oblivious to anything around her.

"I have to go." Sam kissed her on the forehead.

"Good bye," she muttered, not bothering to look up.

He stopped at the doorway, turning to look at his wife, wondering who she had become.

***

The dining room at Marco's restaurant was dimly lit with murals of several Italian cities painted across the interior walls. The wall Nicholas was facing, exhibited the coliseum spread out, making it look exceptionally wider than he remembered. The wall behind him was a poor attempt at capturing the Vatican as it had appeared many years earlier to the very old and partially blind painter.

He sat in wait for Franco with a glass of red wine, which was nearly finished. Franco had called Nicholas asking him to meet, stating that he had news about Christopher's death. Neither of them mentioned having dinner, which was unusual. Franco assumed Nicholas wouldn't be hungry after he delivered what he was going to tell him.

Franco arrived six minutes after Nicholas had taken his seat. He was dressed in a dark blue pinstriped suit and a dark red tie with tiny dark blue specks. One could see their reflection off his black wing tipped shoes. His stomach had expanded and his shoulders had decreased and rounded with time. His frosted hair was neatly tucked under his black brimmed hat. He wore a gold watch and a two-carat diamond ring on the opposite hand.

Nicholas sat watching him as he approached, feeling underdressed. He straightened out his golf shirt collar under his jacket and stood to embrace his friend.

"Have a seat." Nicholas said, motioning to the waiter, who came right over. He was an odd-looking character who could have won first place in a Groucho Marx look-a-like contest.

"Scotch on the rocks," Franco ordered.

Nicholas studied his friend, anxious to hear the urgent news. "I'll have another wine," he said.

"Yes sir, right away," The waiter nodded his head respectfully and took three steps back before turning and heading toward the bar.

"Nicky, what I have to say is not good news, but I don't want you to be hasty and jump to any conclusions until we find out the whole story."

"What is it Franco?" It was apparent to Franco that Nicholas was impatient. When he was anxious he tended to rub his palms together.

"It's about Nick. It seems he won the big game a couple weeks ago."

A surprised and confusing look changed the shape of his face. "What? The nine million dollar ticket that was sold at the neighborhood quick mart?"

"That's right. Nick was the winner," Franco hesitated before continuing. "Nicky, we can't find him. The last time he was spotted, he was bouncing around town throwing cash at everyone."

"There's more isn't there?" Nicholas asked.

Franco's face also took a different form. "Yes, the ticket was actually sold to Chris. Nick was with him when he bought it, but Chris never had the chance to cash it in."

Nicholas didn't respond as the information began to set in. He sat in silence looking across the table at the messenger, and could feel a nauseous pain in the pit of his stomach beginning to take hold. His temperature began to rise and a heat flash set in pushing water from his pours. Nicholas' mind was racing as he began to understand the magnitude of the situation. He started to think of his wife and daughters and how the news would affect them. He wanted to get his hands around Nick's throat and choke the truth out of him. Yet, he also hoped it was just a coincidence and that Christopher's death had nothing to do with Nick winning the lottery. His mind began drifting as he thought about his dead boy, and how he wanted him back.

"Nicky, are you alright?"

Nicholas sat looking at Franco with a blank stare as if he had just undergone a lobotomy.

"Nicky!" He reached out patting his friend on the back of his hand.

His friend instantly snapped out of it, like a person waking up from a bad dream. "Yeah, I'm alright." His reality set in as things became clear again.

"What else can I do for you? Tell me and it's done."

He looked into Franco's eyes and knew he meant it. "Help me find Nick and bring him to me."

Franco squeezed the back of his hand. "I'll find him. You just take it easy. Your family needs you now. I'll find him."

"Thanks, Franco. I appreciate all you do."

"Hey, you are like a brother to me. It's my pleasure, besides, you would do the same for me, right?"

"Without question," Nicholas responded. "I have to go. Thanks again."

They both stood and embraced each other. Nicholas walked out and Franco sat down to his scotch. When Nicholas reached his car, he got in and before he could turn the key, he broke down in tears. Deep inside, he felt Nick was somehow involved in the death of Chris.

Franco was on his third drink when Dennis joined him at his table. Unlike Nicholas, they greeted each other with a handshake. They each respected the other, but for very different reasons. Franco respected Dennis' ability to get things done when he asked, and Dennis respected Franco because he was a captain in the Patriarca family. Franco always treated Dennis fairly and with respect, and that meant everything to Dennis. And for this, he would kill for Franco, without question.

"Any word on our friend's whereabouts?"

"Not yet, still looking," Dennis answered with reluctance.

"When we find him, he is to be treated with respect, you understand?"

"Absolutely."

Franco nodded his head slightly. "Is everything all set for tomorrow night?"

"Yes, everything is in place."

"Make sure there are no mistakes. I don't want any of our guys hit. Gunshot wounds bring attention."

"We will be careful. I have a plan in place, so things will go smoothly."

"Good. This is a big score. We can all do very well on this."

A smile sprouted on Franco's face and Dennis was nodding his head.

"Yes, we can."

"Alright then, good luck."

"Thanks," he said to Franco even though he didn't believe in luck. Dennis believed everything that happened to him was a direct result of his actions and nothing more.

They shook hands and both walked out acknowledging people they knew as they passed the bar. Wherever they went, they were treated like royalty, and that was very easy to get accustomed to.

The black van had been stolen just thirty minutes earlier. The plates were changed in case the van was discovered missing and reported. Dennis figured the police would be looking for the plate that matched the van, so it was an extra precaution. One of Dennis' guys walked the long-term parking lot at Kennedy airport, and within fifteen minutes, he found just what they were looking for. The Van was dark in color and had very little dust on it, which meant it hadn't been sitting for more than a day or two. Dennis and three of his guys sat in waiting and double checking to make sure their weapons were locked and loaded. Two of them had sawed off twelve gauge shotguns, and the other two, including Dennis, carried forty-five automatics. Each had some type of a disguise, whether it was a hat or dark sunglasses. One of his men had a fake mustache which he had stolen from a props table on a movie set in New York City. He boasted about the story while they sat in the van preparing to make their move. Dennis was one of two men that had a gold badge hanging from a chain around his neck. He didn't bother to tell the story about how he obtained the authentic police badges.

"Everyone ready?" Dennis called out, like a platoon sergeant leading his men into battle. They all acknowledged him. "Remember, we move fast and no gunshots."

The four men exited the van and moved in a quick shuffle toward the building. They marched up the stairs with Dennis leading the way. When they reached the third floor of the building, Dennis motioned for them to slow down. They quietly scaled the wall in single file with their weapons in the ready position. Once in front of the door to the apartment, Dennis counted in a low whisper, extending a finger with each number. He moved aside, and when he said the number three, one of his men swung the battering ram, knocking the door open with one crashing blow.

"Police!" Dennis yelled, as they stormed in with their guns held high, looking like professional lawmen.

The three men inside the apartment didn't know what hit them. Two of them sat at a table that was situated in the center of the room. They were weighing heroin on a scale and making quarter ounce packages to sell to street dealers. The third guy was sitting on a couch in the corner of the room watching television. As they hit the room, he started moving his hand under the couch cushion where his piece had mistakenly fallen. Dennis was on top of him in seconds. Before he could get a hold of his weapon, Dennis hit him on the left side of the head with the barrel of his forty-five, causing him to see stars and fall back onto the couch in pain. The two men at the table were thrown to the ground, and cuffed with their hands behind their back.

"You aint no mother fuckin Five O," the man on the couch yelled, while holding onto the side of his head, as it began to swell up. "If you was, you wouldn't be wearing no surgical gloves, motherfucker."

Dennis reached out grabbing him by the throat. "We wear gloves, so we don't contract any diseases from your black asses. Now, where's the money?" Dennis placed his piece against the drug dealer's temple and cocked back the hammer.

"See, I told you, they ain't no cops," he said in a calmer voice.

"Okay, smartass. Let's see if you can fly. Dennis cuffed his hands behind his back, and led him to the open window. "Grab his other foot," he commanded one of his guys. They lowered him out the window as he cried out, begging them to pull him back in. Both men struggled to hold onto the man hanging out of the window upside down.

"I'm going to count to three, and then we drop you. You will find it very difficult to break your fall with your hands cuffed behind your back. Where's the money? One, two," before the third count he yelled out, "It's in my bedroom, in a box in the closet!"

Dennis looked at one of his men. "Jackie, check it out," and he headed to the bedroom as he was told.

Less than ten seconds later, Jackie called out from the bedroom. "I got it Dennis. I found the money."

"No shit!" Dennis said just before letting go of the guy's foot. He turned and smiled at Shawn, who couldn't carry the weight by himself. Shawn held on for two seconds before releasing him. They all stood listening to the short scream, followed by a thud. "I guess he can't fly."

They all started laughing. The two cuffed guys on the ground were both trembling, praying they weren't next.

Dennis took a quick peek into the big, heavy box. It was filled with stacks of nicely packaged ten and twenty dollar bills. "Grab the dope," he ordered, and his men quickly started filling a bag with the heroin. A couple minutes later, they were finished, and Dennis ordered his men to the van. Once they all cleared the room, Dennis took one last look around to make sure they didn't leave anything behind, and then he abruptly stopped before walking out. He towered over the two men lying on the floor. Both were looking at him square in the eye. He was holding the shiny gun in his hand, and the drug dealers feared they were going to die, right there on the floor. Dennis raised his weapon and leveled it at one of the terrified men; he cocked back the hammer and hesitated as the man closed his eyes, avoiding witnessing his own fate. "Bang!" Dennis yelled. Both men jumped at the sound and Dennis started laughing. "You two better look for a new line of work." He smiled, winked at them and walked out, closing the door behind him.

13

It has been said, that when a parent suddenly loses a child, the grieving ends only when they, themselves, are planted into the earth. Every parent deals with the anguish in their own unique and personal way. It's also true that for any parent of sound mind, there is no greater love, than that of a parent for their child.

Maria Gennaro was coping with the loss of her son by gravitating towards her living children. She kept herself occupied by involving herself in their everyday lives. Her appreciation for them was stronger than it had ever been, *now*. She avoided being alone, because her thoughts would catch up to her, and she would experience the deep, nagging inner pain that consumed her whole being. The fond memories of Christopher would come to haunt her and she would break down in a fountain of tears and misery.

With one son departed, she needed to keep her remaining son close to her, so she could protect him. In her eyes, he was a good boy. She knew he had his troubles growing up, but deep down she believed he was good, and she loved him unconditionally. Nick's absence was weighing on her, and she couldn't understand why he hadn't come to visit, or at least called her.

Standing in front of the mirror, she attempted to apply eye makeup. It was a task that took much longer than usual, because her tears kept pushing the black eyeliner down her cheeks, creating a gothic appearance. She stopped to sit for a moment to gain her composure, when the phone rang. She was going to let it ring until the answering machine kicked in, but something told her to get up.

She cleared her throat. "Hello."

"Mom. It's Nick, how are you doing?"

She remained silent while processing his voice. "Nicholas?" She answered with a surprised tone.

"It's me, Mom." He sounded full of energy and enthusiasm, as he did when he was a child

"Nicholas, where are you?"

"I'm in Newport, Mom. There is something I got to tell you."

"What, honey?"

"I hit the lottery for nine million bucks."

She could hear the excitement in his voice. "Stop kidding, Nicholas."

"I'm serious, Mom. Did you read about the winning ticket being sold at the Quick Mart in town?"

She thought for a few seconds before responding in a low tone of voice. "Yes."

"That was me, I won." The phone went silent. "Mom, are you there?"

"Are you serious?" she asked.

"Yes, I'm rich Mom, and I bought you something really nice."

"Nicholas, I don't want you to buy me anything. I just want you to come home."

"I will Mom. I'll come over this week and see you. Wait till you see what I bought you. I have to go. I'll see you soon. I love you, Mom."

Before she could speak, the phone went dead. Once again, she sat down, and began to process what she had just heard. She was happy he called and relieved that he was alive and well, yet concerned that if he did hit the lottery, it might change him for the worst.

Back in front of the mirror, the task of putting on her makeup resumed without disruption. She looked at her reflection, wondering when all the lines on her face had come to life. Maria was pleased with her recent weight loss. Since Christopher's death, her appetite had subsided and eventually her clothes began to hang off her body. Nicholas kept pushing food on her, but she rejected it, like a deadly poison. She could tell by the look on his face, he was extremely concerned, but what could she do? She was seldom hungry.

In her closet, she pushed through her clothes searching for something that would fit. Finally, an outfit that had been hanging there for several years caught her eye. She pulled it out, took off the plastic-wrap and put it on. It fit like a glove. She forced out a smile and found matching shoes.

***

Nicholas was behind the counter ringing up a customer, when Maria entered the store. He glanced over as she walked in, thinking how wonderful she looked. Over the past ten years, she had gained about forty pounds and in a matter of weeks, it was nearly gone. She was an attractive woman with jet black hair and walnut eyes. The loss of weight had brought back the curves that had captured Nicholas' attention many years earlier. He was pleased with the way she looked, but knew it was for all the wrong reasons. He was worried she was on the edge of a breakdown and resigned himself to remaining strong for the family.

"Hey Babe, what brings you here?" He came around the counter and kissed her on the cheek.

"Nick called." She said with a bright smile.

He stopped what he was doing. "What, when?" He asked with less excitement.

"About a half hour ago. He told me he won the lotto. I think he was serious."

"Did he say where he was?"

"Yes, he's in Newport. He said he bought me something nice." Nicholas went silent as he was absorbed in thought. "Did you know anything about him winning the lottery?"

"I heard something to that effect, but I wasn't sure it was true."

Her face was showing life as she continued. "He said he's coming to see us this week."

"When?" Nicholas was thinking he would avoid him, if possible.

"I don't know, he said this week, sometime."

Nicholas went back on the other side of the counter to assist a customer. "Where are you going all dressed up?"

"I'm going to the store to get some clothes. All my clothes are getting too big, they don't fit anymore."

"The clothes aren't getting to big, you're getting too thin," Nicholas responded.

"Yeah, that's what I meant. I'll see you later." She leaned over the counter and he kissed her.

"Okay, I'll see you tonight."

He watched her leave. Then he finished packaging meat for his customer and rang him up. He walked the customer out, locking the door behind him. He put up a sign that read, be back in five minutes and he started toward his office. As he made his way past the register, he stopped to look at an array of family pictures that hung framed on the wall at the end of the counter. He found himself focusing on a photograph of him and his son. Nick was wearing a cap and gown, but unlike most kids graduating from high school, he wasn't smiling. He thought about how happy he was on that day, and how proud he felt. He reached out and removed the picture from the wall, leaving behind a clean square space. He continued into his office, threw the picture into the trash can and picked up the phone and called Franco.

14

The bar was unusually busy for such an early time of the day. A crowd of people had gathered around Nick, as he continued to set the bar up with drinks. He and Zollo had been on a drinking and eating binge for nearly two weeks. Wherever they went, Nick would buy the bar a round. He soaked up the attention like a kid hitting his first home run.

"Give us another round here," Nick ordered. The bartender hopped to it. "Get me a different drink this time. I've had enough beer."

"What can I get you sir?" The young bartender asked.

"Let me get Chopin vodka and tonic, no fruit." The bartender went off to his shiny bottles. When he returned with the round of drinks, Nick immediately noticed the lime floating at the top of his glass. His smile faded to a frown and he slid the glass down the bar nearly knocking it over. "Hey, what are you stupid? I said no fruit."

"Sir, there is no reason for you to talk to me like that." It was apparent he had a proper upbringing, possessing an Ivy League demeanor.

"Fuck you. I ordered a drink and you fucked it up."

The bartender leaned forward resting his hands on the bar, responding in a firm voice. "Sir, I'm going to have to ask you to leave."

"You're asking me to leave? Do you know how much money I've spent in this shit hole?" The crowd that had gathered around for free drinks had now dispersed and Zollo was the only one standing near Nick.

"Let's get out of here, Nick," Zollo pleaded.

"Yeah, to hell with this asshole."

The bartender's complexion was changing as he placed the check on the bar in front of Nick.

"I'm not paying this. You're throwing me out. Stick it up your ass."

"If you don't pay the check, I'll call the police and have you arrested for larceny."

"Well, listen to Perry fucking Mason." Nick was looking directly into the bartender's eyes like a bull staring at the matador.

"Nick, just pay him and let's go," Zollo begged.

Nick counted out three one-hundred-dollar bills on the bar and then another twenty-three covering the exact amount on the bill. When he was finished, he slapped a nickel down on the bar. "Here's your tip dickhead."

"Don't even think about coming back in here. You're barred."

"Fuck you. I'll come back anytime I want. And you better hope I don't see you on the street," Nick added, as he and Zollo strutted toward the exit. As they spilled onto the street, Nick turned to look at the establishment they had just terrorized.

"The Cookie House. What kind of a name is that for a bar? I think I'll buy this place and shit-can that punk-ass bartender. The second thing I'll do is change the name. I'll call it, *The Pour House*." He shot his middle finger into the air adding closure to the ordeal.

As they walked up the street, Nick started chasing a flock of pigeons, trying to kick them. The birds flew away without injury and the two drunkards continued walking in search of the next bar.

In the gallery across the street, two well-dressed men stood watching, through the window as Nick and Zollo made their way up the street. Once they were a distance away, the two men exited the gallery and followed behind. They were in their early thirties, well-built and standing over six feet tall. Both were wearing dark two -piece suits with cuffed pants draped over shiny black shoes. Their overall appearance made people step aside as they walked passed. Both men were carrying handguns concealed behind their jackets, and they were prepared to use them, if necessary.

Nick and Zollo found another hangout at the Mooring Restaurant that overlooked the water, a block west of the Cookie House. Nick went into the men's room and was in the stall snorting coke, when he heard someone enter the room. He took one last sniff and flushed the toilet. When he opened the stall door, the two men in suits were waiting for him.

"Nick Gennaro?" The taller of the two asked.

"Yeah, what do you want?"

"I'm detective Rondo and my partner Detective Nester with the Rhode Island State Police. We would like you to come with us."

Nick's tough guy demeanor instantly changed. "For what, I haven't done anything wrong. That bartender was an asshole."

"This isn't about a bartender. This is in regard to your brother, Christopher. We have been looking for you for quite some time. There are a few unanswered questions. It shouldn't take too long." The detective motioned toward the door.

Nick stopped in his tracks. "Are you arresting me?"

"No, we just need your help in solving your brother's murder. Don't you want the person responsible brought to justice?"

"No, I want him dead. I'd kill him myself, if I knew who it was."

Detective Rondo looked at his partner, then back at Nick.

"We appreciate your cooperation. This has to be done. Why not just get it over with. You can be back here in a few hours drinking with your pal."

"I'm busy right now. Why don't you make an appointment with my helper and I'll consider coming down next week." Nick tried passing through them, but was stopped in his tracks by Rondo who grabbed onto his shirt, pinning him against the wall.

"How about we go through your pockets and see what you've been doing in the stall."

Nick had a quick change of heart. "Okay, where are we going?"

"We'll drive you to our office in Providence and drop you off when we're done."

"I'll go with you, but I'll take a limo back. Just let me tell my friend at the bar."

"Okay, I'll follow you to the bar and my partner will bring the car around," the taller detective said. Nick agreed with a short nod of his head and they moved out of the men's room.

A few minutes later, they escorted Nick to the awaiting unmarked police car. He thought about how he would hire a bodyguard or two, when he was done. He didn't want to be bothered anymore, and certainly not snuck up on, while he was having a good time. He figured the cops were harassing him because he was a millionaire. *They have nothing that could tie me to Chris's murder. I'm innocent and they are on a fishing expedition.*

Rondo and Nester were standing outside the interview room watching Nick through the two-way mirror, as he sat impatiently waiting.

"Now, there's a guy who is really in pain with grief over his brother's death," Nester said.

"Yeah, the only thing on his mind is getting back to the bar and continuing the party."

"Do you think he did it?"

"I have never been surer of anything in my life," Rondo replied. They were joined by Sam and Donny who stormed in as if they had just hit the lottery.

"Where did you find him?" Donny reached out shaking hands with the two men and Sam did the same.

"In Newport, drinking and doing drugs in the men's room at a bar," Rondo said, shaking his head side to side. "He just lost his brother and he is having the time of his life."

"Well, let's hear what he has to tell us," Sam said as he and Donny went for the door. "Oh, by the way, which bar did you find him in?"

"The Mooring," Nester answered.

"Thanks, good job guys. We owe you a beer."

As the two detectives entered the room, they both figured he would be a hard nut to crack, but they were the types of detectives who didn't have to catch a fish in the first hour. They would stay on the boat as long as it took.

"Hello Nick. I'm Detective Carra and this is my partner Detective Burke." Sam reached out to shake hands and Nick flattened his hand out onto the table in defiance. "Nick, I want you to know we are not your enemy. We are here to find out the truth. We're trying to find out who killed your brother. Don't you want the person responsible brought to justice?"

"I want him dead," Nick slammed his palm down on the table.

"I understand how you would feel that way Nick," Sam said in a patronizing tone. He already had a bad feeling about Nick Gennaro, and Donny felt the same.

"Do you? Have you ever had a brother murdered?" Nick asked.

"No I haven't." Sam responded knowing where he was going with the question.

"Then you don't understand, do you?"

"Alright, I'll give you that. But, what I don't understand is how you're acting like you're on a holiday when you just buried your brother a couple weeks ago."

"I guess people handle stress in different ways – I drink."

"Okay, let's talk about the money."

Nick started tapping his fingers on the table. "What about it?"

"Congratulations. I understand you hit the lotto for eight point nine million dollars."

"That's right, I did," he said raising his chin up a notch.

"And you were the sole winner, right?"

He shifted his weight to the right. "That's right."

"Are you sure about that?" Sam took a seat across the table from him. Donny was standing in the corner behind Nick, just out of his view, and Nick didn't like it.

"Of course, I'm sure. I got the entire check, didn't I?"

"Yes you did, and you haven't wasted any time spending it, have you?

"That's right, I believe in living every day as if it were my last."

Sam stood up and walked around the table without speaking, and then he stopped right next to Nick and leaned over him. "Where were you the night of April twentieth, Nick?"

"How the hell do I know? I can't remember that far back. I can't remember where I was last night."

"That was the Friday night your brother Chris was murdered."

"I went out for a while and then I went home." Nick looked up toward the ceiling and then scratched his head. Sam knew he wasn't telling the truth. His physical gestures were textbook indications of fabrication.

"Did you go home alone, or is there someone who can vouch for you."

Nick moved to his left, attempting to find comfort in the hard chair. "I was alone."

Sam backed off and slowly circled around him, like a hungry shark. "Where were you prior to going home?"

"I was out having a couple drinks after work."

"And where was that?"

"I was at Shaky's bar in South Walton," Nick began cracking his knuckles, as Sam circled around the table, once again and stopping at his side staring into his left ear. "What time did you leave?"

"I don't know, around seven or eight. Why are you asking me all these stupid questions? You're treating me like a suspect. I thought I was here to help you find out who killed my brother?"

Sam retreated, pulled up a chair and slowly situated himself in it. "Calm down Nick, I have to ask everyone the same questions. It's the process of elimination. When was the last time you saw Chris?"

He rubbed his nose in a quick side-to-side motion. He wanted to get out of the uncomfortable chair and go fill it with coke. "I don't know, a few days before he was found."

"Where were you when you last saw him?"

"We went bowling."

"Do you remember what night that was?"

"Yeah, we bowled on Tuesdays."

"So that would have made it April seventeenth, right?"

"I guess, if you say so."

Sam glanced over at Donny who stood quietly in the corner. "I need to hit the head for a few minutes. Is there anything I can get you?" Sam asked.

"Yeah, you can get me the hell out of here." He looked at Sam directly in the eye for the first time.

"We just have a few more things to go over and then you're free to go."

"Can I get a smoke?"

"I'm sorry, no smoking in the building, new rule. We'll be right back."

Both detectives left the room. Ten minutes later, the interview room door opened and Donny walked in alone. He took the chair that Sam had been sitting in, turned it around, and sat down across from Nick with his arms resting on the back of the chair. Without speaking, he just sat staring directly into Nick's eyes. Nick had a bad feeling in the pit of his stomach. He wanted badly to replace it with a shot and beer.

"I know why you killed your brother, but what I don't understand is why you would jeopardize losing everything by getting caught. Why not just take your half and allow your brother to enjoy his cut. I guess it just comes down to greed. That's what is destroying this country, greed."

"Fuck you! You think I killed Chris? He was my brother." He glanced at the two-way mirror and then looked at Donny directly in the eye. "I loved him." He said in a calmer voice.

"Enough of the lies, Nick, why don't you just admit it?"

"Kiss my ass. I want my lawyer." Nick lowered his head, staring down at the table like a reprimanded child.

"I recommend you get one Nick, because you're in big trouble. Let me ask you this, what did it feel like to bash in your kid brother's head and leave him floating face down?"

"I'll bash your fucking head in." Nick jumped onto his feet and went after Donny, grabbing him by the tie and attempting to throw a punch. Donny covered up blocking the punch, and used his weight to force Nick up against the wall. Sam came plowing through the door and got in between the two men as they struggled for ground. Sam pulled Nick away, slamming him back down into his chair. Donny straightened out his tie and moved toward the table.

"I didn't kill my brother, you son of a bitch!" Nick was breathing heavy and spit shot out of his mouth as he yelled.

"Nick, you have been lying to us from the beginning. If you had nothing to hide, why would you lie?" Sam asked.

"Why would I lie? What are you talking about?"

"First of all, we have your brother on video tape buying the winning ticket. How is it, that you end up with the ticket, and he ends up dead?"

"That's because we split the cost of the ticket and he gave it to me to hold."

"We have him on tape at the store putting the ticket into his wallet," Sam moved his head closer to Nick to try and get better eye contact.

"Yeah, and when we went outside, he took it out and gave it to me to hold."

"Why the hell would he do that?" Donny asked.

"Because, I convinced him to let me hold it, he has bad luck when it comes to gambling."

"Nick, what are the chances that you and your brother buy a winning lottery ticket for nine million bucks and he ends up murdered, and a few days later, you cash it in for the entire amount. Yet, you have nothing to do with his death? Nick, what do we look like, idiots?

Nick looked up at Donny and then a quick glance at Sam. "You look like a couple of assholes to me."

"Alright, smartass. You say you were at Shaky's until eight o'clock. We have witnesses who say you received a phone call, and after hanging up, you bought the bar a round of drinks. The bartender told us he has never seen you set up the bar. He said you looked like you just hit the lottery. Those were his exact words. Who called, Nick? Did your brother Chris call to tell you about the winning ticket? Then after you heard the good news, you bought a round of drinks for the entire bar, had your celebratory drink, went to his boat, killed him, and took the ticket," Sam recited it, as if he were there.

"I'm not saying another word until I speak with my lawyer. Am I under arrest here?"

"No, not yet. You're free to go. Don't leave town, we're going to want to talk with you again. Who is your lawyer?"

"I'll let you know when I find one."

"You do that." Sam grabbed onto Nick's elbow to get his full attention. "Nick, I don't want to have to come looking for you again. You better check your messages at home in case we call." Nick got up and walked out without responding.

Donny looked at Sam with a disappointed expression. "So he just walks out?"

"We have no choice. We don't have a witness that puts him at the scene of the crime and we don't have a murder weapon."

"We should have enough to get a judge to issue us a warrant to search his house, right?"

"Let's hope so." Sam said. "Let's hope so."

15

The early sun was reflecting off the long-black limousine as it came to a stop in front of Nick's parent's house. In the back, Zollo was adding whiskey from a silver flask to his Starbucks coffee. Nick folded the newspaper he had been reading and placed it on the seat. He took one last puff from his joint and stubbed it out. "You're drinking already? It's eight thirty in the morning."

"Hair of the dog, Nick, hair of the dog."

"Hair of the dog my ass, you're an alcoholic."

"And you're not?"

"No, I'm not," Nick said in a self-convincing way.

"No, you're just a drug addict."

Nick picked up the newspaper and swung it in a backhand motion swatting Zollo directly in the face.

"What the fuck, Nick, I was only kidding."

"I didn't like that joke. Next time remember who paid for that flask. Stay here while I see my mother."

Nick retrieved a small box and got out of the limo. As he made his way up his parent's walkway, he thought about how small their house was. He stopped at the front door and turned to look around the neighborhood. He knocked on the front door and went in.

"Ma," he called out.

His mother came to greet him from the kitchen. "Nicholas, where have you been?" She approached her son with open arms. He hugged and kissed her on the cheek.

"I'm sorry, Ma. I've been busy looking at some new business ventures."

"Business ventures? What kind of business ventures?"

Nick hesitated while he thought of an answer, "Real Estate. I'm rich, Ma." He handed her the box he was holding.

"What's this, Nicholas?"

"It's for you, Ma, open it."

She slowly opened the box, as he watched. "What, do you think there's a bomb in there?" Nick was disappointed with her reaction. He was expecting her to jump up and down or scream, but she simply responded by stating it was a nice necklace.

"What, you don't like it, Ma?"

"I do, Nicholas; it's beautiful. I'm happier to see you." She gave him another hug and held on longer than the first time. "I have fresh coffee, come in and sit down."

"I don't have much time." He was already thinking of an exit strategy.

"What? I haven't seen you in how long? You don't have time for coffee with your mother?"

"Okay, one cup, and then I have to go."

She poured two cups of coffee and they sat at the kitchen table. "Your father is pretty upset with you. Why haven't you gone to see him or at least called him?"

"He doesn't want to talk to me. He hates me."

"That's not true. Your father loves you. He just wants what's best for you, that's all."

She has always been in denial of my father's feelings about me. "Did you tell him about my winning the lottery?"

"He knows. Everybody knows about it, now."

"What did he say?" He asked with the enthusiasm of a child wanting to please his father.

"You know your father, he hasn't said much about it. Since Christopher passed, he hasn't said much at all." Tears were welling up in her eyes.

"I miss him too, Ma. He was my kid brother."

She reached over holding his hand. "I know, honey. We all miss him."

"I went in to see the cops and they don't have shit. They were questioning me, like I was a suspect," he said changing the subject.

"They will catch whoever did this. With the grace of God," she added.

"If I find out first, they will be dropping him in a hole."

"Nicholas, let the police handle it. That's why we pay them."

"They are a bunch of clowns. You think they give a shit about Chris? They are fishing for anything they can hook. I have no confidence in them."

"Now you sound just like your father." She got up and poured the coffee.

"I guess that's one thing we both agree on."

"Nicholas, why don't you stop by the store and see him?"

"He doesn't want to see me."

"Yes, he does. Please, Nicholas."

"Alright, I'll think about it. Here, I have something for you." Nick reached into his inside jacket pocket and took out a fat envelope. He handed it to his mother and waited like a kid at Christmas for her to open it.

She looked inside, and her eyes expanded, as she gawked at a huge stack of hundred dollar bills. "Honey, I can't take this."

"What are you talking about? It's thirty thousand dollars, Ma."

"I know, but that's a lot of money."

"Mom, I won nine million. I want you to have some of it. Why don't you look for a bigger house? I'll give you more, if you need it."

"A bigger house? I love my house, I don't want to move." Her tone was defiant.

"Whatever. Buy yourself a new car, then. Spend it however you want."

He got up from the table without taking in any coffee. "I have to go, now." He moved closer, hugged and kissed his mother, before heading toward the door.

"Honey, promise me you'll stop and see your father."

"Okay, Ma."

She watched from the front door as her boy walked toward the long stretch limousine. It was out of place in her neighborhood, she thought. The driver got out and opened the door for Nick. He was wearing a black suit and white gloves and he conducted himself in a professional manner, just as Nick had demanded. The limo drove off and his mother stood watching as if it were a dream. She had never thought Nick would ride in the back of anything other than a police cruiser. She looked down and squeezed the envelope in her hand. So many bills, she thought.

Nick pushed the button that initiated the intercom. "Take us to Shaky's. I need a drink."

"Yes sir," The limo driver responded.

The bar had just opened its doors and there were already a half dozen people sitting in front of their glasses. When Nick and Zollo walked in, the room came alive. The very same people who despised Nick just weeks before, were now acting as if they were his best friend.

"Set the bar up," Nick barked, "except for that piece of shit, Archie. I wouldn't buy him a glass of water, if his stomach was on fire." Everyone laughed, except Archie. Nick hated Archie because he was a know-it-all. He was always talking and he had an answer for everything. If someone asked him for the time, he would tell them how to build a watch. Many times, he drove Nick to the brink of committing murder.

Archie got up without saying a word and walked out. "And don't come back! I might buy this place just to bar that bastard," Nick hollered.

After pounding down four glasses of whiskey, Nick was ready to confront his father, as he had promised. He and Zollo got back into the limo and drove into town. He ordered the driver to stop at a jewelry store on the way and he and Zollo went in together.

A short bald man, wearing a white shirt and red bow tie stood behind the counter watching, as the limo pulled up in front of his store. He buzzed the two men in with an electronic door opener. There were rows and rows of glass cases lined up against both walls. The cases were filled with diamond, ruby and emerald rings and necklaces. Nick greeted the bald guy with a nod and stopped in front of the case with the tennis bracelets.

"These are nice."

"Yes, some of the finest bracelets made. I bring many in from New York, but also Europe."

"Where are your best watches?" Nick asked.

"Over here," the owner motioned to the last case in the row and walked over, stopping behind it and resting his hand on the glass, exposing the gold Rolex he was wearing.

Nick didn't pay any attention to his modeling effort. Which is the best men's watch you have?"

"Well, Sir, we have many very fine watches."

"Don't dance with me, pal. Which is the most expensive?"

The bald man's expression changed. He realized he was dealing with an asshole, so he went right to one particular watch, took it out of the case, and rested it on a black felt pad. "That would be this one, the Rolex President. It's a fourteen carat gold Swiss piece with diamonds encompassing the face. It's the finest watch we have."

Nick picked up the watch and began looking it over; it was heavy. "How much?"

"This watch is twenty-six-thousand." He cleared his throat.

"I'll give you twenty-four, right now, cash."

"You have a deal," a smile sprouted on the old man's face.

"Wrap it up nice. I'll wait in the car." Nick pulled out two stacks of bills in ten thousand dollar increments and set them on the case. He counted out another forty bills and placed them on top of the pile. "Bring the watch out when he's done," he ordered Zollo.

A few minutes later, Zollo returned with the gift-wrapped box and crawled into the limo. Nick was snorting a line of coke with a rolled up one-hundred-dollar bill. He pushed the button alerting the driver.

"Take me to 1663 Main Street. Gennaro's meat market."

"Yes Sir," the driver came back at him.

As the limo rolled up in front of the store, Nick hesitated before getting out. His heart was beating faster, and his palms were beginning to perspire. He didn't understand why. *I'm the one with all the money, and now, all the power. Why should I care about what anyone thinks? Most of my life has been spent disappointing my father, but now, things are going to be different. I will finally get the respect I deserve.*

He exited the car holding the gift for his father. Nicholas was alone in the store when the limo pulled up. He figured Nick was inside, and when the limo door opened, he realized he was right. He was uncomfortable as he stood behind the counter waiting for Nick to enter his store.

Nick pushed open the door and closed it behind him without taking his eyes off the doorknob. Once inside, he finally looked up at his father. "Pop." Nick nodded his head.

Nicholas looked up at his son without saying a word.

"Pop, I wanted to stop by to tell you things are going to be different. I can do good things with my life, *now*. I want to help you and Ma, too."

Nicholas began arranging cold salads and casseroles in the case and didn't stop to look up. He could tell his son was intoxicated. He wasn't sure from what, but he knew it wasn't from too much coffee.

"Have you been drinking or taking dope? Christ, it's not even noon and you look like shit."

Nick rubbed his eyes. "I haven't slept much, lately."

"I bet. It looks like you've been having a big party."

Nick placed the gift on top of the meat case. "Pop, I got you something."

"I don't want it," he said without looking at it.

"You haven't seen it, yet." Nick opened up the box and pulled back the black velvet lid exposing the watch. His father glanced at the gift without emotion. "Pop, this is a gold Rolex. The best watch in the world. I bought it for you."

"I told you, I don't want it. I don't want anything from you."

"What is it with you?" Nick's voice was escalating. "Chris is gone and I'm the only son you have left."

"Don't you *ever* mention his name to me again."

"He was my brother, Pop, and I loved him too."

Nicholas stopped what he was doing. He looked up at his eldest son with hatred in his eyes. "I saw the tape from the Quick Mart. Chris was the one who bought the ticket, not you," he said, slamming his palm against the glass case. "How is it that he ends up beaten to death and you cash in the ticket?"

"I already explained it to the cops, and they cleared me of any involvement. After we got back to the car, he gave the ticket to me to hold because we agreed that I had better luck than him."

"I don't believe you. I know in my heart that somehow you are responsible for his death."

"Fuck you!" Nick shouted.

"You get the hell out of my store. I don't want you coming around here or the house again. You stay away from me. You are dead to me. I don't have any living sons. Get out and take your fancy watch with you." Nicholas walked into the back room leaving his son standing alone. They were both trembling, one slightly more than the other.

16

Since the murder of his son, every day seemed to drag on into the next without a lick of excitement or even an entertaining thought. Nicholas was like a walking zombie and it hadn't gone unnoticed by his customers. Word had spread fast and most people knew about the murder of Chris and many had heard that his oldest son had won the lottery. News coverage on the murder had slowed, but occasionally popped up from time to time. The death of his son was an unbearable pain that he had never quite experienced before. Feeling that his surviving son may have been involved or possibly killed Chris was even more torturous. Nicholas felt helpless, not knowing what he should do next.

With a bottle of Windex in one hand and a paper towel in the other, he wiped down the glass display cases. This was one of the last chores he did every day, before closing the store. The door alarm rang, alerting Nicholas, as Sam and Donny entered the store. Nicholas looked up briefly and then continued cleaning the glass.

"Good afternoon, Mr. Gennaro," Donny greeted him. Sam nodded his head when Nicholas looked up again. Nicholas recognized Sam from the start and knew he was Italian, but he was a cop and couldn't be trusted.

"What's so good about it? Have you come here to tell me you arrested my son's killer?"

"No, I'm afraid not. Not yet anyway," Sam said.

Nicholas pointed toward the street. "Then why are you here, instead of out there trying to catch him?"

"We thought we'd stop in and touch base with you. To see if you've recalled anything that might help us. Also, to bring you up to speed on the progress of the investigation," Sam said.

Nicholas rested the Windex and towels down. "So you finally decided to come around and tell me that Chris bought the winning lottery ticket, yet Nick cashed it in a few days after

Chris was murdered?"

"Yes, that's true. We spoke with Nick and he said Chris gave him back the ticket outside the store just after they purchased it. What do you think?"

"I think you are a few days late telling me this. Why is it I hear this information from the street before I hear it from you?"

"I apologize about that, Mr. Gennaro. This is not the only case we're working on," Sam said.

Nicholas quickly dismissed his excuse and continued on the glass without saying a word.

"So what are your thoughts on this? Have you spoken with your son, Nick, about this?"

Nicholas stopped once again, putting down the bottle, looking up at Sam. "I spoke to Nick and I believe what he told me. Now if you guys don't mind, I have to close the store and meet somebody for dinner."

"Sure. No problem. The glass looks nice. You take care." Sam said, walking toward the door. Donny followed behind, not saying anything. They went back out onto the street feeling like they hadn't accomplished anything by the visit.

The detectives got into their vehicle and drove off.

Nicholas watched them drive away and then picked up his phone and called his wife. He told her he would be home a little late.

***

Lorenzo's Sicilian Restaurant had a reputation for excellent veal and notorious wise guys. Seven years earlier, it was the scene of a mob hit. Vincent "wrecking machine" Rizzo was an Underboss who had big dreams of taking over the top spot. When it became known that he was plotting to hit the boss of the Patriarca family, he was killed by one of his own guys, while he sat on the toilet in Lorenzo's restroom. He took a bullet to the forehead and one through the heart with a .38 caliber handgun. One would think that would have been bad for business, but the restaurant became busier after the hit. The murder was all over the front page of the newspapers in Rhode Island, Boston, and New York and the murder also made national news.

Carmine Lorenzo, the owner, had been known to say, "If I get a couple more hits in here, I could retire early." It was an ongoing joke with him and some of his wise guy friends.

Nicholas joined Franco and Dennis who were sitting at a table in the rear of Lorenzo's dining area. Nicholas knew Dennis was someone who could be trusted, so he felt comfortable talking in front of him. He and Franco were the best of friends, but Nicholas had many other friends in the family all the way up to the Capo di Capa. Even though he was not a made guy, he was well respected. It was understood that if he had chosen a life in the La Costa Nostra, he would be an important member of the family. Both men stood to greet him as he approached their table and Carmine came right over and greeted Nicholas as well, taking his drink order as Nicholas sat with his friends.

"How are you, Nicky?" Franco asked.

He situated himself into the chair. "I'm surviving."

"Any word from the cops?"

"They just left my store," he said, shifting to one side. "They got shit."

"They are fucking useless. Have they brought Nick in yet?"

"Yeah, they said they spoke with him. Same story we got."

"Where do we go from here?" Franco asked.

"I'd like to bury his ass."

Franco had never heard him talk like this before and he didn't like the sound of it. The Nicky he knew was a solid family man that would protect his children with his life. "Nicky, this is your son we're talking about here."

Nicholas's color began to change. "He is no son of mine. Both my sons are dead."

"We don't want to jump the gun here, Nicky. Let's give it some time. We will keep our eyes and ears open on the street and see what the cops find out. There is always the chance that he didn't have anything to do with this."

"Yeah about one in nine million." Nicholas said.

The waiter came over and greeted the men and placed down Nicholas's drink.

Franco motioned toward his friend.

"I'll have the New York strip, rare." Nicholas ordered.

17

Sam sat in his favorite chair reading a cloak and dagger novel. He had read every Ludlum novel at least once and was on his second round with this one. He turned a page and glanced at his watch. It was one-thirty in the morning and Susan hadn't come home yet. He read a couple more pages before putting down the book. Wondering where his wife was, he was no longer able to concentrate. Sam knew he had to make an effort to spend more time at home with his family, but it was a hard thing to do with such a heavy caseload.

In the past few months, he had noticed that his wife had been staying out later at night. When he questioned her about it, she would become defensive, stating she was out with her friend, Lois – asking him, "What do you care anyway?"

Homicide detectives sometimes become absorbed with their work and Sam knew it was a problem for him and his relationship, but like an addict he couldn't stop. He had an overwhelming need to rid the world of bad people. It was his obligation, and it was all he knew, and he was good at it.

It was two-fifteen when the door opened, and Susan quietly crept into the house. Sam switched off the light, sitting still in the dark family room. He watched, as she quietly walked by toward the staircase and went upstairs to the bedroom; soon after, he followed.

"Did you have a good time?" She was startled and turned to see her husband standing in the doorway.

"It was alright. Lois and I went to the movies and then out for an early breakfast. I thought you were in bed."

"I was reading downstairs. What did you see?"

She hesitated before responding. "Are you interrogating me?"

"No, I was just making conversation," he responded in a calm voice.

"We saw Seven Daggers," she said, while undressing.

"I heard that was pretty good."

"It was okay."

"It was a long movie, about three hours, right?"

"Yeah, it was long." Her short responses raised concern.

"How's Lois doing?"

"She's fine. I'm going to take a quick shower then go to bed, I'm tired," Susan said, closing the bathroom door behind her.

Sam sat on the bed and picked up a framed picture of his kids that rested on the bed stand; their son was eleven and their daughter eight. The photo brought him back to that day when they had gone on vacation to Niagara Falls. Everything seemed so clear and simple back then. They had such a happy family and he and Susan had a very solid connection. He remembered the way she used to look at him. He would glance across a room, catch her eye and her smile would say it all. She was totally in love with him and this instilled a sense of content and security in him, at that time. Sam placed the picture on the nightstand and got down on his knees and began to pray.

Sunday morning came early for Sam. He already had two cups of coffee and was reading the paper when Susan came down stairs.

"Hey, what do you say I take you out to brunch today?"

"I have to meet Lois. I promised her I would help her move some furniture. She is giving a couple of chairs, a table, and some other stuff to her son; he just got a new apartment."

"Why can't her son help her?"

"Because she asked me, that's why. He isn't going to be around."

"Okay, when will you be home?"

"Probably not till later this evening. We're going shopping after we're finished moving, there's a sale at Talbot's."

"That's great. I have the day off and you've made plans all day and night."

"You didn't tell me until this morning. I already made plans."

"Fine, I'll spend the day by myself."

Sam retrieved his off duty weapon from the closet and clipped it onto his belt; he put on his jacket and walked out of the house without speaking another word. He drove to the shore and found a diner that he used to frequent for breakfast several years ago. The building was tiny and sat alone on the main street — it was as if nothing had changed in twenty years.

The chimes came alive when the door opened, and it was the same sound he remembered. Everything from the menu board to the grill had remained intact. The only thing that had changed was the digital cash register and the faces of the employees.

He sat alone in a booth, ordering breakfast and watching people come and go. When his food came, he took his time eating his sausage and eggs. He found himself fixed on a family sitting in a booth across the aisle. The father sat next to his daughter and the mother next to her son. They were talking and laughing and seemed contently happy together. Sam noticed the way the woman looked at her husband. A faint smile and a subtle flirtatious look brightened her eyes. It was the same way Susan used to look at him, and for a brief moment, he was envious of the man sitting in the booth across from him. He took one last sip of his orange juice and carried the check to the register.

For the next two hours, Sam walked around the town looking into windows, occasionally stopping into a store that displayed something that appealed to him. When he exhausted the window shopping, he moved on without purchasing anything; he decided to go to the beach.

Sam always felt at peace when he spent time near the ocean. It was endless and unchanged and one always knew where they stood when staring out into the open sea. Somehow it helped him put his life into perspective and made his problems seem insignificant. One day he hoped to retire near the ocean.

He looked at his watch and it was nearly noontime, so he got back into his car and drove down the street. As his car stopped at a red light, Sam noticed a theater across the street. The light changed, and he took a hard left and pulled in front of the theater. He rolled down his passenger window for a closer look and noticed that Seven Daggers was playing – the next showing at twelve-fifteen. After parking his car on the street, he went in, bought a single ticket, and walked straight past the concession stand and to the theater. He found a seat in the middle of the theater and sat alone watching the suspense film. He hadn't been to the movies in years, and didn't realize how much he missed it. It was quite different than he remembered. The screen was curved and there were holes in the armrests for placing a drink. Large speakers were lined up along the wall and his feet didn't stick to the floor like he had remembered they had.

The time he spent watching the movie on the silver screen was a time free from his everyday life and daily worries. He didn't focus on anything but the story. Being absorbed in the plot brought him to another place, where he didn't think about all the dead bodies, and the killers, or the bullshit at the office. His mind was completely free, at least for a short while.

When the movie ended, Sam just sat watching people file out, and within a few minutes, the theater was empty. He thought about the movie and how much he enjoyed the story, and then his mind drifted back to his wife. He looked at his watch, the movie was shorter than Susan had said, it wasn't a long movie at all – it was only one-fifty-nine.

18

Silks gentlemen's club sat in the heart of Providence. On weekends, they charged ten dollars to walk in, offering a coupon at the door for a free drink. The promotional idea came from Johnny Silk, one of the owners. He knew it would favorably catch on with the customers. Drinks started at five-dollars and his cost averaged less than two. He still got his eight-dollars and the customers would feel better about reaching into their pockets, he rationalized.

Nick's coupon was balled up on the floor where he threw it after walking in.

Zollo sat drooling, as a dancer dressed up like a squaw moved around in front of him removing one piece of clothing at a time. Earlier in the day, Nick had stopped by the bank to load up, and he was holding twenty five thousand in cash.

"I wonder if Eden is working tonight," Nick said. He had watched her the last time he was there and he became infatuated with her. Nick had given her four hundred dollars in tips and she later found out through the grapevine that he was the big lotto winner.

"I hope so, she is hot." Zollo said without taking his eyes off the squaw. Nick was less impressed.

"Hey," Nick called out to the bartender.

The bartender turned and came strutting over. She was a good-looking woman in her mid-thirties with a great body that came with a dead personality. As she grew older, she had been demoted from twirling around the brass pole to tending bar. She was receiving much less attention and tips in her current position, and she hated it worse with every passing night.

"Is Eden working tonight?"

"Yes," she answered as if she had been asked that question a hundred times already.

"Good, let me get Chopin vodka and tonic, no fruit. Make it a double, and get this clown whatever he wants," he motioned to Zollo, who was still fixed on the girl with the long, black hair like a horses' mane. Her hair was tied tight around her head with brown rawhide that erected a feather that looked like a colorful antenna sticking up from the rear of her head. With the exception of the feather, she was now completely naked.

"I wish they would play more rock instead of this Rapp-crap."

"Yeah, I hate this shit," Zollo added.

The song ended and Eden was announced. As she climbed up onto the floor, she drew the attention of nearly everyone in the place, including the other dancers. She had long, silky-blonde hair that rested on a perfect body. Standing five-feet-eight, and weighing a solid one-hundred-and-twenty-seven pounds, she was flawless. Eden didn't display any tattoos or visible scars, at least not on the outside. Her body contained less than eight-percent fat, and that was fat unseen to the naked eye. She began gliding across the stage, grabbing onto the pole and spinning around it, sending herself in the other direction. She caught Nick's eye as she turned, and with a quick smile, she dropped to the floor into a full split.

"Did you see that? She likes me."

"What she likes is that wad of cash in your pocket," Zollo responded.

"Shut the fuck up, she doesn't know how much money I have. She likes me."

Eden began her performance and Nick was now the one drooling. He loved the way she commanded the stage. Her big blue eyes and full lips surrounded by her silky soft skin moved him like no other woman. She was dressed in pink lace and her pink high heel shoes made her appear even taller.

"Man, would I like to get in Eden's garden," Nick said without taking his eyes off her. Zollo knew enough to keep his mouth shut. There was something about this girl that caused Nick's emotions to stir, and when Nick got emotional, people got hurt. Nick reached into his pocket peeling off a hundred dollar bill. He waited until she looked his way and he placed it on the bar in front of him. She danced over and her smile grew wider as she got closer realizing it was not a one or a five-dollar-bill.

Eden began her dance in front of Nick, slowly removing one garment at a time. When she was completely naked, except for her heels, she bent over looking at him from between her legs. She reached out snatching up the bill in one quick motion. With a wink of the eye, she moved on to dance for another guy. Feeling betrayed, Nick pulled out five one-hundred-dollar bills and spread them out on the bar. A few minutes later she returned, and he motioned for her to come closer, and she knelt down next to him. He could smell the sweet scent of her perfume, and she looked even more beautiful up close.

"Four of them are for you, and the other one is for you to buy me a drink, after you finish your dance."

"What's your pleasure?" She asked with a perfect smile.

"We can talk about that later, but for now, I'll have a vodka and tonic, no fruit."

"You got it." Once again, she began her dance for Nick, and it was even better than the last. When she finished, she moved on with the five bills. Nick was so mesmerized, he hadn't even noticed her take them off the bar.

When her set was over, Nick watched her go into the dressing room, and a few minutes later, she came out wearing a black outfit. She went to the bar and was quickly served two drinks, and she carried them over to where Nick was sitting. Handing Nick his drink, they both raised their glasses, as she offered a toast.

"Live long, love hard, and die laughing."

"Saluda," Nick said, before pouring down the whole drink.

"Easy cowboy."

"Don't worry babe, I have a liver made of stone."

"I'll remember that."

Nick motioned to the bartender and she went off to make him another drink.

"Listen, I'm going to be completely honest with you. I think you are the most beautiful woman I have ever seen. I am very rich, and if you walk away from this tonight, with me, I'll give you five-thousand-dollars.

"Let me get this straight. If I leave with you tonight you'll give me five grand in cash?"

"Yes, but you can't come back. I want you to be my girl. I'll show you the best time of your life."

"Yeah, just how rich are you?"

"I have millions," he said with a proud and cocky smirk on his face.

"Five grand —I can make that much here on a good weekend."

Nick reached into his pocket and pulled out a wad of bills wrapped in a rubber band. "I'll give you ten grand right now if you leave with me. My limo driver is waiting outside."

Eden looked down at the large roll of hundred dollar bills without speaking; she pinched her nose before responding. "Thanks for the offer, but I don't think so." She walked back to the dressing room leaving Nick behind, disappointed.

"Man, are you crazy? You were really going to give her ten grand?" Zollo asked.

"What I do with my money is not your business, so just shut up and drink whatever drink I bought you."

Zollo could see he hit a sensitive spot, so he did as he was told. Nick shrugged it off and ordered a shot of tequila with no lime.

Inside her dressing room, Eden sat in front of the mirror looking at her reflection. She didn't see what the others saw when looking at her. She saw a scared child named Tammy Backland living in a small white house with the curdled paint, cracked windows and a buckled roof. The house sat on the outskirts of Redwood Cove, Indiana. Being an only child and living in a secluded area, she was left alone, playing by herself, most of the time.

Just short of her eighth birthday, her father decided he wanted more out of life than a demanding wife and needy daughter. The morning he packed up and left, he placed a note on the kitchen table stating that he would return once he earned enough money to provide a better life for them. Tammy held onto the note with hope, as if it were a tangible promise that couldn't be broken. Her mother knew better. She was stubborn and beautiful; her husband used to say that was a dangerous combination.

Not long after her father left, Kyle Moan came into her life, and it wasn't a gradual transition by any means. Her mother had met him at the diner where she worked as a waitress, and shortly thereafter they began dating. Kyle was ruggedly handsome, wearing a thick mustache and a face that felt like sandpaper most of the time. He wore jeans and flannel shirts with steel toed construction boots. His hands were strong and callused from pounding nails on a roof six days a week. Much of the time he had a cheap, skinny, cigar clenched between his teeth, and both Tammy and her mother hated the nasty smell. Loneliness has a way of thickening ones tolerance, so Tammy's mother learned to live with it.

It was a sunny summer afternoon when his car pulled up in front of their house. Kyle got out retrieving a suitcase and an old green army duffle bag that stood nearly as tall as Tammy. Even though her mother had told her Kyle was moving in, she wasn't prepared for this change in her home life and what was to follow.

As summer turned into autumn and fall into winter, Tammy felt something was different with Kyle than she had experienced with her father. He never played with her or read to her, but he always showed her physical affection. Kyle would ask for kisses and he would constantly hug and pick her up, sometimes twirling her around in the air. The affection she felt from Kyle felt strange to her. It didn't feel genuine, similar to the affection she remembered getting from Santa Claus in the lobby of a department store.

Tammy was eleven years old when her mother started working double shifts on Tuesdays and Thursdays. She would work until eleven at night placing Tammy under the sole care of Kyle for several hours a week. The abuse began with subtle touching and compliments about her body regarding how quickly she was sprouting into a woman. The following summer Kyle could no longer contain his urges, and he forced himself on her, reassuring her that he loved her and that everything was going to be all right. The sexual abuse became a regular occurrence and Tammy coped by learning to detach herself from her body. The years passed by and Tammy had blossomed into a beautiful young woman. Kyle had become obsessed with Tammy, and her mother had eventually become sexually and emotionally neglected. Kyle would decline her advances telling her he was tired or not in the mood, all the while his mind was on Tammy.

When Tammy refused his advances, he threatened to tell her mother the truth about their affair. Not wanting her mother to endure the pain and disappointment of learning what Kyle had been doing with her on the nights she was working at the diner, she kept it all a secret, not telling anyone. As Tammy grew older, she knew she had to get out. The burden she carried was drowning her and she felt like crawling out of her skin. She felt as if she was dying a slow agonizing death.

Thursday night had arrived and Tammy's mother was feeling sick to her stomach. She asked her boss if she could leave early and he agreed, so she collected her things and punched out. It was eight-thirty when she made it home and entered the house. Once she closed the door behind her, she could hear a moaning sound coming from her bedroom. It was a small house and sound carried through the paper-thin walls. There was no mistaking the unique sound Kyle made while having sex. When she opened the bedroom door, she never expected in a million years to see what she did. It wasn't a bimbo or a lounge lizard from the bar, it was her daughter and she had just turned seventeen.

The sickness Tammy's mother felt at work had now tripled. She ran straight to the bathroom where she vomited all over the floor and toilet. When she was finished, she went directly into the kitchen where she picked up a carving knife. Kyle was fully dressed when she returned to the bedroom and Tammy had crawled out the window half naked.

Kyle started attempting to convince her that he loved her and it was all a big mistake. He didn't have the chance to finish his sentence when she thrashed the blade back and forth slicing into his right forearm. She attacked him in a frenzy screaming out like a wild animal. She was totally out of control and was desperately trying to kill him. The second strike was a straight plunge into his right shoulder. Kyle fell back against the dresser with severe pain shooting down his arm. Blood was gushing out of his wounds and he was starting to get dizzy. He managed to get onto his feet before she came in for another attack. She swung the blade toward his mid-section and he pulled back avoiding a near hit. With a quick left hook, he punched her in the jaw knocking her to the floor. As Kyle hurried toward the door, she plunged the knife into the back of his thigh. He yelled out with a high-pitched sound as the blade sliced through his hamstring. Kyle knew if he didn't get out of the house, he was going to die. He snatched up two towels before hobbling out of the house, leaving a trail of blood behind. He made it to his car, crawled in and drove off.

Tammy had been hiding in the woods and was listening to the commotion. She watched Kyle run frantically from the house; she could see he was badly hurt. After Kyle drove off, she went back into the house where she found her mother on the bedroom floor crying. Kyle's blood was spattered all over the bed, walls and floor. She observed the bloody knife lying on the floor next to her mother, so she picked it up and slid it under the bed. She sat down next to her mother and put her arms around her. She wanted to tell her mother how sorry she was and that it wasn't her fault. She wanted to tell her how Kyle forced himself on her when she was just eleven years old. Tammy wanted to tell her how she hated it, and that she only did it to deny her from knowing the truth. She wanted to tell her all those things, but she didn't have the chance. Her mother pushed her away, calling her a whore. When Tammy tried consoling her, she began screaming out of control and demanding that she pack her things and leave immediately. Tammy tried to explain, but her mother wouldn't listen. Without any hope of reconciliation, Tammy did as her mother said; she packed her bags and left. With the few dollars she had saved, Tammy bought a one-way bus ticket to Los Angeles, California.

That night, Kyle admitted himself into the hospital, but refused to give any explanation regarding to his injuries. He knew he could be criminally charged for what he had done to Tammy, and deep down, he understood he deserved every laceration from that knife he endured and more. His wounds were so severe that he would never be able to properly swing a hammer again. The tendon and nerve damage had taken away his livelihood. Kyle had led himself through a path that could only end with darkness.

The next day, Tammy's mother put on her diner uniform and went to work. When her shift ended, she went home to an empty house and cried herself to sleep.

Tammy found herself lured into an acting scam that put her in front of a camera having sex with strangers while other strangers watched and filmed her. Once again, she felt like crawling out of her skin. After three pornography movies behind her, she met Robby Silk. He had a stake in the pornography production company, and after watching Tammy on the set, he knew she was special. He wanted to have her, and he got her by offering her a way out. Robby made it very clear to Tammy that he was well connected with the mob and that he would take care of her, but that she could never leave him. She agreed and he took her back home with him to Providence where he got her a job at his brothers club.

As she gazed into the mirror of her past, Tammy noticed a tear rolling down her face. She wiped her eyes with a tissue, retrieved her bag, and returned to her familiar world. Nick was still sitting at the bar when she returned. He was surprised when she came walking over.

"Is the offer for the ten grand still valid?" She asked without a smile or any real emotion. Nick reached into his pocket and handed her the roll of bills without speaking.

"Let's go then," she said.

The three of them walked out with Tammy leading the way. Standing near the office door, Johnny Silk watched as Tammy left with her bag in hand. Her shift was not over by any means.

19

Dennis bent over peering down the well-groomed green slate, examining the two balls left on the table. One was pure ivory white and the other a tainted coal black. The opposing balls had fought a battle time and time again had tested the skill of men.

"Cross corner," Dennis declared. He carefully aimed his cue at the white ball, sliding the long stick between his fingers and with a quick snap of his wrist, the ball shot out pushing the eight ball against the rail. The eight ball moved elegantly as it bounced off the bank and rolled to the opposite corner finding its destination in the leather pocket. The white ball had stopped in its place after meeting its counterpart and sending it off to victory.

"Nice shot, Dennis." The defeated player reached into his pocket and handed Dennis a fifty-dollar bill before packing his stick into a black leather case. His nose was pointing downward as he walked past Franco retreating from the back room of the Sons of Italy social club.

"How much did you take that fool for?" Franco asked with a nod of his head.

"A buck and a half in three quick games."

"Rack em up. I'll play you one game. Not for scratch, I'm no fool."

Dennis racked the balls and Franco found a cue that felt right and he broke the rack sending balls in every direction, without sinking one.

"So what's going on?" Dennis asked as he took aim.

"We have a problem with Stark again. He's been ducking us for too long."

"What does he owe this time?"

"With points, he's into us for eighteen grand."

"How far is he behind?" Dennis handed Franco the chalk.

Franco chalked the tip of his cue. "He was supposed to pay over a month ago."

"He has been pretty good about paying on time in the past, right?"

"Yeah, but he doesn't call me, and he keeps mouthing off to my collector. It's always next week with him." Franco took aim at the nine-ball and missed.

Dennis moved into position. "What do you want me to do?"

"We need to set an example. Don't break any arms or legs. If he can't work then how the hell will he ever pay us back?"

"I'll take care of this one myself." Dennis sank the six-ball and moved on to his next conquest.

"Good," Franco said through a half smile.

"I got news of a shipment of Xbox units from my guy at the trucking company. I'd like to take it," Dennis said.

"Is it a teamsters run?" Franco took a seat as Dennis ran the table. He sank his third ball in a row, "No."

"Save a few for my nephews." Franco said.

Dennis ran the remaining balls and sunk the eight-ball.

"This is why I don't play you for money. Let's sit down for a minute." Franco motioned to a booth and they took a seat. "I'm getting a little concerned about our friend at the meat store. Is there any news on the street about his boys?"

Dennis took a seat and found the chair to be unsteady, so he switched. "I haven't heard anything."

"I need you to keep your ears open on this. Nothing from our people in the police department?"

"All I'm hearing is that it's still under investigation. They are looking hard at the brother."

"That's what I'm afraid of, the look in Nicky's eyes when I mention his son, Nick." His thumb and four fingers met creating a beak and he gestured back and forth with his fingertips pointing up. "I don't want him doing anything crazy. I never saw a man who hates his own son as much as he does."

"Maybe he has good reason. Franco, they have no other suspects."

"I don't think his wife could take the loss of another son. You know how mothers are. They're little boys can do no wrong."

Dennis thought about his mother for a moment without speaking and Franco knew it wasn't a good subject for Dennis.

"Anyway let me know how it goes with Stark." Franco got up and landed two gentle pats on Dennis's shoulder before walking out.

It was drizzling outside and every couple of minutes Dennis hit the switch to clear his windshield. He looked at his watch and lightly pounded his steering wheel with the bottom of his clenched fist. He had been sitting in his car outside the Cornerstone Bar for an hour and a half.

He watched as a couple walked out the bar. It was obvious they were having a fight. The woman was walking a couple of steps ahead of him and she had a look that could kill. He followed behind wearing an invisible leash.

The door opened again and Stark came walking out alone. Dennis quickly and quietly exited his car following Stark as he walked toward his truck. Stark heard someone coming up from behind him and he reached into his waistband for his .38 revolver. Dennis stopped his draw with his left hand and gave him a hard right uppercut to the kidney. The gun fell to the ground and Dennis kicked it under the truck. Producing a thick plastic bag out of his back pocket, Dennis quickly wrapped it over Stark's head pulling it tight around his neck, while standing behind him with his knee in the small of his back. Stark began thrashing attempting to take in air, but there was none to be found. Dennis pulled him to the ground holding the bag tight until Stark began moving slower. Once his fight was over, in one snapping motion, Dennis tore the bag off his head. Stark began gasping for air, surprised, yet relieved to still be alive.

"You are way behind in your payments. You have two days to come up with the entire eighteen-grand or next time I won't be so nice. Do I make myself clear?" Dennis was now looking directly into Stark's eyes. He knew by the look in Dennis's eyes, he was dead serious.

"Yes, I'll get the money," he said in a scratchy and convincing voice.

"I know you will. Just in case, here is a little reminder." Dennis hoisted him up just enough for a clean shot. With a fierce right hand he punched Stark in the side of his face, breaking his jaw. Dennis saw that he had knocked him out cold. Letting him fall to the ground, he walked back to his car.

Two days later, Stark made a phone call asking Franco's runner to meet him the next day. It was a real challenge understanding what he was trying to say through his wired jaw, but Franco's collector finally got it and agreed to meet him the next afternoon, where he paid him the eighteen- thousand in cash.

Stark had robbed his brother's house the night before in order to avoid the ultimate penalty. He vowed never to gamble again. It wasn't the first time he made that vow or the last.

20

The gleaming boat moved on the water with incredible grace. At fifty-nine feet long, the pure white, with teal-cut-pin striping and matching interior, the Viking yacht was a true eye catcher. It was definitely, a wallet emptier. Written across the stern in italic teal was the name Nick had thought of long before he wrote the check to purchase her. She was officially named *Ticket to Paradise*.

Nick sat on the deck in a leather swivel chair drinking a vodka martini while Tammy knelt down between his legs pleasuring him. Zollo was in the cabin with Dana and Kirsten, two dancers from the club who worked with Tammy. Nick had ordered Zollo to go inside, so he and Tammy could spend some time on the deck alone. Zollo welcomed the idea because it gave him the opportunity to snort coke with the girls and cop an occasional squeeze of a breast.

Nick's glass was depleted of liquid, as he sat in the sun feeling like a king. "Get me another one babe, while you're up." As Tammy shook the martini shaker, her natural bare breast jiggled back and forth. Nick watched from the corner of his eye. They were perfect, he thought. When she finished, she came over holding two martini glasses filled to the brim. Wearing only a yellow thong bottom and black Oakley sunglasses, she had more clothes on than Nick desired. The bright yellow thong barely covered the small patch that thousands of men at the club dreamed of exploring up close and personal. The yellow brought out the beauty of her copper toned tan, Nick thought.

She handed Nick his drink, kissed him on the neck and sat down. "How was that, baby?" She asked.

"Unbelievable, as usual." Nick raised his glass and leaned toward her and the sound of pure Waterford crystal colliding was heard and then lost in the sea air. "Do you think Zollo is getting laid?"

"I wouldn't bet on it," Tammy responded without any thought.

"How about if I gave each of them a couple hundred?"

"I think it would have to be more like a thousand."

"A thousand! I want to rent them, not buy them."

"No offense Nick, but take a look at him. He's a loser."

Nick took a long sip of his martini. "Yeah, you have a point there."

"Save your money, baby. Wouldn't you rather spend it on something that will give you a return for your investment?" She moved closer reaching down and caressing him between the legs.

"Another good point. I think a nice three-carat-diamond would look good on you." Nick's smile was as wide as his wallet.

Tammy got up and put her breast in his face and he began shaking his head side-to-side with his face in between them.

"Now, that's what I'm talking about." He said, feeling the softness against his cheeks. "I think I'm in love."

"You ain't seen nothing yet." She turned and bent over like she had on stage.

"I can't wait," He said like a young boy waiting for the ice cream truck.

She stood and spun around in one smooth and elegant motion. "So, Tuesday we are going house hunting, right?"

"Yeah, I saw a house in the paper in Tiverton that looks nice. It's right on the water,"

"How big?" She asked with enthusiasm

"It's a five-bedroom white colonial. I think it's just over five-thousand square feet."

"That sounds expensive." Her concern seemed genuine to Nick.

"It's not bad. It lists for two point three million."

"Oh, that's all." He could sense the sarcasm in her tone.

They sat in silence for a moment, both looking out into the open, blue Atlantic. She finally broke the silence with a question that had been dangling from the tip of her tongue for quite a while.

"Nick, you never talk about your brother. How are you coping with everything?"

"Tammy, my brother was a great kid. He was my best friend and someone killed him and the cops think I did it. Hell, my own fucking family probably thinks I did it. How do you think that makes me feel?"

"Pretty bad, I would think." He had her full attention as she looked into his eyes for reassurance.

"You can't imagine. If the cops don't come up with something soon, I'm going to hire a private investigator and try to find out who did it. And if I do, I'll kill the son of a bitch myself."

"Don't do that, baby. If you're in prison, how can you have this?" Tammy pulled her thong aside exposing herself. Nick looked at her with a dazed glare, as if he were somewhere else. Then he snapped out of it and moved down in front of her getting onto his knees. It was now his turn.

"Life is good," he said. "Life is good."

Soon after, Zollo and the girls came up from the cabin. All of them were topless. Tammy was the only one of the three that had natural breasts, and Nick wasn't afraid to boast about it.

"Zollo, turn up the music. It's party time!" Nick pulled out a bag of coke and the girl's eyes all lit up. All except Tammy, she had bigger things in mind than a quick, white powder high.

"What about our trip to Block Island?" Tammy asked.

"Soon we will be on our maiden voyage, my ladies. Very soon," Nick said as he rolled up a hundred dollar bill.

PART TWO

21

The Buck and Bull lounge was situated on a main country road in Walton, Rhode Island – nine miles north of South Walton. The establishment was known for attracting a rowdy crowd with fights and disturbances occurring on a regular basis. Most went unreported to law enforcement under the strict directive of the owner, Hank Reynolds. If a patron was seriously injured and needed an ambulance, then it would be reported to the police by the EMT or hospital administration. Other than that, what happened inside the Bar, stayed inside the bar.

Reynolds had been sued on two different occasions by customers who had suffered injuries on the premises, but was settled in both cases. Reynolds, an avid biker himself, was a groupie of the notorious biker gang that occupied his establishment. The Rhode Island chapter of the Hells Angels Motorcycle Club had declared the Buck and Bull their territory and it remained so for several years. Although, Reynolds owned the bar, the Hells Angels ran it and called the shots. From the beginning, it had been made very clear that Reynolds could easily disappear, should he decide not to play ball with the vicious gang of bikers. For this reason, and the fact that Reynolds enjoyed a certain sense of power and protection being affiliated with the gang, it never crossed his mind to betray them.

He was never inducted into the gang, but he was made an honorary member and was awarded a leather jacket with wings expanding across the back. The night the jacket was presented to him, he was told he should never wear the colors on the road or he'd be smothered to death with it. Reynolds knew the Angels' leader, Victor Mender, was dead serious the night he pissed on the jacket and put it on Reynolds. The jacket never left the bar and Reynolds wore it proudly whenever he was inside his establishment. Most patrons not affiliated with the biker club considered Reynolds to be a member of the Hells Angels.

***

Sharon Satowski had been a bar maid at the Buck and Bull for nearly two years. She tried to keep her promiscuity quiet while enjoying playing the filed, mainly because her boyfriend of eleven months, was second in command of the Rhode Island chapter. Whenever she had the chance, she would sneak a fuck with any guy she found attractive or uniquely interesting. She was drawn to the rough and tumble type and she enjoyed riding on the back of motorcycles. This alone, was the main reason she applied for the position at the Buck and Bull.

It was Thursday night, and like most Thursdays, the bar was crowded. Once again, Sharon caught the eye of a good-looking biker with long hair and a black leather jacket. He wore tight black leather gloves with the fingers cut off and that turned her on. With a few passing words and a smile, it didn't take long for her to slip him a note asking they meet up the road after her shift ended. She knew that all eyes were on her when she was at work and she had to be very discreet. When her shift ended and she finished cleaning off the tables and gathering her tips for the night, she said goodnight to the bartender and left. Up the road in the designated meeting spot, the man with the black gloves sat waiting. As Sharon pulled up to meet him, her heart began beating faster. The combination of sneaking out on her boyfriend, and the thought of getting humped by the good looking stranger, had filled her with a sense of excitement that seemed to get her blood flowing to all the right places.

The trailer Sharon lived in was old and beaten up but it was located on a corner lot, which was the main reason she had bought it. The sun had risen to smile on a new day and the birds were chatting away like old ladies enjoying their morning tea.

Luther Banks sat in the distance watching from the comfort of his soft tail Harley-Davidson. To onlookers, his frame appeared to be much too large for the bike he rode. Standing six-foot-six and weighing three-hundred-and-forty pounds, he would have fit much nicer on a Custom Cruiser.

He watched, as the puny guy in the black leather coat, came strutting out of his girlfriend's trailer and straddled his Fat Boy and began to kick start it. Luther wanted to go over and cut his throat with his double-edged stiletto and watch him bleed to death in the dirt, but he decided that could wait until another day. He sat watching, as he started his bike and rode down the dirt path, leading the way out of the park.

Dismounting his Harley, Luther quietly approached the trailer. He carefully spied the area to make sure no one was watching and he opened the door and went in. When he opened the door, it made the familiar screeching sound he was accustomed to hearing every time he came and went.

"Bobby, did you forget something?" Sharon called out.

Luther walked into her bedroom that was set at the end of the trailer. As he entered through the threshold, he saw her lying naked on the bed smoking a cigarette. The second she realized it was Luther, her complexion turned to a pale white.

"Yeah, Bobby forgot to ask you if you had a boyfriend." His voice was low and raspy, which was an indication to Sharon that he had been up all night drinking. His body consumed the entire doorframe and his head nearly touched the ceiling.

She started thinking fast as her mind scrabbled to recover. "Turk, nothing happened! He's just a friend – he's gay."

He stood over her like a mad Neanderthal over his prey. "You're a fucking lying whore! How long have you been making a fool of me?" Spit was shooting out from his thick, dark brown beard, as he roared in anger.

"I haven't, he's only a friend." She said through trembling lips.

"Don't you fucking lie to me!" He reached out grabbing her by the ankle and pulled her toward him. Then grabbing onto the other ankle, he jerked her legs apart spread-eagle and stood motionless, glaring at her exposed privates with dull eyes.

"Please don't!" she cried out.

"There's God damn smoke coming out of there." His voice resonated through the trailer like a giant in a cave.

"Okay, it only happened once, I'm sorry." Tears were flowing as she pleaded with him for forgiveness. Still holding onto her ankles he tightened his grip and shifting his weight backwards, he spun around throwing her through the air like a rag doll. She was thrown into the wall, knocking the television over during her travels. As she lay on the floor gasping, attempting to find air, Luther stood looking down at her with eyes lacking any indication of remorse or pity.

"You feel like watching some TV? Hey, Oprah's on, your favorite show." He picked up the nineteen-inch television and holding it up to his forehead, he threw it down with one sudden crashing blow. The glass tube shattered on impact and killed her instantly. Turk laughed, as she lay slumped against the trailer wall twitching with the television smashed over her head like she was wearing a hat.

"Well, you always wanted to be on television, didn't you?" He chuckled once again watching the blood flowing down her chest. After rifling through her pocketbook and taking what little cash she had, he went into the kitchen and pulled a beer out of the fridge. With one long swig he downed the beer before walking out of the trailer leaving behind a belch and a corpse.

22

Luther Banks, alias Turk, was not always dead inside. It was a place he resigned to after a long and unforgiving journey. His threshold for tolerance had reached its limit just after his twenty-fourth birthday.

When he was seven-years-old, his mother walked out on him. She brought him to her sister's house outside of Mobile, Alabama, along with two large green trash bags filled with clothes, most of which were hand-me-downs. His mother used to tell him "You can dress up a trash can, but you can't hide the handles." Luther wasn't sure exactly what she had meant by that, but figured that it was degrading. He watched as his mother and her sister argued about what the right amount of money was to assume custody of a seven-year-old that was the size of an eleven-year-old.

"Look at the size of the boy." His aunt blared out pointing at him. "He'll eat the fucking couch if I don't bolt it to the floor. You better give me more money than that."

After his mother gave his Aunt Carrie enough money, she shuffled over and gave him a quick, cold, hug, telling him to be good before getting into her beat up station wagon and driving off. That was the last time he saw his mother.

Luther never knew his father. He was sentenced to life in prison for killing a gas station attendant when Luther was three. He had a distant and foggy memory of his father, like the way he smelled and the feel of his hands. As he grew older, the memory became clearer. The smell was that of stale whiskey and the touch of his hands was consistent with sandpaper. The day his father was taken away in handcuffs was the last time Luther had seen or heard from him.

The boy's new home was a torn up ranch that his aunt bought from a woman who was devastated by a tornado and didn't have property insurance to cover the repairs. Even after seven years, it stood pretty much the way she had purchased it, for the exception of a few new windows and a patched-up roof.

Luther felt like a stranger and an outcast since the first day he arrived at his Aunt's ranch. Two years earlier, his aunt had taken in a guy named Jim who worked part-time cleaning out septic systems. He used to brag about being into shit. "There's good money in shit," Jim used to say, as he poured down a glass of straight vodka. He would come home from work and creep around the house drunk, still donning his shitty work clothes, until he passed out on the couch.

Jim had four kids of his own and Carrie had two boys, ages fourteen and six from two different fathers. The three-bedroom house was seldom quiet with kids crawling the walls and loud parties disturbing the weekends. Luther had been ordered to sleep in the unfinished basement, so he set up a spot in the corner, which was the driest area he could find. He used an old, musty, stained mattress that had been discarded a year earlier. He used an old army blanket to cover it up that Jim had given him; he found his place in the house.

The school Luther attended was a half-mile walk and a bus ride away from the ranch. His aunt would yell at him from the top of the stairs and tell him to get his ass up before he missed the bus. The days she didn't, he would skip school. Most days, Luther hoped his aunt would drink heavily, because when she did, she would sleep in and he would have the next day off. As time passed on, he missed more and more days in the classroom. Luther hated school, but when he reached the fifth grade, he started liking the attention he was getting by the other kids. Being much larger and not having a care in the world set him apart from most of the others. His first suspension came after he beat a kid up so badly, that he was taken to the hospital with a broken nose and a sprained arm. The kid was thought to be the toughest in the schoolyard, but Luther destroyed his reputation in less than a minute. Now holding the schoolyard title, Luther enjoyed a certain sense of power and respect. He accumulated half a dozen groupies that hung around him and he used them to extort lunch money from the timid and weaker kids. Luther never had to worry about lunch money or cigarettes since his schoolyard victory, and he was really enjoying his new status. He didn't catch the eye of very many girls, but he didn't care. To Luther they were whiney and annoying and he didn't bother with them.

The clothes he wore were seldom clean and he had a reputation of carrying a bad odor. Everyone knew Luther smelled bad, except Luther. When the school nurse brought it to his attention, he lost control, throwing things around her office, telling her she smelled and she should clean out her pussy — which caused him another suspension.

A month before his tenth birthday, Luther was lying in his corner of the basement, avoiding a loud party Jim and Carrie were throwing upstairs, when suddenly, a friend of Jim's came stumbling down the stairs. He was drunk and belligerent when he began telling Luther his views about the meaning of life. Describing it as hell, he explained that the best anyone could do was to accept it and embrace it. Not long after his sermon, he produced a pocketknife and forced Luther to perform oral sex on him while holding the knife to his throat. He warned Luther that he would cut his head off, if he yelled out. When he was finished, he slowly brushed the tip of his blasé across Luther's face warning him he would come back and kill him if he told anyone what had happened. Even though Luther was scared and humiliated, he decided to tell his Aunt what had occurred. The next day, Luther approached his hung over Aunt Carrie and told her what her guest had done. She responded by slapping him in the face, calling him a liar and threatening to have him sent to an orphanage if he ever mentioned it again to anyone.

That very night, he removed a kitchen knife from the silverware drawer and brought it downstairs to keep under his mattress. Luther never cried about what happened to him, and he was resigned to the reality that he was completely on his own. In his mind, he told himself over and over, the next time someone came down the stairs with bad intentions, he would bury his knife into them and watch them die. Luther never had the chance to carry out his fantasy, and deep down inside, he regretted it.

By the time Luther attended the eighth grade, he weighed over two-hundred-pounds and was nearly standing six-feet tall. Jim and Carrie had gotten into a bad fight which was a regular occurrence, except this time, she stabbed him in the neck and he nearly died. After Jim was released from the hospital, he came by the house, collected his things, and was never seen or heard from again. Luther didn't care one way or the other. It was business as usual for him, and his business was now selling marijuana at school.

Life for Luther took a huge turn when he was arrested for assault and battery by means of a dangerous weapon, a handgun. He was fifteen, when he put his gun to the temple of another student who was also selling pot in the schoolyard. Luther had warned him once before that the school was his territory and he wouldn't tolerate competition. The boy didn't get the message, so Luther took it to the next step, which landed him in juvenile lock up for six months.

During his tour in juvenile hall, Luther learned that power was realized through fear. The second day he was incarcerated, he found out who had the reputation of being the toughest kid and he beat him senseless in front of several other boys. He claimed self-defense and was put on punishment duty, but was spared any additional time.

When he was released, Luther had been elevated to an even higher status among his trouble-making peers. For the next two years, Luther had expanded his business to other local schools, and was dealing pot on the street, as well. He moved out of his Aunt Carrie's house after she threatened to call the police and turn him in for beating the shit out of her two sons. They had eaten the Kentucky fried chicken Luther had stored in the fridge.

Luther moved into an apartment with one of his regular customers – an older guy with little ambition, who smoked pot all day long. Luther enjoyed getting high occasionally, but was not one to get stoned on a daily basis. His drug of choice was beer and he was beginning to find girls more attractive.

In his junior year, he dropped out of high school and was hanging out with a crew that were a few years older than him. This is when his love for motorcycles began. In Luther's mind, if it wasn't a Harley Davidson, it was a piece of shit. He loved the loud roar it made when turning the throttle – it commanded respect. He bought his first bike at eighteen, a used Sportster that needed a paint job from being dumped several times by a drunken rider, who didn't know how to downshift properly. Luther fixed it up the best he could, and learned how to ride by trial and error.

Soon after, Luther began hanging out with a group of local bikers that called themselves the Renegades. He bought a brown leather jacket with their logo on the back. It was a Grim Reaper wielding a long sickle with blood dripping off the tip.

One hot summer day in July, they all hopped on their bikes to attend a biker's weekend rally, five hours away in the State of Georgia. Once they arrived, Luther was amazed at how many bikers were in attendance. He was in awe of hundreds of Harleys lined up with the sunshine detailing the brilliant colors like an eternal rainbow. He loved the custom paint jobs and the shiny chrome pipes and spoke wheels Harley Davidson offered. He felt at home and was ready to party.

The beer and whiskey was flowing heavily and joints were being passed around like candy on Halloween. Luther, being one of the tallest people in attendance, was asked to participate in a volleyball game. Normally, he would have rejected the idea, but the girl asking had very large breasts so he engaged. The game had been underway for ten minutes, when a player on the other team spiked the ball hitting Luther on the side of his face. Everyone began laughing, mostly because he wasn't paying attention and had a funny and surprised look on his face. When Luther saw that the guy who spiked the ball was also laughing, his blood began to boil. He walked directly to the end of the net, grabbing onto the long pole, circling round-and-round, like he was stirring a large pot of soup. Then with a loud grunt, he pulled the pole out of the ground. The pole's dirt covered end had a sharp point. The other players thought he was just disrupting the game and many were asking him to calm down. Luther had an evil look in his eyes – a look that warned people they should stay clear of him, if they wanted to remain intact.

In a split second, Luther charged like a warrior in the Macedonian army with his spear in the ready position. The player who was responsible for hitting Luther didn't have a chance to run away. By the time he realized what was happening, it was too late. Yelling like a lunatic, Luther impaled him through the stomach with the business end of the volleyball pole. Then he proceeded to lift him up into the air with the end of his weapon. Luther's arms were nearly the same size as his victim's thighs, and he had the strength to hold him high in the air with the pole embedded into his mid-section. The guy was screaming in pain and his blood was pouring down the pole covering Luther's arms, chest and beard. When Luther finally dropped him, everyone had dispersed and watched from a distance. Luther stood in the open field still holding his weapon, looking down over his fallen enemy like a proud soldier. This is how he earned the nickname, Turk, because of the way the Turkish would impale their victims on the end of long stakes during the reign of Vlad the Impaler.

The mayhem that occurred in the field was ultimately the demise of the volleyball game and the end of Luther's freedom for the next seven years. His victim survived the attack, but was paralyzed from the waist down due to complications from the spinal cord having been pierced.

Luther had been sentenced to a term of fifteen years, but was released after serving less than eight, due to overcrowding in the Georgia state prison system, and it having been his first offense as an adult.

During his incarceration, Luther met a fellow Harley enthusiast, Ray Butler. It was quickly determined that they shared a passion for motorcycles, while lifting weights together on a sunny afternoon in the yard. With their shirts off and the sun baking their skin, they displayed an array of tattoos on their arms and upper torso. Both inmates had tattoos signifying the Harley Davidson motorcycle and it immediately became a topic of discussion. Luther had a tattoo of a dagger piercing a bloody heart on his upper left arm and Ray had the grim reaper riding a hog on his back, just above his right shoulder blade.

Ray Butler had been sentenced to five years for trafficking in heroin. Standing three inches shorter than Luther and weighing ten pounds more, he was named "the bull" by his fellow Hells Angels. Ray had killed two people while he was a member of the notorious biker gang and one prior to his induction. They instantly became friends and spent much of their time in the yard together lifting weights and sizing up the other inmates. They were well respected inside and nobody dared to mess with either one of them.

Three years had passed and it was time for Ray to be paroled. The day before he was released, Ray assured Luther he would introduce him to the right people when he was back on the street. Most friends would have parted with a hug or a simple handshake - they said goodbye by head butting each other. The cracking sound was loud enough to draw attention of several inmates in the yard and it left Ray with a nice gash above his right eye.

The next four years seemed to drag on and Luther was counting the days until he could carve out his place in the world. When his day arrived, he was all business, gathering his things, signing his release paperwork, and walking out into free air, without looking back.

He rode a bus to Providence, Rhode Island, where he was met by Ray and two other Hells Angels at the terminal. They drove him to a farmhouse where he was introduced to the leader of the Rhode Island chapter, Vince Mender. After several hours of drinking and getting laid by a local biker slut, Ray and Mendor took Luther into an old barn where they gave him a gift, a stolen shiny, dark maroon Heritage Softail Harley.

Luther was not one to show emotion, but he displayed a half smile when he laid eyes on his new bike. They celebrated the rest of the day toting shotguns and pistols. Drinking up a storm and shooting everything in sight, they were totally out of control, like a bunch of drunken cowboys.

It didn't take long for Luther to be initiated into the gang. Mender knew he had the right stuff, and he was exactly the kind of member he wanted in his gang.

Nearly five months after he was released from prison, Luther was sent to make a buy from a heroin dealer that was coming up from New York City. He and Ray drove to New Haven, Connecticut where they met in a remote area outside city limits. Ray was holding the case of cash with a hundred-thousand-dollars inside and Luther was holding a sawed off shotgun concealed under his long trench coat. The two men they were to meet were twenty minutes late and Luther wasn't happy about it. Once they determined the heroin was genuine, and the cash was all there, they began to make the exchange. Just before the money was handed over, Luther pulled out the shotgun and blasted the taller guy in the face spattering his brain matter all over his friend. Surprised by what had happened, the other guy never had time to react, before taking a slug through the heart. Both men died instantly. Ray turned to Luther with a confused look on his face, "Turk, what the fuck!" - was all he said.

Luther picked up the case of heroin, looked back at Ray who was still standing over the bodies, and repeated what Mender had said to him just before he left Rhode Island for the exchange, "Three can keep a secret, if two are dead." His evil look in his eyes, even frightened Ray.

The two men left Connecticut with the heroin and the money. Three months later, Luther was promoted to second in command of the Rhode Island chapter of the Hells Angels

23

The car was parked and the engine turned off in a dimly lit corner of a Motel 6 parking lot. Sam sat slouched down, watching the one-story building from a distance. He had begun following his wife three hours earlier, after leaving their house, and this is where she ended up. Sam kept a safe distance behind her, as she stopped at the liquor store, leaving with a brown paper bag and then continuing on to her final destination at the motel. As he watched her pull into the parking lot, his vision began to blur with eyes clouded by tears. When she entered room number nine, and the door closed behind her, he broke down crying. He knew someone was waiting for her when she went directly to the room without checking in.

Sam's suspicions about where she had been going at night had been consuming his thoughts and he knew it was interfering with his ability to focus at work. He tried to push it out of his mind, but it was an impossible task, so he resigned himself to finding out the truth before he lost his mind.

Through itchy eyes, Sam sat watching the building that had slipped out of focus as the night grew darker and quieter. Occasionally, he brought the green binoculars up to his face for a closer look, but there was nothing to see with drawn curtains and the darkness behind them. Like so many times over the years, Sam was once again on a stakeout from behind the wheel of his car. Only this time it was different. This time he was afraid of what he might uncover.

The light in room number nine became illuminated, and Sam could hear his heart sounding out like African drums. He picked up his binoculars for a closer look, and a couple minutes later, the door opened. His wife came out first followed by a tall, black man wearing a jacket and tie. Sam was feeling extremely warm and began perspiring, followed by nausea. He was able to contain himself long enough for them to kiss goodnight and drive away in separate cars, before he frantically opened his driver side door vomiting into the parking lot.

Sitting in the parking lot for over an hour, Sam swept away the tears that snuck out of his eyes in deceit. His mind was racing as he thought about his young bride on their wedding day. The vows she recited were as clear as if it were yesterday. He remembered the day their son was born and then the birth of their second child. So many happy and loving memories they shared. *How could she do this to him - to them?* He had to kill the pain so he started his car and slowly drove away heading directly toward a bar.

Standing alone at the bar, Sam went over and over in his mind what he observed at the motel. As the alcohol started to take control, he did all he could to maintain his composure. When he felt like crying, he would grunt and shrug it off with a shot of Wild Turkey. After the bartender pleaded with him to go home, he finally gave in, taking a cab and leaving his car in the parking lot.

When he arrived home, Susan was in bed and sound asleep. He stood in the doorway watching her motionless body as she lay in the bed they had bought together many years ago. He was about to wake her, and then he quickly came to his senses, remembering what his father had once told him when he was a teenager. *"Never argue with a woman, when one, or both of you, have had too much to drink. Wait until the next day when you are thinking much clearer."* He turned and went downstairs and fell into the couch, he didn't dream.

24

Pam Sanders decided to pay her friend a visit with the intent to burn a few cigarettes and catch up on the latest gossip. It was nearly noontime, so she figured Sharon would be up and about. Her trailer was only a short walk across the park and she would stop by on a regular basis and they would spend time complaining about life and the men that caused the complaints.

Whenever she saw the maroon Harley parked outside, she would turn around and go home. On this particular morning, it wasn't there, so she continued onward and began knocking on the door. After a minute of knocking, she decided to try the door as she always did when Sharon didn't answer. Unlike most other times, the door was left open. Sharon always locked her trailer when she wasn't home, so she decided to go in and wake her. What she saw was a vision that would remain with her for the rest of her life. On that same night, for the first time ever, she knelt down alongside her bed and prayed for Sharon, her family and herself.

As Sam and Donny's car pulled into the trailer park, they noticed the absence of many people outside, which was unusual for such a nice sunny afternoon. While continuing on, they observed a large gathering of people standing outside the yellow crime scene tape that surrounded the trailer of Sharon Satowski.

The resident trooper and a few other troopers in uniform were already on scene and waiting for the homicide investigators to arrive. Walton, being such a small town, didn't have their own police department. They had a resident trooper who worked an eight-hour shift Monday through Friday and was on call the rest of the time. If anything serious occurred in town, he would call for back up from troopers assigned to the closest barracks.

The troopers did a good job preserving the crime scene, keeping the spectators under control and away from the trailer. Sam and Donny used their car as a wedge moving slowly through the crowd, dividing them with their vehicle, before coming to a stop and getting out.

"Hey Dan," Sam greeted the resident trooper with a handshake and Donny followed suit. His head was pounding and he was hoping there would be a vile of aspirin inside the trailer.

"Sam, Donny, it's pretty ugly in there. Whoever did this was pretty damn strong. He literally killed her with a TV," the Trooper said with a grin.

"Who is she?" Donny asked. The other troopers came walking over and they all greeted each other.

"Her name is Sharon Satowski. She is a waitress at the Buck and Bull."

"Why doesn't that surprise me?" Sam said. "We should have closed that place down a long time ago."

"Believe me, we tried." Dan said while running the yellow tape between his thumb and fore finger.

"Who found her?" Donny asked with a pen and notebook in hand.

"Her friend that lives in a trailer just down the road, Pamela Sanders. She said she came over to visit this morning and found her. She called it in immediately."

"Dan, do me a favor and keep her here until we can interview her. Let's go inside and take a look." Sam patted the trooper on the shoulder, took out his latex gloves, and entered the trailer with Donny following behind. They walked into the bedroom, stopping dead in their tracks once they observed the scene. The detectives saw her small frame slouched in a large pool of dried blood, in a semi- sitting position and leaning against the wall with a portable TV over her head.

"Jesus, have you ever seen anything like this?" Sam looked toward his partner.

"Never," Donny responded with a look of disgust.

"He crashed a TV set over her head, like something you might see on the Three Stooges," Sam said.

"Yeah, except she doesn't get up and walk away on this set."

"No she doesn't." Sam concurred.

"Looks like she has been dead about a day or so," Donny said.

"The print squad has been notified, and the coroner too," a young trooper standing behind Donny advised them.

After examining the body, they took their time and went through the entire trailer looking for clues. Sam found a bottle of Tylenol in the bathroom and without anyone watching, he quickly slipped three tablets into his mouth, swallowing them down without water. Donny had a plastic evidence bag with a set of tweezers and was gathering up any evidence considered relevant to their investigation.

After an initial thorough sweep of the crime scene, Sam and Donny went outside for some fresh air. The photographer and the print squad had arrived and were kind enough to bring a couple bottles of water for the investigators. Sam and Donny knew they were sucking up in hopes that someday, they too, would be working in the homicide division.

Dan came walking over to notify them that Pamela Sanders wanted to leave and Sam agreed to speak with her right away. She was leaning against a cruiser smoking a cigarette, when Sam and Donny approached. Her hair was dark brown and pinned up into a poorly shaped bun. She had a pockmarked complexion and wore thin rim glasses. Her dark brown sweatshirt had a noticeable stain on the left lapel.

"Ms. Sanders."

"Yes.

"I am Detective Carra and this is my partner Detective Burke." Sam handed her his card. "We will be heading the investigation into Ms. Satowski's death."

"Nice to meet you," she said as she attempted to straighten out her hair.

"How well did you know Ms. Satowski?" Sam was asking while Donny took notes.

"We were good friends. We used to get together at least twice a week for coffee and drinks."

"When was the last time you saw her alive?"

"Three days ago, Tuesday morning."

"Did she seem like anything was bothering her, was she acting differently than normal?"

"No, she was the same as always. She was such a nice person, a free spirit."

"A free spirit?" Donny asked.

"Yes, Sharon loved life. She liked to have a good time."

Sam made a quick glance in Donny's direction. "Was there a particular boyfriend that she spent most of her time with?"

"She had many guys chasing after her, but there is one guy she was with a lot. He's a real asshole. He goes by "Turk". He's in the Hells Angels.

"When's the last time you saw this, Turk?" Donny was writing fast, as if he was back in college trying to keep up with a rambling professor.

"It's been a while, maybe a month ago. We had a little argument and I haven't seen him since. I avoid him. Anytime I see his motorcycle parked out here, I turn around and go in the other direction."

"The guy really rubbed you the wrong way, Huh?" Donny asked.

"That guy is an evil prick. I don't know what she sees in him. The way he looked at me that day I called him out, if looks could kill."

"What did you argue about?"

"He was very crude. He was pushing for a threesome and not in a very nice way, I might add. I told him he would be the last person on earth I would have a threesome with and he didn't take the rejection well."

"Do you know what his real name is?"

"No, just Turk, that's all I know."

"Did he ever display violence towards Sharon or did she ever tell you he did?"

"No, not that I can remember."

"What color is his bike?"

"It's a maroon Harley Heritage Soft Tail."

"I'm impressed, Sam nodded. You really know bikes."

"Not really. That's all he ever talked about. You know these biker types. If their motorcycles had a pussy they would marry them."

Donny chuckled. "Yeah, we know the type." Sam kept his poker face. He was focused on getting a description of Turk.

"What does this guy look like?"

She pushed a strand of hair away from her left eye. "He's humongous. Stands about six eight and he probably weighs about three-fifty. This guy hasn't missed many meals. He has long, brown hair and a full beard. He looks like a cave man, and acts like one, too.

Sam bit his lower lip. He had seen someone that fit this description before, but he couldn't recollect when or where. "We'll be in touch if we need anything else. Thanks for your help and we're sorry about your friend," Sam added.

She looked into his eyes and knew he meant it. "Please find whoever did this and put the maniac behind bars."

"We will," Sam assured her.

Both detectives walked over to where Dan was standing. "Do you know a Hells Angel named Turk?" Sam asked him.

"Yeah, I know who he is. The guy is a mountain. His real name is Banks, Luther Banks."

"Well, it would take a mountain to smash a TV over someone's head this way." Donny concluded.

"He's ranked pretty high up in the gang. I pulled him over once for speeding. He ate the ticket right in front of me. He paid it on time, though. We have Intel on him from an undercover task force we put together about a year ago, and then, someone took our guy out with a hammer, remember that?"

"Yeah, I remember. He was working undercover at the biker bar when someone threw a hammer at him, splitting his head open." Donny was rubbing the back of his head as he spoke.

"That's right. His name was Dave LaBerge. He was undercover for about six months and then one night when he was walking out of the bar, a hammer came flying through the air and clocked him in the back of the head. He had a serious concussion and some brain damage. The poor bastard had to retire. We never found out who was responsible, but he had accumulated some good information on the gang and some of its major players. He must have gotten too close. In any case, it's all on file, if you need it."

"Yeah, we'll check out the file." Sam reached out his hand to thank him.

When the coroner arrived, the fingerprint team was busy dusting away. Sam gave them some direction before he and Donny left the scene. The uniformed troopers had interviewed everyone they could locate in the park, and no one saw anything out of the ordinary. A couple of people heard the roar of a motor cycle, but that wasn't unusual in the park.

Sam and Donny were in their vehicle driving straight to State Police headquarters. Donny reached out to the dash, turning the music down to a whisper. "I would assume we're going to archives?"

"Yeah, let's see what we can find out about Luther Banks."

"From what it sounds like, he is a real bad ass." Donny said, while tapping the steering wheel with his thumbs.

"If he is responsible for killing that girl, he's nothing more than a coward."

"Well, I guess there is such a thing as a bad ass coward, isn't there?"

"I don't know about that. Maybe he is just plain sick in the head, assuming he did this," Sam said.

"Those Hells Angels are crazy bastards. I remember during an organized-crime-training class a few years ago, they covered a segment on them. Many of their senior members are veterans of foreign wars. Did you know that?"

Sam looked at Donny with his familiar stare, which was an indication he had knowledge of the gang. "Yes, that's true. They have been around since after the Second World War. Back then they were mainly a bunch of bikers that were attempting to escape from society. Many felt our government had turned their backs on them after the war. After Vietnam, the club grew in size with chapters expanding the globe. They grew more disgruntled regarding our government's policies and treatment of returning war veterans. I can't say I blame them, but I don't think it's an excuse to deal in illegal drugs and extortion." Sam rubbed his eyes. Donny could tell he had a hard night, but didn't mention it. "I think many of the newer members like this guy Banks aren't veterans. They are just a bunch of out of control criminals. Some of these guys are serious sociopaths and would cut your heart out, without blinking an eye."

"I guess when we find Banks we should be extremely careful," Donny suggested.

"Yes, we definitely should be careful. We can't take any chances with this type of person. There is a retired undercover trooper that will attest to that." Sam turned the music up and sat back into a comfortable position and he closed his eyes.

25

The drive back to Rhode Island from upstate New York was by far the best drive Nick had ever taken. He sat in the cockpit of his new Lamborghini Diablo cruising up route 95 in the passing lane. Every now and then he would shift from third gear into fourth just to feel the power underneath him. He wasn't able to keep the car in fourth gear for long, because it easily pushed the speedometer over the one-hundred-mile mark. He had chosen the Diablo for many reasons, but the power it deployed was the main one. He had done his research before making the call to the dealer in New York. The fact that the car was powered with a V12 and 520 horse power was impressive enough for Nick. He knew what he wanted, and it was a bright yellow Diablo that went from zero to sixty miles per hour in 3.8 seconds, with a top speed of 208 miles per hour. He tried his best to beat the salesman down on the price, but ultimately ended up paying nearly the full price of two hundred and twenty nine thousand dollars.

Nick was cruising along doing 80 miles per hour, when a red Corvette convertible quickly pulled up alongside him. The driver looked at Nick and smiled just before nodding his head. The young man with short, blond hair punched it and began to take off. Nick could feel the adrenalin come alive within him. He hit the clutch and shifted into fourth and then fifth gear passing the Corvette in a flash. He glanced at his speedometer and saw that he was doing 140 miles per hour. He quickly downshifted into third gear and returned to his cruising speed. The Corvette passed him on the right and then pulled into his lane in front of him. The driver didn't bother to look at Nick this time.

All heads turned, as Nick drove through town in his new machine. He knew it wasn't very often one observed a Lamborghini being driven through town, maybe in Beverly Hills California, but not in South

Walton, Rhode Island. He felt like the king of the road, winking at a couple young girls, as he turned the corner like he was on rails.

Pulling to a stop in front of his apartment, he still couldn't get used to the way the doors opened upward. He got out, set the alarm and stood admiring his new car in awe. It looked like something out of the future, he thought.

As Nick turned the key to open the outside door to his apartment building, he figured it would be the last time. He walked up the stairs, and as he turned the corner, he noticed some things piled up in front of his apartment door. He hadn't been to his apartment in a couple weeks, and the hallway seemed narrow and dingy to him *now*. As he got closer to his apartment, everything was coming into focus. Neatly placed in front of his apartment door was a bouquet of flowers with a small envelope attached. Someone had placed a fruit basket with apples, oranges and pears that were beginning to rot. There was a box of candy and several envelopes scattered about with his name written on them. At first, he thought it was a shrine – maybe someone was sick or had died. He bent over picking up a card that rested on top of the cheap carnations that were beginning to wither away. Opening the card, he began to read the note.

Dear Mr. Gennaro, congratulations on winning the lottery. My name is Marilyn Comenski and I live in the neighborhood. My daughter, Donna, is twelve years old and has been diagnosed with Hodgkin's disease. We have no insurance and are unable to get proper treatment for her. Please help us to stop her suffering. You have millions of dollars and all we need is ten thousand dollars to begin her treatments. We appreciate your generosity and wish you the best of luck with your new-found fortune. Enjoy the fruit basket. Our address is on the back of the envelope. God Bless You. Marilyn.

Nick picked up an apple, disturbing several fruit flies that were resting on the fruit bed. He swatted at them and then dropped the apple back into the basket. He picked up another envelope, opened it and began to read. It was the same thing, just a different person looking for a hand out. He kicked the debris aside and entered his apartment where he found a few more envelopes that had been pushed under his door. He looked around his place and realized there was very little he wanted to keep. He retrieved some personal items and made a short list of the few pieces of furniture he wanted to keep. There was an old saber from the Civil War his uncle had given him. A couple pictures that hung on the wall and his VCR and color TV he could use as a spare. He would give the list to Zollo and have him come by and move everything out.

Once he was finished, he went downstairs to the mailroom to check his mailbox. He pushed the key in, and as he turned it, the mailbox door sprung open as if it were being pushed from the inside. His mailbox was completely full with at least a hundred letters. A sticky note from the postman was glued to the inside of the mailbox door, notifying him that there was no more room and the rest of his mail was at the post office. He gathered his mail and left the building. He would sift through it for anything important and throw the rest out. Nick had been warned at the lottery commission about people coming out of the woodwork looking for a piece of his new fortune; but he never thought it would be this bad. He had hired a lawyer so he could keep his identity confidential, but eventually people began to find out, and not long after that, the press had been notified. It wasn't long before his identity was made public and people attempted to locate him with the hope of getting their hands on a piece of his gift from the State.

Once outside, he found a couple kids hovering over his car. One of them was running his hand over the hood. "Hey, get your fucking hands off my car or I'll break them!" The kids both gave him a nasty look and went on their way. Nick got in and turned the key, once again coming to life.

Sunday arrived, and Nick had been invited by his mother to have dinner with the family. After leaving his apartment, he drove to his parent's neighborhood, slowly passing by their house wondering if he should stop by. He saw his sisters' cars parked out front and he assumed his father would be there, as well. He shifted his car into second and it lurched him back. Burning rubber in front of their house, he tore down the street.

Inside, Nicholas sat with his wife and daughters at the dining room table. At least twice a month, Maria made sauce and they would all sit together for a filling meal of pasta and homemade tomato sauce. The fresh sausage and hand rolled meatballs came from Nicholas's butcher shop. The difference now was the two empty seats that Chris and Nick use to occupy. Maria tried her best to put it out of her mind, but she felt like an amputee. They bowed their heads as Nicholas offered grace, ending with a gesture of the cross. Grace to Nicholas had become routine and he had long forgotten the meaning of the words he spoke.

"I saw an article on the investigation in the paper today. It said that Nick is a suspect in the murder." Ashley glanced at her father after speaking and didn't like the look on his face. She started to twirl the pasta around her fork in silence.

"They will write anything to sell a newspaper these days." Her mother said, as she carved a slice of Italian bread off the loaf. "They should be ashamed of themselves."

"They said that Chris was the winner of the lottery and they have him on tape buying the ticket. What if he did do it?

Marybeth stopped eating and put her fork down. "Shut up Ashley. Just shut up! Nick loved Chris and he would never do anything to hurt him, right Pop?"

Nicholas just looked at her without speaking. Everyone at the table was glaring at Nicholas expecting him to comfort them with a positive response, but he couldn't speak. He just sat with a blank face.

26

Rhode Island State Police Headquarters was located in a three-year-old building in Cranston. It was a palace compared to the old headquarters in Providence, which was now abandoned and covered in anti-police graffiti. The two detectives sat in an air-conditioned office specifically dedicated for criminal offender file search and review. Donny had just downloaded the file on Luther Banks and was browsing through it.

"Can you print that out? I hate staring at a computer screen. It's bad for the eyes." Sam asked, squinting like an old man confined to a retirement home.

Donny hit the print icon and they sat in wait as the laser printer spit out what they were looking for. Once the printer stopped singing, Donny retrieved the documents and handed them to his older partner.

"Here, you can browse through the hard copy and I'll go through it on the screen." He took a seat, covering the mouse with his large hand. "This is one disturbed individual," Donny commented, as he scrolled down the file. "He impaled a guy with a volleyball pole."

"And almost killed him too," Sam added. "This reads that the interviewing officer was fearful they would lose the victim before he had a chance to identify his attacker and there were no other witnesses."

"Look here on page four." Donny pointed at the screen with the eraser end of a pencil. "He has been a suspect in two murder investigations, but we could never get enough evidence to convict him. This guy is pretty slippery and lucky I might add."

Sam briefly examined his partner. "I'm thinking his luck may soon run out. It looks like he resides in Cumberland. At least that's where his motorcycle excise tax bill was last sent. His address is listed as 649 Landsong Drive. What do you say we pay him a visit and see where he was yesterday morning?"

Donny moved his mouse around in small circles, finally placing his curser on the icon to turn off the system. "Sounds like a plan." He got up and gestured toward the door and followed Sam out.

The drive took nearly half an hour. While pulling up to a stop in front of the address, it occurred to Sam that the residence was exactly the type of place he would expect a guy like Banks to live. The house was a beat up three family in a low income neighborhood. The light, green paint was falling off the face of the house and the porch was leaning to one side like a drunk in a Saint Patrick's Day parade. They got out of the car, negotiated the decrepit brick walkway leading to the porch and carefully ascended the stairs. There were three mailboxes and one of them had a huge dent in it that could have been caused by a large fist. That was the one that had a black sticker that read, Banks. The number two was faded, but legible enough to determine he lived on the second floor. Sam opened the door and started up the stairs when he heard the first floor door opening. Donny was the closest, so he peaked his head around the corner to see who was there.

"He's not home." A woman in her mid to late fifties was stood in the doorway. She was wearing a faded blue bathrobe and tightened it up around her throat as she spoke.

Donny wasn't surprised by her appearance. "Hello, how do you know he's not here?"

She looked at the two well-dressed men and knew right away they weren't there for a friendly visit or social gathering.

"Because, when he pulls up on his motorbike, it shakes the house. It's so damned loud. Why are you looking for him anyway, did he kill someone?"

Sam shot a look at his partner and then moved down the stairs to get a closer look at the woman. "Well, I hope not. We just need to speak with him about an urgent matter. What time does he usually get home?" Sam asked.

"Who knows, sometimes it's very late. Sometimes he doesn't come home at all."

"Did he come home last night?" Donny asked.

"Yes, I heard him come in around one in the morning. He was drunk."

"How do you know that?" Sam inquired.

"Because he bounces off the hallway walls and he talks to himself. He's not a very nice person at all."

"Alright, we appreciate your help. If you would Miss?"

"Campbell, Iris Campbell." She proudly finished his sentence while fixing her hair.

"Ms. Campbell, please let this be our secret. We don't want Mr. Banks to know we were here." Sam handed her his card.

"Detective, I knew you two were cops. Mums the word." She put her finger vertically over her mouth.

"Thank you Iris." Sam said in a whisper and they turned and went back to their vehicle and drove off circling around the block before coming to a stop further up the street. They sat in wait for Banks to return for nearly four hours. The sun had gone down and Donny was dozing off while Sam read a Robert Ludlum novel.

The roar of a motorcycle could be heard for blocks and it grew louder and louder as it got closer to their position. Donny woke up when the Harley turned down the street their car was parked on.

"My money says this is our man heading home." Sam said.

Donny was rubbing his eyes. "How should we handle this?" He asked.

"We question him before he goes into the house, because once he's in, he probably won't answer the door."

"I brought this along just in case he becomes unruly," Donny said while producing a stun gun.

"Great, that's all I need, to be brought up on charges for using unauthorized equipment."

Donny squeezed the weapon and raised it up high. "There is an old saying; I'd rather be tried by twelve than carried by six."

"You do have a valid point. We'll stop him as he pulls up to the driveway. Be careful with this guy," Sam warned his protégé.

27

As Luther pulled up to the driveway, the two detectives came up from behind him, as he got off his bike to open the gate to the driveway. Luther saw the two men sneaking up from behind him, and for a split second, a voice in his head was telling him to attack. His mind began racing and his eyes darted from the men to the pouch strapped to his bike. He knew they were the police and they weren't there soliciting for the policeman's ball. *I will go for the tall, young cop first, striking him with an open palm to the nose. Then I'll pull out the hunting knife I have concealed under my leather coat and bury it into the older cop's chest, before finishing the tall cop by slicing his throat. If that fails, I'll dash to my leather pouch, pull out my revolver, and end it in a blaze of glory.*

Luther gained his senses and calmed himself. Something told him they had nothing on him. If they did, they would have come with a small army of cops equipped with guns in the ready position.

"Luther Banks?" Sam called out holding his gold shield up high.

"That's right, what do you want?"

"Turn off the bike for a minute, so we can talk."

Luther kicked the stand down and killed the engine. "I'm very busy today, what do you want?"

"I'm detective Carra and this is detective Burke with the State Police. We are investigating the murder of Sharon Satowski."

"Sharon is dead?" The huge bearded man said without a hint of remorse.

"That's right. She was killed yesterday morning. I understand you and her were dating?"

"Dating, no, I dropped a few nuts in her, along with half the dudes in Rhode Island."

Sam was agitated by his coldness. "Well, someone dropped a TV on her head in Rhode Island. What do you know about that?"

"I don't know shit about that!" Luther's tone was becoming louder.

"Where were you yesterday morning between nine and twelve noon?"

"I was here, sleeping."

"Were you alone?"

The hair on his face parted and allowed a half smile to peak out. "No, I was with your mother."

"You're a funny guy, Luther," Sam said, controlling his temper.

Donny had his finger on the stun gun trigger and was ready to light him up.

"I got nothing more to say to you. If you have anything else to ask me you can talk to my lawyer." Luther opened the gate and pushed his bike through and closed it behind him.

Donny relaxed his finger and spoke to Luther's broad leather back as he moved away. "We'll be in touch, Luther."

Luther quickly spun around and looked deep into Donny's eyes. "Next time you come here you better have a warrant," he barked out.

"Next time we will," Sam replied. The detectives began walking back to their car. Halfway there, Donny turned his head, peaking over his right shoulder.

"Let's go home and get some sleep. Tomorrow we'll go see the judge and petition for a warrant." Donny concurred and they got in the car and drove away.

The next morning they returned to Luther's house with a warrant in hand along with three other state troopers. It didn't take a lot of convincing to get the judge to issue a warrant. With Luther's violent history and his relationship to the victim, the judge agreed there was cause.

At first Luther was hostile, but he calmed down after Sam advised him that they would gladly lock him up for obstruction, if he didn't play ball. They went through his entire apartment tagging clothes, and before leaving, they took the boots off his feet. When they were finished, the apartment didn't look any worse than it did before they arrived.

Luther was fit to be tied and knew he needed to blow off some steam before he did something crazy. He jumped on his bike and rode directly to the Buck and Bull and began downing shots of Jack Daniels with beer chasers. He sat alone at the end of the bar, and when he did that, nobody came near him.

***

Jonathan Taylor Blaine had his nose down and eyes fixed on a two lens microscope, as he normally did throughout any given day. Being the Chief Forensic Scientist for the State of Rhode Island is what defined him. With a degree from John Hopkins and an undergrad from Princeton, he was respected more than understood. Jonathan was considered by most as the ultimate nerd whose entire existence is based on his work. Never married and very few girlfriends, he lived alone and saved every nickel he earned. His thin frame and matted down brown hair gave him a look that might win him a Pee Wee Herman look-a-like contest.

Throughout the past five years, his goal was to disprove Dr. Kim, his nemesis from Connecticut. Whenever Dr. Kim offered his theoretical conclusion of a murder or cause thereof, he would try to discredit the famous scientist with his own conclusion.

"Good morning, Scope." Donny said, as he and Sam entered the lab.

The doctor was alarmed for a second, until he saw the familiar faces of the detectives. "What do you say, fellas?"

Jonathan had earned the nickname "Scope" several years earlier. Many people thought it was because he was always peering into a microscope. However, the real reason, was because of his unbearable halitosis. Due to a lack of saliva flow, he suffered from a condition, which caused his mouth to dry up, and in turn, it produced bad breath. In the past, cops and other state employees would discretely leave bottles of mouthwash in the lab, hoping he would get the hint and start rinsing on a regular basis. It took quite a while, but eventually he caught on and began using it several times a day. Once this process began, the whole issue came out in the open and it became a subject that created many laughs at his expense. At first he took it offensively, but in time he became calloused and let it roll off his shoulders.

"Can you take a close look at these items we tagged from a suspect's house in the Satowski case?" Donny asked.

"Sure, I'd love to help you bag the perp that ruined a perfectly good RCA. You know there aren't many American made televisions anymore. Everything is labeled Sony, Hitachi or Panasonic. What has happened to this great country of ours?"

Donny wondered if Scope even owned a TV. "I guess we forgot that exporting is better for our economy than importing," he said.

Sam's cell phone began vibrating in his pocket. For a brief moment, he thought about the stun gun that Donny had taken along in case he had to zap Luther. "I'll be right back." Sam walked into an adjoining room to take the call. A few minutes later he returned. "That was the print squad. Banks has his prints all over the trailer and the TV as well."

"That doesn't surprise me," Donny said.

"Me neither, but it's not enough. He was seeing her on a regular basis, so his prints are expected to be there. We need more to bag this creep. Let's grab some lunch and we can come back after you have had a chance to examine these items. Start with the boots. Scope, can we bring you back a sandwich?"

"I'm all set. I brought my lunch, thanks anyway. I'll make this my top priority."

"Thanks Scope, we owe you a beer."

"Sam, how come you keep saying that even though you know I don't drink? You have been saying that for years."

"Because I figure eventually you'll start."

Scope pushed out a laugh, as his favorite investigating duo walked out of the lab.

During lunch they discussed the Gennaro case and their frustration with the lack of progress. The murder cases just kept falling on them like so many snowflakes during a blizzard. Once they felt traction on a case, another body would surface. Sam was beginning to feel the weight and his body wasn't getting any stronger. It was weakening with time.

Donny was scanning the paper looking at alternate employment options. His dream of being a novelist was dying a slow death with every literary agency rejection. He hung them on a spike that was sticking out of his kitchen wall. He knew he had a winner, maybe even a best seller. If he could just get someone to read his work, he might have a shot to sell his book and move on with his life.

After they finished lunch, they went back to their office to take care of paperwork that was piling up faster than manure at a race track. They were both sitting at their desks pushing a pen when Sam's cell phone rang.

"Sam Carra."

"Sam, its Scope. I have something here you and Donny are going to like."

"Scope, what have you got?"

"I found tiny traces of blood on the suspect's boots and guess what?"

"They match the DNA of the victim," Sam finished his sentence.

"Bingo."

"Scope, you are a genius. Document it in a report with all the bells and whistles buddy."

"I'm on it." The phone went dead.

"We got him. Her blood is on his boots. His prints are all over the television. We can prove the age of the blood evidence and it's a perfect DNA match. With his history, it shouldn't be hard to get an indictment." Sam reached out and shook Donny's hand. "Good work partner."

As Donny shook hands with his friend, he wasn't feeling quite as optimistic. He had a feeling bagging Banks was not going to be so easy, and he was right.

28

The bright, golden smile of an awakening sun was warming the glass table, as it peered through the window lighting up Sam's kitchen. He sat alone at the table behind his half-empty cup of coffee. He didn't notice the brightness or the warmth of the sun. In his mind's eye, it may have even been a gloomy and cloudy day. His thoughts were totally consumed with his wife and what he had witnessed outside the motel. It was like his mind had a playback button and he kept rewinding it again and again going back to the night he suffered the ultimate betrayal. He tried pushing the forward button, but it was broken. In his mind, he went through all the different ways he could possibly handle his approach with Susan about what he had seen. At first, he thought about telling her to pack her bags and get out. Then he thought about slapping her senseless and throwing her out. As time evolved, he calmed and thought about suggesting counseling. If that didn't work, he might even pack his things and leave it all behind. He wasn't sure what to do. His heart was in pain, but he knew he didn't want to lose his wife. She was a huge part of his life and he was comfortable with her. Without her, he would be lost, because what he had with Susan was all he knew. He thought about the kids and how they would handle it. How would a divorce affect them, and what would they think of their mother if they found out what she had done to the family? Sam had always been faithful to his wife, even through the hard times. He truly believed if you cheated on your spouse, then you are also cheating on your children.

His thoughts snapped back to reality and he stood up, as he listened to the floorboards warning him Susan was up and out of bed. He paced the kitchen floor a couple of times before picking up his cup to replace the remaining coffee with cold water. He couldn't remember the last time he was so anxious, and then it hit him. His mind drifted back to his childhood when he stood behind the corner in his father's shop watching as two men were threatening and degrading his father. He had the same uncomfortable and helpless feeling now that he had just before the magnificent police officer came to their rescue. He thought about the officer and the strength he possessed and he knew he had to be strong just like the officer had been on that day. He gained his confidence as she walked down the stairs and into the kitchen.

"Good morning," she said, as she headed directly toward the pot of coffee warming near the stove. He didn't respond at first, and then he thought he should say something positive.

"How did you sleep?"

"Like a baby, and you?"

"I slept fine," he lied.

"I have to move quickly this morning; I have a lot to do today."

He didn't like the way she was always rushing out the door.

"Susan, I would like to talk to you about something."

"Can't it wait until later? I really have a busy day."

"No, this can't wait."

With a roll of her eyes, she let out a sigh. "What, what is it?"

Sam rubbed his eyes before looking at her. He had to get the picture out of his head of her in bed with another man. "I know what you have been up to."

"You know what I have been up to. You know what? What are you talking about?"

"I know that when you say you're going out with your girlfriend, you aren't always telling the truth." Sam immediately noticed a change in her demeanor. He had seen that same look, so many times before in the interrogation room, after disclosing incriminating evidence against a suspect that would close the book on them. It was a look that said, I have been nailed.

"Sam, what are you talking about?" her voice softened.

His eyes began to water and then he thought about the police officer in his father's shop and he regained his composure. "I followed you the other night to the motel and I waited until you came out. I saw you Susan. I saw you come out of the motel with a black guy."

Susan sat down at the kitchen table without saying a word. She knew she was caught and deep down inside she felt maybe she wanted to be caught. "You followed me?"

"Yes. I had to know the truth."

"So now you know," She said in a cold uncaring tone.

"Who is he?"

"Why, does it matter?"

"It's bad enough that you betray me, but with a black guy too."

"Here we go with the prejudice cop bullshit."

"You know I'm not prejudice, Susan, but how do you think the kids will feel if they find out?"

"Are you going to tell them?"

"Of course not, but what if they found out on their own?"

"He's a judge for Christ sake," she busted out.

Sam stopped and thought about what he had just heard. He started to think about all the judges he knew in Rhode Island. It wasn't a very big state and he knew of most of them. He thought about all the black judges and there was only two that stood as tall as the man she came out of the motel with. "It's Benson, isn't it? Judge Donald Benson from family court in Providence."

Susan didn't answer, but Sam knew her well enough to know he was right; her expression alone was answer enough, and he was right.

"How long have you been seeing him?"

She reached to the back of her head and toyed with her hair. "A few months."

"Let me get this straight. You and Judge Benson, from family court, of all things, have been having an affair for three months?"

"That's right. You weren't there for me. You were hardly ever around."

"That's because I was out earning a living." Sam's voice was becoming loud and broken. "I was working so we could afford to put our kids through college and pay our mortgage. So you could go and have your nails done and go to the movies."

Susan sat quietly looking down at her cup of coffee.

"Isn't he married?"

"Yes, but he's going to leave her."

"Are you in love with him?" He asked in a softer tone.

"I don't know, I think so."

He walked over to the window looking out into the back yard, speaking with his back facing her. "What do you want to do here?"

She started to tear up. "I don't know."

He quickly turned and looked directly at her. "It ends right now Susan, and it can't happen again or you can pack your bags. Am I clear?"

"Yes."

Sam pounded his hand on the counter and left the room. She could hear the front door slam shut and the sound of his car engine starting. She sat wiping away the tears, thinking how she was going to get him out of the house.

29

Luther Banks had disappeared. The grand jury came back with an indictment for murder and a warrant for his arrest had been issued. Iris Campbell, the woman that lived in the first floor apartment told Sam and Donny that a few hours after they had searched Luther's place she heard the roar of his Harley leaving the property and she had not heard or seen him since. A national all-points-bulletin was in effect with clear instructions that Banks was extremely dangerous and most likely armed to the teeth. It went on to read that any law enforcement officer should not attempt to apprehend him alone. It was clearly a call for backup situation and a joint force engagement. The FBI had been notified, and in turn, forwarded the lookout to their national gang and organized crime units for special consideration.

The day after the warrant was put into effect, Sam and Donny along with two uniformed State Police Troopers sat outside the Buck and Bull in Sam's unmarked vehicle and were going over how they were going to conduct a search for Banks.

The sound of a bike approaching interrupted them and they all turned to watch a very large man slowly riding through the parking lot wearing a Hells Angels jacket. As he passed by their car, his eyes were fixed on the officers for a longer than normal period.

"We might as well get rolling. In a minute, everyone in the place is going to know we're here." Sam suggested.

All four men exited the vehicle and quickly walked toward the door following the Hells Angel who had moved off his bike in a hurry and shuffled to the door. The front of the building was a shiny column of metal and rubber. There had to be over thirty Harley's lined up in front of the establishment, Donny estimated. The bar was quite busy for such an early time of the day. Donny looked at his watch and it was a few minutes before noon on Saturday. As they entered through the threshold, all eyes inside were glued on the four men. They walked in single file directly to the bar with Donny leading the way. The bartender stood waiting, and as they approached, he turned and spit on the floor as a gesture of insult.

"What do you boys want?" The bartender asked in a nasty tone.

"We are looking for a biker who drinks in here. His name is Luther Banks, do you know him?"

"No," he quickly answered and began running a towel across the surface of the sticky and scratched up bar.

Sam produced a photograph from the inside of his jacket and turned it facing the bartender. "This is a picture of him. Are you sure you haven't seen him?"

The man took a quick glance at the photograph and once again replied. "No."

"How long have you been a bartender here?" Donny asked.

"This is my first day. I just started this morning." A few biker types, along with a heavy woman with bleached blond spiked up hair started to laugh, and the bartender joined in. The bartender had a scar that ran from his left eye down to his chin. He was a large man with a shiny, bald head that displayed a couple more scars where he had been clocked over the head. He wore a black, leather vest with his chest hair sprouting out from the top and sides. On his right forearm, he had a large tattoo that read "Born to Lose" and below it was a skull with a dagger penetrating all the way through it and a noose wrapped around its neck.

"I wonder how many of your friends in here would appreciate it, if we lined them all up and did a weapons and drug check? Donny asked. "Because it's your first day and all, we would want to make sure you get off to a nice, safe start."

The smile on his face dropped and the laughter ended in an instant. "Look man, I'm just a bartender. They come in and I serve drinks. I don't ask questions and I'm not looking for trouble."

"I'll ask you again," Sam was interrupted by Hank Reynolds who came out of his office and walked to the bar where the officers were standing.

"What's the problem, Rock?" Reynolds asked while moving behind the bar wearing his Hells Angels jacket and a maroon beret concealing his graying hair.

"These cops are asking about a guy named Luther."

Sam produced the photograph for Reynolds. "Who are you?" Sam asked.

Reynolds looked at the picture. "Who am I? I am the owner of this establishment. Who are you?"

"I'm Detective Carra with the State Police. Do you recognize this man?"

Reynolds hesitated before speaking. "Yeah, he comes in once and a while. He goes by the name Turk. Why, has he done something wrong?"

"We just want to have a word with him, that's all." Donny said.

Sam noticed it was getting quieter and the crowd was starting to move closer to them than he was comfortable with. "Can we take this into your office?"

"It's over there." Reynolds pointed toward the wooden door he came out of a minute earlier.

The two detectives followed Reynolds into the office, while the uniformed troopers guarded the door from the outside. Reynolds took a seat behind his cluttered desk and the two detectives stood towering over him, just as they preferred it. The room was small and windowless. To their left hung a very large mirror with a Harley Davidson logo. The rest of the walls were covered with unframed posters of naked women, the kind one might find in a Hustler centerfold. Sitting on his desk were three six-inch models of Harley Davidson motorcycles, all in different colors.

"Do you know Sharon Satowski?" Sam asked.

"Of course I know her, she works for me. Well, she used to work for me."

"What do you know about her death?"

He turned his eyes away from the detectives and fixed them on one of his posters. "Just what I read in the paper, she was killed."

"How long was she employed here?" Donny picked up one of the Harley models and was checking it out.

"I don't know, about two years, maybe less. Don't touch that, put it down." Reynolds scolded him.

Donny looked directly into his eyes while placing it back down. It was apparent he didn't like Reynolds' tone. Reynolds quickly looked away.

"Did she have any trouble with anyone in here recently?" Sam asked. As he picked up a different model and began twirling it around.

"No, everyone liked her. Please put that back." Sam did as he asked.

"Not everyone." Sam concluded. "Was she good about showing up for work?"

"Yes, she hardly ever called out."

Sam looked at Donny and then, back at Reynolds. "If she didn't show up for work, wasn't that out of character for her?"

With a confused look on his face Reynolds answered. "Yes, it was."

"Then why didn't you check up on her, maybe call her when she didn't show up after she was murdered?"

Reynolds sat thinking for a moment before responding. "I don't know, I thought she might be hung over or something. I think someone did call for her, but couldn't get a hold of her."

"Not true. We checked her voice mail at her place and there were a few messages, but none from here, or anyone asking why she hadn't shown up for work."

"I must be mistaken, then." He said, shaking his head side to side.

Sam stopped and turned to look at one of the posters on the wall. "Nice décor. Do you have a general disrespect for women?"

"No, I just love pussy. Don't you?" He said through brown stained teeth.

Sam didn't respond. "When was the last time you saw Luther Banks?"

"Maybe three or four days ago."

"You don't know the last time you saw him? Banks is way up in the chapter ranks and you're a Hells Angel. I would think you would know every time he walks in the door. I know when my boss is around."

"I don't pay attention to who comes in and when, and he's not my boss." He spoke with his head down. Sam knew he was lying.

"Well, what is the word? Where is he?"

"I have no idea." This time he looked up.

"I guess that's it for now. We'll be in touch, if we need anything else."

Sam opened the door and Donny followed him out. Reynolds straightened out the models on his desk, putting them back in a straight line. The two uniformed officers were standing just where they had left them. As the four men filed out the door, Donny noticed a guy wearing a jean jacket and a cowboy hat standing at the end of the bar. He turned away avoiding eye contact with them as they walked out.

Once outside, they thanked the uniformed troopers for their assistance, shook hands and watched as they each made their way to their own vehicles that were parked at the very end of the property.

Donny got behind the wheel and turned to Sam. "I spotted a guy in the bar I arrested on a drug sting a while back. I can't believe he is back on the street already. We hit a house in Warwick along with narcotics and bagged four guys with over a key of coke, and he was one of them. They also had two handguns and a shotgun in the house. That was only a couple years ago. I can't remember his name. Let me make a call and find out."

Donny pulled out his cell phone and called one of the narcotics officers that had been on the raid, and a few minutes later, he had a name and address. "His name is Michael Harmon, and guess what, he's still on parole. He's not supposed to be mingling with known felons and he isn't supposed to be in a bar drinking. I'd say he's in violation of his parole."

"Is that right?" Sam said.

"Yes, and he spotted me. I could tell by the way he turned away after we made eye contact. Why don't we stick around here for a while and see if he comes out. I don't think he wants to get caught violating his parole."

"Yeah, if it were me I'd get the hell out of dodge before you figured out I was still on parole and came back to grab me," Sam said. Donny nodded in agreement. After so many years working together, they began to think alike. Sam thought, if he had spent more time with his wife, maybe they would be on the same page, instead of being on different book shelves altogether.

30

As the detectives had figured, a few minutes later, the bar door swung open and Harmon peaked his head out scanning the lot before darting for his car. He quickly got in, started the engine, and spun out of the parking lot without looking back. A few minutes later, as he drove up the road, he looked into his rear view mirror only to realize the scenario he had been avoiding. A vehicle occupied by two men was following him. He nervously watched as an arm protruded out from the passenger side and placed a blue bubble on the roof. Then he heard a loud bullhorn siren that was unique only to police cruisers. Harman pulled over and briefly thought about his .38 revolver under his seat. He began to reach for it, thinking it was one way out of his situation. If he didn't take care of these cops, he would end up back in prison for another three to five years, and that was not an option for him. *I'll wait until they approach my car. One would come to the driver side window and the other would be by the passenger side rear window. I'll wait until they are in place and surprise them. I'll shoot the cop next to my window in the face and then quickly turn the gun and shoot the other cop in the belly right through the rear window. It will take all of two seconds and it will be over. If they are still moving, I'll finish them with one more round through the forehead for good measure, then I'll be on my way.*

As he moved toward the gun under his seat, his hand was shaking and his mouth was becoming dry. Sweat was creating bullets on his forehead and he could hear his heart pounding inside his shell. He realized he couldn't go through with it, so he stopped, sitting still and watching as the two officers approached his car just as he imagined they would. The only difference was that the officer on the passenger side had a gun in his hand in the ready position. He knew now that he had made the right decision. He rolled down his window.

"Is there a problem officer?"

"License and registration please," Sam requested with one hand tickling his weapon.

Harman reached into the glove box and then into his wallet, producing the documents. He handed them to Sam, his hand was still shaking. After a quick glance, Sam nodded to Donny.

"Mr. Harman, please step out of the vehicle."

Harman did ask why he asked. Donny came around to the driver side while Sam patted him down for weapons.

"Hello Michael, do you remember me?" Donny asked in a condescending tone.

"No," Harman said without making eye contact.

"Yes, you do. I busted you for drugs a couple years back in Warwick, remember?"

He took a quick glance at Donny and responded with a faint mumble. "Yeah."

"Michael, I just saw you at the Buck and Bull and I made a call, and guess what I found out? You are in violation of your parole. You're not supposed to be in a bar, and certainly not with known felons such as Hells Angels gang members."

Harman still didn't have bracelets on and he was wondering why. The cops had gone to the bar for a reason, but he wasn't sure what they wanted. "What do you want?"

"We want information. If you cooperate, we will forget about what we saw today and you can be on your way, but it better be good."

"What are you looking for?"

"Do you know a Hells Angel named Luther Banks?"

Just hearing his name made Harman swallow hard. "Yes, of course I do. Everyone knows Turk."

"Well, we are looking for him and he seems to have disappeared. Where did he go?"

"I don't know." Harman answered in record time.

"You're not cooperating." Donny reached for his handcuffs.

"Wait, I heard he took a vacation down South – to Alabama somewhere."

"Why such a quick exit, Michael?" Donny asked.

"You know why, because of Sharon, the waitress."

"What about Sharon? I assume you mean Sharon Satowski right?" Donny tugged on his arm to get his full attention. It worked, because he was now looking into the eyes of the tall trooper.

"Yes, he thinks the cops are on to him and he split."

"What else do you know about the murder of Ms. Satowski?" Sam asked.

"That's all. Only that Turk left the state to avoid the cops."

"And do you think Turk committed the murder?"

Harman didn't answer at first, until Donny began rubbing his cuffs. "Man, Turk is the craziest dude I have ever known. He's just plain nasty. If he knew I was talking with you guys, he would kill me, and it wouldn't be a quick death either."

"You didn't answer the question," Sam said.

"I don't know. Sharon was his girl and everyone knew she was banging everyone she could get her hands on. Everyone who didn't know Turk, that is. Anyone who knew Turk wouldn't be stupid enough to go near her. Not if they wanted to live."

"So, you think maybe Turk found out someone was banging his girl and he flipped out?" Donny asked.

"I don't know for sure, but that's the rumor on the street." He responded with reluctance.

"Okay, is there anything else you haven't told us?" Sam asked.

"No, that's all I know." He looked Sam in the eye and Sam was comfortable with his answer.

"We have your address and know where you live, if we need anything else." Donny said.

Sam handed him a card. "If you hear anything else, you call me. Now you're free to leave."

Harman was surprised and delighted that they were actually giving him a break. He had never gotten a break from the cops before. "Thanks a lot," he said in a goofy way before getting back into his car. He didn't wait around for them to change their mind. He drove off thinking how nice it felt to be a free man.

31

Nick's new house was a magnificently architected structure, originally designed and built for the lead guitarist with a two time platinum rock band called Pencil Thread. The rolling green lawn ascended upward from a secluded side street and passed an iron-gate to the stairs that led to the front door.

Both sides of the property were flanked with a four-foot-high stone wall with assorted mums and pansies, spread out in long flower pots covering the top all the way to its end, which concluded just past the deck and patio area in the rear of the house. The back yard overlooked a salt water bay that flowed into the Atlantic Ocean. A thirty-six-foot dock had a small fishing boat on one side and a speed boat tied to the other.

The house consisted of an open floor plan with five bedrooms, three and a half baths, and a total of eleven rooms. All kitchen appliances were stainless steel, including a subzero refrigerator and a double oven. The countertops were laid with the finest Italian granite with beveled cut corners. Custom cabinets were handmade white birch with stainless steel knobs and fixtures. Recessed lights were strategically placed on nine-foot-ceilings that spanned throughout the entire house. The house was wired with a custom sound system and alarm unit which included several motion detectors and all windows and doors were wired. The entire house was constructed with Pella windows and Anderson sliding glass doors. Many of the windows in the rear of the house consisted of custom rounded windows which allowed for a spectacular view of the bay. There were three fire places, including one in the master bedroom, which could be enjoyed while bathing in a six-foot Jacuzzi with a crystal chandelier hanging above it. The other two were situated in the family room, which was open to the kitchen, and to the formal living room that was set in the front north section of the house.

Inside the dwelling, sat the finest furniture, money could buy, and all his artwork were original artists and signed and numbered prints from some of the world's greatest masters, including Picasso and Van Gogh. Several sculptures sat on pedestals adding to the décor and class that made Nick's place nothing less than a small palace in its own right.

Zollo sat on the deck gazing out at the open water with his feet up and a beer attached to his left hand. His vision was fogging as his eleventh beer was clouding his ability to see straight. He sat with his new girlfriend who was bought and paid for by Nick. They sat together in silence and both were wondering what it would be like to own such a beautiful place.

"What do you think the taxes are for a place like this?" Jeanie asked, before slugging down half of her Grey Goose martini.

Zollo shifted his glassy eyes toward her without moving his neck. "Like Nick says, if you have to ask, you can't afford it."

"But, what would be your guess?" she asked again.

"I would guess around thirty grand a year, maybe thirty-five."

"Wow, that's more than I made in a whole year before I started dancing."

"Well, if you hit the lottery like Nick for nine-million, then you wouldn't need to bend your ass over in front of strangers anymore. But, that isn't the case, so you're fucked, just like me."

She pondered what Zollo said and knew he was right. It gave her a feeling of hopelessness. She hated her job, but it was all she could do to make the kind of money she was accustomed to.

Zollo turned as the sliding screen door opened and Nick and Tammy came out after enjoying an afternoon adventure in the master bedroom.

"Man, it's a beautiful day." Nick popped open a Sam Adams logger. "Shall we take a cruise to Block Island on the yacht?"

Zollo turned in his chair nearly falling over. "I'm up for that," he said.

"I was talking to the ladies, dickhead."

"Sure, but why don't we relax here for a while and then head down to the boat later," Tammy suggested while straightening out her bathing suit top and situating herself in direct line of the sun in her lounge chair.

"What are you going to do about Robby?" Jeanie asked, unaware she was opening up a can of worms.

Nick looked at her in surprise. "What do you mean, what am I going to do."

Tammy lowered her Ray Bans to examine Jeanie.

"He keeps pressuring everyone for answers on where Tammy disappeared to. He said nobody walks out on him and gets away with it."

Nick's blood began to boil. "Who does this punk think he is? He is nothing more than a wise guy wannabe. He probably sits home all night watching The Godfather over and over again. You tell Robby Silk that Tammy is with me now, and if he has a problem with that, he can come and see me. I'll rip his fucking heart out and eat it for lunch!"

"Why don't you just settle for a Caesar salad instead?" Tammy said attempting to lighten up the situation.

Nick stood up, pushing his chair aside. "What does this guy think, he owns you or something?"

"He is just a possessive asshole, that's all." Tammy responded, shrugging it off.

Nick downed the rest of his beer. "If he contacts you in any way, I want to know about it."

"Alright baby, can we talk about something else?"

"Yeah, who's up for a line?" Nick pulled a vial out of his pocket and started shaking it loose.

Zollo's eyes lit up "I'm up for that."

Nick just looked at him with dead eyes. He was getting tired of Zollo's drunken ass. He wanted to punch him in the face, but restrained himself. He knew he may need Zollo in the future.

They all participated in a snorting frenzy, except Tammy. She wanted to keep a clear head and not lose focus on what she wanted out of her relationship with Nick. She wanted it all, the house, the boat and the money. It was her time and nothing would fog her vision, especially not white powder.

***

Johnny Silk walked into his club, as the custodian was just finishing up and preparing to leave. He walked past the shiny brass poles and fine polished mirrors and went into his office to find his brother, Robby, sitting behind his desk with two cups of coffee.

"I got you a coffee, black with three sugars."

Johnny reached over, scooping it up and took a sip. "Did you use the sugar in the brown packets, the natural ones?"

Robby looked confused for a second before responding. "Yes I did," he lied.

Johnny didn't believe him. "Thanks, that's the way I like it."

"Did we have a good night last night?" Robby asked.

"We did okay, twelve grand." It was really fourteen, but Johnny didn't think Robby needed to know that, he wanted his cut, but never did any work at the place.

"What's the word on Eden?"

Johnny knew his older brother didn't drive all the way down for just a social visit and expected Eden to be the main topic of conversation. "Word has it she ran off with a guy who hit the lottery."

"What, are you fucking kidding me?" Robby nearly choked on his drink and brought a napkin up to his mouth, dabbing away the spillover.

"No, I'm not. I'll tell you this, though. Customers are asking for her and it's not good for business. She is our biggest draw."

"What are you telling people?"

"I'm telling them she is on vacation and will be coming back soon. The dancers all know the truth, but I warned them to keep their mouths shut."

"Yeah, fat chance of that." Robby picked up the switchblade Johnny used as a letter opener. He pushed the button opening up the blade with a sharp clicking sound. "So who is this guy and how much did he hit the lotto for?"

"I hear nine million. His name is Nick Gennaro. Supposedly his father is connected to the family here."

"Gennaro…" Robby sat carving a hole on his coffee cup lid. "I know who the father is. He has a butcher shop in Walton."

"Yeah, that's him."

"I want her back and I mean now." Robby demanded.

"What do you suggest?" Johnny asked.

"Find out where this guy lives and where they hang out. I think we may need to pay him a visit and explain to him it's not nice to take something that isn't yours."

"Yeah, and Eden needs to know she doesn't just walk out on us. We made her who she is, and she owes us." Johnny added, while pointing to a poster of Eden tacked to the office wall.

Robby got up holding the knife and placed the point of the blade against the bare nipple of Eden's photograph. "She will come back to us, even if it kills her."

32

The biggest mistake Luther ever made was riding south on his Harley wearing his Hells Angels colors. He was so proud of being a Hells Angel, and second in command of the Rhode Island chapter, that his arrogance consumed his common sense.

With the wind in his hair, he beamed through a back woods road in Riverwood, Alabama, with the afternoon sun reflecting off his black mirrored sun glasses. He was headed to Mobile to meet his contact Sean Soderhouse, the leader of the Alabama chapter of the Hells Angels.

Sitting off the side of the road, in his beat up twelve-year-old cruiser, was Lyle Kensington. He sat flipping through a Penthouse magazine, waiting for some poor slob to cruise passed him exceeding the thirty-five mile an hour speed limit. Every day, he sat in one of two spots for a few hours along the same country road, pulling over drivers who broke the law by driving over forty-miles an hour. He was kind enough to administer verbal warnings for those who were clocked at thirty-nine or below.

Lyle was not the brightest of officers. He carried along with his shiny badge and .357 magnum a sense of duty and a false sense of invincibility. He was a homely man of thirty-two-years with a crew cut and a wrinkled uniform that was pasted to his large frame.

As he sat with his window rolled down, he could hear approaching vehicles in time to drop his porn and pick up his radar gun. The warning he got from the sound of the motorcycle gave him plenty of time. He could hear its loud roar from nearly a half-mile away. He positioned his radar gun toward the curvy road waiting for the bike to round the curve and fall into his trap.

As the biker came into view, he looked at the digital read out which read forty-six. He locked it in place with a simple push of a button, started his cruiser, and watched as the bike passed by him.

As he negotiated the curve, Luther noticed the cruiser partially hidden along the side of the road. He immediately hit his foot break slowing the bike down. He wasn't really speeding, so he thought he was safe.

Lyle watched the biker pass by and he noticed the logo on the back of the speeder's jacket and it put a smile on his face. He had never pulled over a Hells Angel before, and certainly never had the opportunity to write one a citation. He would have a great story to tell at the end of his shift.

Luther looked in his side mirror and saw that the cop car had pulled out behind him. His mind started to go into a tactical mode. His forty-caliper bulldog revolver was tucked into his saddlebag, so it would be a challenge getting to it in a pinch. He figured he could always get to his hunting knife that was tucked inside his boot and bury it into the cop's throat if he had to.

The lights on top of the cop car were switched on, spinning blue and red colors across the trees and the siren started to holler. Luther pulled over to the side of the road and sat waiting. As Lyle came walking toward him, Luther was sizing him up through his mirror.

"Turn the bike off," Lyle shouted.

Right away, Luther knew he didn't like him and he began to tense up. He did as he was told.

"License and registration," Lyle commanded.

"Did I break some kind of law?" Luther asked as he tugged on his beard in anger.

"I said, license and registration, boy."

Luther gave him a look that could kill. "It's in my bag." He pointed to the back of his bike.

Lyle glanced at the leather bags hanging off the back of the bike. "Well go get it, nice and slow."

Luther climbed off his seat and stepped to the rear of his bike.

Lyle took a couple steps back after seeing the enormity of the man. Luther had two bags attached to his bike. He opened the leather bag that was on the driver side – the one with his unregistered handgun in it. He took out an envelope, retrieved the registration, and then took his license out of his wallet and handed the documents to Lyle. The officer turned and walked back to his cruiser. He ran the identification through a local and (NCIC) national criminal check. A few minutes later, the dispatcher from the records bureau came back on the air.

Luther's license and registration were legal and valid; however, the dispatcher warned Lyle that he was a fugitive from Rhode Island and was wanted for murder. She also advised him that he was considered armed and extremely dangerous and not to be taken alone. She immediately called for back-up and advised him to wait until another cruiser arrived in approximately fifteen minutes.

Lyle sat for a minute and thought about it. *Why do I need to wait fifteen minutes? The guys at the stationhouse will think I'm a stud if I were to bring in a Hells Angel wanted for murder by myself. I have a gun and I'm as tough as nails – to hell with waiting.*

He got out of his cruiser, leaving the documents behind. Luther knew right away something was wrong. He could tell by the look on the cop's face, and when Lyle reached for his holster, it was confirmed.

Lyle cautiously approached Luther with his hand on his gun. "Well, Mr. Banks, it seems we have a small problem here. You have a warrant in Rhode Island and we need to go to the station and clear it up."

"You must have me mixed up with someone else." Luther responded, his mind racing.

"I'm afraid not, Mr. Banks." Lyle slid his revolver out and pointed it at Luther. Turn around and put your hands behind your back, right now!"

Luther was beginning to see red. He didn't like anyone pointing a gun at him, especially a redneck cop. Luther turned and put his left hand behind his back. Lyle, while holding his weapon in his right hand, reached and took out his handcuffs with his left. In an instant, Luther spun around to his right with his right hand up deflecting the gun pointed at his back, knocking Lyle's gun hand across his chest towards his left shoulder. Luther reached out grabbing Lyle by the throat and head butted him with a fierce blow fracturing Lyle's cheekbone. Lyle's eyes flashed with a painful spark that knocked him back, and his gun fell to the ground.

Lyle knew if he didn't get his senses back quickly, he was in big trouble. He shook off the shock and pain and pulled out his mace, spraying Luther in the face. Luther screamed like a warrior in battle, charging Lyle and delivering two crushing right-hand punches into Lyle's face, breaking his nose. Blood was pouring down covering Lyle's badge while he continued to spray Luther who was now blinded. In a sudden fury, Luther grabbed the mace and peeled the canister out of Lyle's hand and began spraying it into his eyes. The officer could no longer remain on his feet. His nose and cheek were crushed and he was unable to see or breathe. He fell to the ground and felt the shod foot of Luther as he kicked him in the ribs three times, cracking two ribs. As Lyle lay in the road conscious, but completely incapacitated, he now realized he should have waited for back up.

Luther walked over picking up the officer's gun that was lying by the side of the road. He cleaned out his eyes with the bottom of his T-shirt, and walked back over to Lyle, who was lying in the road and just beginning to catch his breath. Luther reached down with his left hand grabbing onto Lyle's shirt collar, pulling him up a foot off the ground. "Do you see this?" Luther put the barrel of the gun into Lyle's left eye socket and pulled the trigger. He walked over to his saddlebag and took out a bottle of water, leaned his head back, and poured the entire contents directly into his eyes, and then wiped them off with a rag. He placed Lyle's gun into his saddlebag next to his Bulldog and pulled the leather strap tight. He got back on his bike, started the engine, and rode off leaving Lyle behind, with his brain matter spilled all over the dusty country road.

***

No matter how hard he worked behind his desk, he could never seem to catch up on the paperwork. Sam was backed up on four progress reports from three different cases. He needed to update all his interview notes and evidence forms. His court cases were continuing to pile up and he needed to go over each case in detail before testifying in open court. Of all his cases, the one that haunted him the most was the murder of Christopher Gennaro. He was ninety-nine percent sure he was killed by his brother, and the motive was one of the oldest since man walked the earth – greed.

He was sitting behind his desk when Rick Maddox, a detective who sat across the room, called out to notify him that he had a phone call from the FBI in the Mobile, Alabama field office.

"This is Detective Carra."

"Hello Detective Carra, this is Agent McDonald from the Mobile field office. How are you today?"

"I'm buried with paperwork, and you?"

"I'm in the same club. I'm calling because I was directed to you by our Providence office. I understand you are the lead investigator in a murder case up there involving one Luther Banks."

"That's correct. We have issued a warrant for his arrest and he has slipped out of our grasp. What have you got?" He had Sam's full attention.

"Well, it seems your boy shot and killed a local deputy sheriff after a traffic stop down here in Riverwood."

"When?"

"Yesterday afternoon. He put a bullet right through his eye at point blank range."

"Did he have children?" Sam asked.

"No, he was a bachelor."

"Were there any witnesses?"

"Nope, it was on a country road and he was alone."

Sam thought for a few seconds. "He must have run a check on him and learned about the murder warrant."

"Apparently that's exactly what happened." He had the voice of an adolescent, Sam thought.

"Why didn't he call for back up? Banks is as big as a polar bear and just as nasty."

"Back up was on the way, but arrived too late."

Sam thought in silence for a brief moment. "Have you got any leads on his whereabouts?"

"Nothing solid yet, but we're working on it. This has been dropped in my lap and is now considered a possible serial murder case. He crossed state lines, so he's mine to deal with now."

"Please keep me in the loop on this," Sam asked.

"You got it."

Sam sat wondering how many more people would die before Banks was caught. "Can I have your number?"

"Sure, here's my cell. You can reach me anytime at this number 206-445-3978."

"Thanks for calling." Sam hung up the phone and then picked it back up and called Donny at home.

33

Tammy was lying face down on a massage table while Victor Castano rubbed warm oil deep into her tanned skin. He was the sole owner of Martens Salon ever since his partner Larry Marten left him for an Irish poet named Scott Linnehan. Castano was heartbroken after the split, but decided to carry on and stay in Newport continuing to run the business. With a small buyout, Marten was on a plane to Ireland, and Castano, an immigrant from Columbia, was working the salon six days a week.

Nick didn't like the idea of a man massaging Tammy's naked body, but after he learned Castano was gay, he shrugged it off with a light joke about homosexuals. Once her massage was finished, they walked around the town going from shop to shop. Nick wasn't into the shopping experience, but for Tammy he endured the agony until it became too excruciating and he would cry, Uncle. He purchased a seven-thousand-dollar emerald necklace from the Smoky Topaz Jewelry Store and slipped it over her head. Nick closely admired it as it rested on her smooth chest just above her defined cleavage. Tammy was ecstatic about her new gift and began enticing him about what was in store for him back in the hotel room later that day.

After making out near the Old Port Marina, they decided to venture to The Mooring for dinner. They were immediately seated after Nick slipped the host a fifty-dollar-bill and within minutes, they sat at their booth enjoying their drinks and playfully flirting with each other. Nick was totally in love with Tammy, and she was in love with her new necklace.

Tammy had a way of bringing out the lamb in Nick. When they were alone, it was like he was a little kid again. As he sat looking deep into her eyes, he was at peace. Suddenly, out of the corner of his eye, his peripheral vision alerted him someone had abruptly walked up on them. He turned his head to see two men standing in front of their booth.

"Hello Eden." Robby Silk spoke with an evil look in his eye, a look that displayed nothing other than contempt. Tammy began to tremble and Nick could immediately sense her fear. The lamb was now replaced by the lion, and in a split second, Nick stood up burying his beer mug into the side of Robby Silks face, cutting deep into his flesh — the force of the blow sent Robby to the floor. Johnny threw a right hand punch, but Nick saw it coming, so he bent his head down causing Johnny to punch the hardest part of his head, just above his hairline. This sent a shattering pain through Johnny's hand. Nick moved away from the booth and the punches started to fly with both rivals swinging in frenzy. Nick, being a seasoned street fighter, was getting the best of him. A quick kick to the groin, followed by a left and two rights' brought Johnny down to meet with his brother on the floor.

Nick stood over the fallen brothers in victory, and delivered a couple more vicious kicks to their ribs for good measure. "You come around Tammy or me again and I'll kill you!"

The manager came over demanding they leave, warning that the police had been called.

"Forget the police, Nick boasted, you better call an ambulance." He took Tammy by the hand and escorted her out. Once they were outside, he pulled her close, kissing her, and then he let out a loud roar like Tarzan in the jungle.

"I feel great," he said. "Will you marry me?" Tammy's heart was still beating at a rate she wasn't comfortable with.

"Marry you?" She was totally taken by surprise.

"Yes, marry me this weekend, today if you want."

After a short hesitation, she reached up caressing her emerald. "Okay, let's do it."

The next morning they flew to Las Vegas, where they, along with several other couples, recited their vows in a strange chapel with strange faces in attendance. They stayed for a week and gambled away fifty eight thousand dollars before jumping on a plane and traveling back to TF Green airport in Providence.

The next day, Nick was advised by his attorney to have a prenuptial agreement drawn up, but he was adamantly against it. He assured his lawyer that he loved Tammy more than anyone he had ever known, and she loved him.

The Silk brothers sat at the wet bar in Robby's house setting back glass after glass of 15 year old scotch. The left side of Robby's face was bandaged from his temple to his jaw. He had taken twenty-nine stitches and his face was badly bruised almost to the point of a fracture.

Johnny had a cut over his right eye, that could have used a few stitches, but he declined, demanding a butterfly bandage instead. His right hand was swollen and soar, from hitting Nick's hard head.

"I'm going to whack that son of a bitch myself, and it won't be painless either." Robby said.

"I say we kidnap his dumb ass and torture him for a few days first, before we clip him," Johnny suggested. "And did you see her, just sitting there watching, ungrateful bitch. We should whack her too."

Robby picked up his nine millimeter Smith & Wesson and began trying the action. "The only problem is his old man is connected, so we need to clear it with Gino Patriarca first."

"So, we go see him and tell him our story." Johnny said.

"Yeah, but I'd be surprised if he'd give us his blessing on a hit. He may give us permission to break his legs, but not take him out."

"Then fuck it!" Johnny sprang to his feet. "Let's just do it and cut him up. Nobody will ever find his body."

Both men were intoxicated and not thinking clearly. "I'll think about it for a couple days and figure it out." Robby said. He was older, smarter, and had more influence than his kid brother. Johnny knew this to be true, so he never argued with his older brother's decisions.

"One thing is for sure, that bastard will regret the day he ever stepped into our lives," Robby said, pointing his gun at the mirror and pulling the trigger, while they both listened to the metallic clicking sound echoing throughout the room.

34

Judge Donald Benson sat in his chamber looking up at his law school diploma that hung dust free on the wall to the left of his desk. He was proud of the fact that he had graduated from Yale Law School, because during his day there weren't many black men who were fortunate enough to realize such an achievement.

Growing up, one of seven children, in the Bronx, added to the difficulty in achieving the goals he set for himself. His father walked out on the family when he was nine-years-old, just at the time when a boy needs his father's attention the most.

His father had never known his father before him, because he was also absent. It was a long legacy in the Benson tradition. Donald was determined to break the chain of poverty and irresponsibility, and as he grew into a young man, his determination had taken control over everything else in his life. Every obstacle that stood in his way, he conquered and moved forward. He was a proud man and was highly regarded by his peers.

Married, with a son of his own, Donald had raised his son to be a driven, respectful and responsible young man. He now had accomplished all he had hoped for. He broke the chain that had imprisoned his family for two centuries. He enjoyed a close relationship with his son and they spent time playing golf, tennis and occasionally attending a concert together. His son was a senior in high school and had recently applied to New York University where he was hoping to eventually attend law school, himself.

The marriage between Donald and Emma Benson had deteriorated over time. She had a chronic weight problem, and as time passed on, she allowed it to get way out of control.

Although Donald loved her as a person, he had a difficult time accepting the extra hundred and thirty-five pounds she had gained since their wedding day. He was a big man himself, but he kept in decent physical condition and was proud of his semi-flat stomach.

The intimacy between Donald and Emma had suffered, and as she got heavier, he withdrew from sexual activity with her altogether. The straw that broke the camel's back was when he came home one evening and she was waiting for him wearing a black Victoria Ssecret negligee. Donald took one look at the fat rolling over her tight outfit and realized he had to find the passion that he once felt. He knew he wouldn't find it with her, so his mind began to wander, and his sexual fantasy began to find a place in his daily life.

Emma was completely drained of the self-esteem that once occupied her soul. She started with weight watchers; that didn't work, so she moved on to the Atkins diet. She lost eleven pounds before she collapsed into a sugar craving frenzy. After gaining back the eleven pounds, plus five more, she tried the South Beach diet, which ended up in failure as well.

Two years after the negligee incident, Donald met Susan Carra at a Sudden Infant Death Syndrome (SIDS) fundraiser. When he first saw her, he was instantly attracted by her nicely shaped curves and shiny black hair. He didn't hesitate to approach her, introducing himself as a judge, and the conversation flourished from there. They spoke about the law, their children and eventually the unhappiness they both shared in their individual marriages. He invited her to have lunch and she agreed. A few days later, they met for lunch at a small diner on the outskirts of the city. That afternoon they checked into a motel.

Beads of sweat were rolling down both sides of his face, and his shirt collar was sticking to his neck, as Sam walked from his car to the old building that was designated as family court. It was extremely hot outside and Sam's air conditioning was due for a good charge. August in Rhode Island could sometimes be very brutal, and once again, Mother Nature was showing off her power.

It had been quite some time since Sam had entered the old building and his ascent up the long staircase had brought back a few distant memories of when he worked in uniform. As he entered the building, he took out his badge and showed it to the court officer standing by the metal detector walkthrough. Sam was waved on through and the beeping sound came to life because his gun was clipped to his belt.

Waiting for the elevator to take him to the fourth floor, Sam took out a handkerchief and wiped the sweat from his face and neck. He got into the elevator thinking what his next move was going to be. *How exactly should I confront the man who has been screwing my wife?*

The doors opened, and Sam got out, looking around to figure out where to go next. His common sense told him to go left toward the two courtrooms at the end of the building. After reaching his destination, he couldn't find any marked doors indicating where the judge's chambers were situated. He approached a court officer standing outside one of the rooms; he identified himself and asked her for help. She indicated that the only way in, was through the courtroom door by the judge's bench, stating that outside doors were locked at all times.

Court was not in session, so Sam walked right in and entered through the old oak door that was labeled Judges Chamber. It led to a hall with three doors and Sam realized it wasn't going to be made easy for him. He walked past the first door and decided to try door number two. It made him think of a game show he used to watch years ago.

He opened the door and walked in finding Judge Benson behind his desk with a pen in his hand. Benson stopped writing, looking up obviously surprised.

"Excuse me, what are you doing in here?" Benson firmly asked.

"My name is Sam Carra."

Benson's face dropped, nearly landing on his desk along with his pen. "Yes." Benson entangled his fingers as if, he was praying. "I knew it was just a matter of time before you would approach me."

"Judge, I'm going to get right to the point. You have been fucking my wife and you're a married man, and a Judge. I don't care how you feel about her, or she you. I don't care what has happened or for how long. It ends right now, this very second. Or I promise you, I will bring so much heat down on you, you'll melt right beneath that robe you so hypocritically wear. Do I make myself crystal clear?"

Benson looked at Sam standing before him, and for the first time in a long time, he was afraid. "Yes, it ends today."

Sam took two steps closer. "No, it ends right now!"

"Yes, right now." Benson calmly responded.

"You should be ashamed of yourself," were Sam's last words before turning and walking out.

Benson sat without moving, soaking up what had just occurred. He was ashamed of himself ... just as Sam had suggested. He began to feel nauseous, and he went for a glass of water.

***

As soon as the door opened, she began yelling. Sam sat in his recliner and calmly put his book down, as she came into the family room.

"You went to his chamber today and humiliated him? Are you insane? He is a fucking judge, Sam."

"He's a hypocrite with no integrity. He sits making judgments all day long on divorce cases, family disputes, and domestic violence. What does he do outside of the courthouse? He screws another man's wife in a cheap motel on the edge of town. He is a disgrace to the bench."

"Well, you really did it now. He just broke up with me. You just hate to see me happy, don't you?"

"So this is all about you? What about us and our kids?"

"There is no us. I love Donald!" Tears began to flow south, bouncing off her red blouse.

"You are nothing more than a whore! You disgust me."

"Fuck you!" She attacked Sam, swinging like a mad woman. He was still sitting, when she came at him with her arms flailing. Sam covered up and got onto his feet. She continued swinging in a rage of anger. Sam grabbed her by the throat backing her up against the wall. He didn't choke her, but attempted to gain control of her so he could leave. He pushed her against the wall and used his body to stop the blows. A few had gotten through, stinging the side of his face. Once he was able to trap her arms, he held her tight and spoke into her ear. "Pack your bags and get the hell out of my house."

"This is my house just as much as it is yours."

Sam finally let her go and took a few steps back. "Not anymore," he said in a soft, sad tone before quietly leaving the room and going outside. He decided to take a walk around the neighborhood and cool down. He had taken hundreds of walks around his neighborhood, but today was a different kind of walk.

Susan sat at the kitchen table thinking about what had just occurred and what she was going to do about it. After a few minutes she picked up the phone and called Donald's cell phone. His voice mail kicked in so she hung up without speaking. She raced to her car and drove to the police station where she filed a complaint for physical and emotional abuse at the hands of her husband. Before signing the complaint the female police officer explained the implications that may arise because her husband was a police officer. Susan told her she understood, but still wanted to move forward with the complaint.

Once the complaint had been completed a temporary restraining order was issued until they were both able to appear in front of a judge. Two police officers followed Susan back to the house where they found Sam sitting on the front steps. As soon as he saw the cruiser pull up, he knew what had occurred while he was taking his walk.

The officers came to escort Sam off the property. They explained to him that he was to stay at least two-hundred-feet away from his wife. Once he appeared in court a judge would decide if there was merit to continue a protective order and to what extent. They gave him a copy of the temporary restraining order and advised him they would have no choice but to arrest him, if he violated the order.

Sam agreed, not bothering to explain his side of the story. He knew they had no choice under the strict domestic violence guidelines that had been put into place a few years earlier. After packing a suitcase and a few other belongings, Sam drove away from all that he had cared about, and worked hard for, most of his adult life. He checked into a motel and sat alone with his thoughts and a bottle of Bourbon.

***

Nick Gennaro was now the only suspect in the murder of his younger brother, Christopher. Any leads they once pursued had since dried up and blew away with the hot summer breeze. The leaves were growing old and the air had brought a refreshing change that came every year like clockwork in Rhode Island.

Sam and Donny had brought Nick in for another round of interviews. They were a little harder on him this time, but he stuck to his story. He brought his new attorney along with him and he mimicked the whisper in his ear before answering every question. He still maintained that the last time he saw his brother was the night they went bowling and bought the ticket. Nick continued to badger the detectives, suggesting they were both incompetent and were wasting time questioning him, when they should be out searching for the real killer. He was becoming irate so they cut him loose. Sam wanted to slap the snot out of him, but with Nick's lawyer present, he had to contain himself.

When the detectives ended their shift, Sam was in his car trailing Donny down the busy street. Soon after he was served the restraining order, Donny offered Sam to stay with him until he got things sorted out, one way or another. Sam was reluctant to move in, but Donny insisted – stating it was more for him then Sam. He told Sam his place was too big and he got lonesome for company and needed to have someone to talk to. Sam knew he was using reverse psychology on him, but Sam gracefully accepted.

Things didn't go well for Sam in the courtroom and he knew exactly why. Judges in Providence were thick as thieves, and with a few inquiries, Sam learned that the judge who heard his case was very tight with Benson. Judge Stolz found in favor of Susan and put a permanent restraining order in place.

Susan was now living alone in the house and she and Benson were back together, bouncing up and down in Sam's bed. Sam knew the justice system was flawed, but until now, he never realized just how much. He conditioned himself to focus on work in order to keep his mind off everything bad that was happening in his life. He and Susan both downplayed the separation to the kids, but Sam could tell by the tone of their voices they were very concerned. Sam decided to take a vacation to the Caribbean and he would ask the kids to go with him. They needed to know the truth.

35

Momma Zeoli's was considered one of the best Italian Restaurants in Providence. The veal was pounded fresh daily, and the seafood came directly off the boats in Galilee every afternoon. Gino Patriarca sat at his favorite table, as he did four to five nights a week. His face was full of pasta when Robby Silk approached, as directed by Gino's soldier earlier that day.

"Hello Gino," Robby dug out a huge smile.

"How are ya?" Gino replied through a full mouth. He sat with two of his soldiers on both of his flanks. "Sit down," he ordered. "Are you hungry?"

"No, I already ate, thanks."

"Best food in Rhode Island. I might even argue New York too."

Robby sat down and the waiter came right over. "Glass of your best red wine," he ordered.

"Yes sir." The waiter scrabbled off and Robby turned to face Gino.

Gino finished swallowing and washed the remainder down with water. "What's on your mind?"

"We have a problem with some a punk named Nick Gennaro."

Gino stopped eating to look up. "The butcher?"

"No, his kid."

"I heard about him recently. He hit the lotto?"

Robby's smiley face turned sour. "Yeah, that's him."

"So, he did that to your face?" Gino gestured with an upward nod.

"Yeah, he's lucky I didn't pop him right in the restaurant."

Gino disregarded the comment and picked up his glass of wine. "What's this all about?"

"He ran off with my best girl at the club. You remember Eden?"

"Yes, Eden. What a fine piece of ass she is."

"And now she's gone. This punk is throwing money at her and he is sticking his nose up at us. My brother and I went to talk to him and he clocked me with a beer mug and cut Johnny's eye pretty good."

"And you want what?" Gino looked at his damaged face.

"I want that mother fucker to pay. I want him dead."

Gino cut into his veal and ate a large piece. When he finished, he wiped his mouth with a red linen napkin. He was a big man, but not fat. Sporting a full head of curly black hair and wearing a dark gray Armani suit, he was a man that didn't go unnoticed. "That is not a fair and even response. He slapped you in the face and you want to whack him? His old man has many friends including my best Captain. I'll talk with my guys and see what we can do to make this right."

"Gino, with all due respect I'd like to take care of this myself."

"It was good to see you." Gino got up cutting his sentence short. They shook hands. "I'll be in touch once I get my head around this problem."

"Thanks Gino, come and visit us at the club. I got some new talent you may like to see." Robby said less than enthusiastic.

"Thanks, I just might do that. I'll see you soon."

Robby walked away feeling like nothing was accomplished. He knew he should have listened to Johnny and just killed Nick and buried him in a swamp.

Gino ate without speaking. It was a time when he did some of his best thinking. When he finished his meal, he ordered one of his soldiers to contact Franco and arrange a meeting at the Italian club later that night.

Gino sat at the card table behind a pile of chips holding three kings. He wore dark sunglasses so the other players couldn't see his eyes. He loved to bluff and was damn good at it. He enjoyed it more when he held a three of a kind or better.

Franco entered the room and went to the bar and poured himself a glass of scotch. Gino saw him through the corner of his eye, but didn't acknowledge him.

"I'll raise you four-hundred." Gino sat motionless waiting for any takers. There were two players left in the game.

"I fold." An old guy named Zippo threw his cards down. He had been named Zippo after setting fire to a building he owned in order to collect the insurance settlement. The second time he did it, he was caught, and it cost him five years.

"I'm in." Fat Matt, an overweight, balding guy, tossed in his chips. "I'll call you."

Gino didn't hesitate. "Three kings." He neatly placed his cards down face up.

"Son of a bitch," Matt cried out in defeat. He slapped his hand down without revealing what he had been dealt.

Gino reached out, pulling the pile of colorful chips toward him. "I need to take a break and talk with Franco. I'll sit back in later."

The other players acknowledged him and continued on. Gino walked over to Franco and gave him a kiss on both sides of his face. He poured himself a scotch and gestured toward the back room. Both men took a seat at a table and placed their drinks down.

"Franco, we have a bit of a problem and I'd like to get your advice."

"Sure Gino, what is it?" Franco took a sip of his scotch.

"It appears that Nicky the Butcher's kid is becoming a little unruly." Franco adjusted his tie. "How so?"

"He smacked a couple guys around the other day in Newport, the Silk brothers."

"I know those guys, what for?"

"It's all about some broad who dances at his club. It looks like she took off with the kid, and they went to have a talk with him and he snapped. Hit Robby with a beer glass, cut him pretty good."

"The kid has been out of control ever since he won the money, Franco said. You know he hit the Lotto for nine big ones?"

"Yeah, I heard. How do you suggest we take care of our problem?"

Franco finished his scotch. "Let me have a talk with his father and see what he says. I'll get back to you."

Gino stood up and they embraced again. "Don't worry Gino. This problem will be taken care of one way or another."

Gino reached into his pocket and took out an Ashton cigar and handed it to him. "Franco, Silky wants the girl back."

"Understood." Franco acknowledged the gift with a nod and left the club. He went home so he could spend time alone and think about how he would approach Nicholas with this problem.

The next morning, Franco called Nicholas and invited him to his house for dinner and a game of pool. That night they had a nice steak dinner at Franco's house with a New York cheesecake for dessert. Nicholas brought the steaks from his store and Franco took care of the rest.

During dinner, they talked about sports and the old days – about friends that weren't doing very well, and others that were. Once they finished eating, they went to the billiards room for brandy and a cigar. Franco racked the balls and watched as Nicholas broke.

"Nicky, we have a problem."

"What is it?" He took his second shot after sinking a ball in the break.

"It's your son, Nick. He has caused a problem with friends of mine, and now Gino is involved."

Nicholas missed his shot. "What did he do now?" He picked up the chalk and began brushing it over the tip on his stick.

Franco took aim and shot, sinking a ball. "He beat up the Silk brothers. One of them took several stitches to the face. Nick hit him with a beer mug." He missed his second shot.

Nicholas stopped to listen. "What was the beef over?"

"Apparently, he took off with Johnny Silk's best stripper, so Johnny and Robby went to have a talk with him and he went berserk and attacked them." Franco chalked his stick. "Gino is pretty upset over this. He's pretty tight with the Silks."

"They aren't made guys." Nicholas reminded him.

"No, but Robby has been nominated and it's going to happen soon, maybe next month, I hear. Nicky, this is a problem. What should we do?"

Nicholas walked over to the bar and poured another brandy. He took a long sip and placed it down. "He is dead to me. Franco, he killed Christopher." Franco didn't respond. "And now he's causing trouble, beating up people who are connected. I never liked him. Even when he was a kid, he always rubbed me wrong. He was always starting trouble and that mouth of his - is the worst." He tapped the bottom of his chin twice with the back of his hand. "I loved him because he was my son, but now, even that has changed. He is nothing to me now. He took away my pride and joy. For what, money? I'd just as soon get rid of him all together."

Franco wasn't sure what he had just heard. "Nicky, this is your son you're talking about."

"My son!" Nicholas raised his voice. "My good son is dead because of him. He is no son of mine. Am I going to spend the rest of my life dealing with his bullshit? Do I have to spend the rest of my life knowing he's out there having a good time laughing it up, taking dope and banging strippers, while my son is lying in a box six-feet under? I've made up my mind on this, Franco." Nicholas picked up his jacket and put it on. "With or without your help, he's gotta go." Franco watched him walk out without saying a word.

The next day, Franco called Nicholas and told him he would take care of it whenever he was ready. Nicholas said he was going to take his wife on a trip, and that would be the best time to take care of it. Franco hung up the phone not feeling good about the whole ordeal. He had known Nick since the day he was born. He never liked Nick, but there was something he didn't like about this. He figured, maybe it was because Nick wasn't in the business. He never clipped a civilian before and certainly not his best friend's son - his Godson.

36

As Sam's eyes opened, he was disoriented, not understanding where he was, and how he got there. His vision began to clear and reality set in. He had an awfully bad taste in his mouth and many of his joints were aching. He rubbed the sleep out of his eyes and rolled left to a sitting position. He sat looking around the room. It was so empty, he thought. The walls were bare and the room was furnished with a bed and small nightstand. This was where his life was now, a small room that was nothing more than a cell with a bunk. He was a man trapped inside an empty room of loneliness and despair. The pain in his heart soon took over, and once again, he forgot about his arthritic joints. He needed a hot shower, so he walked across the guest room to a hallway leading to the bathroom. Moving like a zombie in a bad movie, he passed the pictures hung on the hallway walls. They were bright and colorful pictures of flowers and fruit baskets. He began to awake from the dead as he climbed into the shower.

Donny was reading the morning paper and sipping a diet coke when Sam walked into the kitchen. "Good morning," Donny's voice was cheerful.

"Hey." Sam went for the coffee. He made enough for one person. He wasn't used to that and he didn't like it. At home he always put enough coffee on for two people. It was a reminder that he wasn't alone. Donny drank soda in the morning and Sam could never figure that out.

Donny had been searching the employment section and quickly flipped several pages to the real estate section when he heard Sam coming into the kitchen.

"Did you sleep well?"

"Yes, thanks," Sam said unconvincingly.

"Sam, how are you doing? Are you going to be alright?" Donny rested his paper on the table.

"Life can be so unforgiving, and it can turn on a dime." He stood by the sink looking out the window. "You know what I mean?" Donny nodded his head in agreement. "The strange thing is that it can happen to anyone at any time. Just when you think life isn't all that bad, and sometimes even good … then, Bang! It slaps you across the face and knocks you to the ground. Then it kicks you while you're down and doesn't stop until your wind is gone."

Donny sat thinking about his dead brother. "I know what you mean," he said while nodding his head.

Sam continued as he glared out the window. "It's not just me. It's the woman who suddenly loses her child, or the guy who gets laid off and can't find work." He turned and looked into his partner's eyes. "It's the people with lost hope."

Donny could feel his pain and knew he was hurting badly. "If there's anything I can do partner, you know I'm here."

Sam walked over and patted Donny on the shoulder. "You already have."

The two men sat quietly reading the paper and sipping their drinks. Sam turned his cell phone on and received a beep indicating he had a new message. He hit the button and listened. After hanging up, he looked at his partner.

"That was Scope. He sounded very excited and asked that we call him immediately." Sam dialed, and a few seconds later, he was connected.

"Sam?"

"Yes, Scope. What is it?"

"I have something here you and Donny will want to see right away. I've been up since four this morning."

"What have you got?"

"It's better if I show you. Can you come down here?"

"Yes, tell me what it's in regards to?"

"I found some evidence in the Gennaro case that may point you in a different direction. Sam, this may show that Nick Gennaro didn't kill his brother."

The detectives made it to the forensics building in record time. Scope was waiting for them in the lab when they arrived and he had a glow about him that added life to his usually dim existence.

"Over here." Scope directed them toward a microscope in the corner of the lab, like a kid in biology class that just discovered a hidden organ in a frog.

"This better be good. I skipped breakfast to rush over here." Donny said.

Scope stopped at the microscope and he turned to Sam. "Take a look." He gestured toward the state of the art equipment.

Sam bent over looking into the eyepiece and saw two long narrow specimens situated vertically next to each other. "What am I looking at Scope?"

"You're looking at two hair fibers. What do you see?"

Sam didn't say anything for a moment, and then he lifted his head up and looked at Scope. "They're identical."

"Yes, they are. One of them came from the head of our victim, Sharon Satowski, and the other came from the boat owned by Christopher Gennaro."

Both detectives were still, as they absorbed the information.

"What made you think to do this?" Donny asked.

"How many bludgeoning deaths do we have in South Walton, Rhode Island in any given year?"

"None," Sam responded.

"That's right. Both victims were beaten over the head and killed only a few miles apart in a three-month period. I decided to take evidence found at Gennaro's boat and compare it to the evidence taken from the Satowski crime scene. "

"What you're telling us is that Sharon Satowski was in Christopher Gennaro's boat?" Donny asked.

Scope displayed a crooked victory smile, "Exactly,"

"And with her history, it's safe to assume they weren't playing scrabble." Sam added.

"That's right. The boyfriend, who is a real bad ass, learns that Gennaro is screwing his girlfriend, so he goes to his boat and clobbers him over the head, and then dumps his body in the water. A few months later, he finds out about another guy, or maybe they argue about her screwing Gennaro, and he smashes a TV over her head. Whatever the reason is, one thing is for certain…"

"She was on his boat." Sam finished Scope's sentence.

"Scope, you're a genius." Donny said.

"Good work Scope. We have to find out more about this boat visit. We'll see you later." Sam gave him a short punch in the shoulder.

Scope took the punch as a symbol of merit, like a gold star on his forehead. "Keep me apprised," Scope requested.

"You got it." Sam raised his arm as they walked out of the lab. Scope went back to his evidence feeling unusually energetic.

***

The marina was relatively busy. It was late morning on Saturday and people were out working on their boats. A few boats were setting sail for a fishing trip, or a leisure cruise on the open sea. Some had decided to begin wrapping their boats to store them away for the season, and were busy moving them into winter storage.

Sam and Donny were sitting on Christopher's boat looking around the marina and taking in the fresh salt air. Nicholas had decided to leave the boat slipped through the summer. It was paid for and he wasn't ready to deal with the pain associated with putting it down for the winter.

"What's the plan? Shall we start here and split up, you go left and I go right? Donny asked.

"That sounds good. Show anyone and everyone the picture and see if anybody recognizes her," Sam suggested.

Both men started out in their designated direction. Some people were not cooperative, but most were happy to speak with them. Nearly two hours had passed when Sam received a call on his cell from Donny asking that he hurry back to Christopher's boat. When he got there, Donny was speaking to a man and woman who apparently owned the boat slip next to Christopher's'.

The couple, Steve and Linda Minor, were in their mid-thirties, and by the look of their forty-two-foot boat they were not hurting for money.

"Mr. and Mrs. Minor, this is my partner, Sergeant Carra."

Sam shook hands with both of them. "How are you today?" Sam was hoping they had something good to say. He had enough of the marina.

"Mr. Minor was just telling me that they heard about the murder of Chris Gennaro a few months ago and were a bit hesitant about sleeping on the boat while docked."

"I think you'll be alright. We have no reason to believe this was a random crime," Sam assured them. "How well did you know Chris Gennaro?"

"We slipped our boats next to each other for two years. Once in a while we would get together for drinks, he was such a nice guy. We don't come down here as much as we would like because we live in Salem Massachusetts, so it's a bit of a ride. Linda is a real estate agent and has to work on weekends much of the time."

"When was the last time you saw Chris?" Donny asked.

"It was early in the season, back in April. We came down to put the boat in the water."

Donny produced a photograph. "Have you ever seen this woman?"

Steve took one look and then Linda did the same. They both looked at each other and Linda responded. "Yes, that's Sharon."

"How do you know her?" Sam asked.

"We had coffee with her and Chris the weekend we came down to open the boat up." Linda said with a confused look about her.

"Why are you looking for her?" Steve asked.

The detectives disregarded the question.

"How is it that you had coffee with them?" Sam asked.

"It was a Sunday morning. They stayed on the boat the night before, as we did. Chris was going out for coffee, so I asked him if he would pick us up two cups. We sat and had coffee and bagels and talked for a while," Steve said.

"Did they seem like they were a couple, or just friends?" Donny asked.

Linda spoke right up. "They were definitely more than friends." She glanced at her husband, who was nodding his head in agreement."

"Let's just say their boat wasn't very still for most of the weekend." Steve offered, with a smirk.

"Did they happen to say how long they had been dating?"

"I think I remember Sharon saying they had recently just met." Linda said.

"Do you remember the exact date that was?" Sam asked.

"Let me get my calendar in my bag." She climbed into the boat and came back with a pocket calendar and opened it up. "That was the weekend of April Twenty-sixth."

Donny was writing down the information as they spoke. "Is there anything else you can tell us about Chris or Sharon?" Donny looked up from his pad awaiting an answer.

"No, they were having a party weekend, that's all." Steve said.

"One more thing," Sam said. Did you notice anything or anyone that seemed out of the ordinary? Anyone suspicious?"

"No, not at all." Steve said and Linda gestured in agreement.

"Detective Burke will take your information. If we have any more questions, we will be in contact. We really appreciate your help."

While Steve was providing Donny with information, Linda asked Sam. "Is Sharon alright?"

"No, she was also found murdered."

"Oh, no!" Linda was clearly disturbed by the news.

Steve overheard Sam and his attention was drawn to him.

"Are the two murders related? Is it the same guy?"

Sam looked at the couple with their shiny white boat docked behind them. "It appears so." Sam was happy to say, without indicating so.

They shook hands and started down the dock. Donny turned and looked back. The couple had not moved. They stood still watching the two detectives as they walked toward land.

37

Sam decided to drive back to the office. He felt a certain sense of relief learning that Nick Gennaro may not have killed his younger brother. His feelings on that were directly related to the burden that would be lifted off the parents of the slain young man. Donny was skimming through his notebook and adding notes as needed.

"What are the chances?" Donny said, tapping his pen on the small note pad. "I guess Chris Gennaro had sex with the wrong woman at the wrong time."

"Yeah, of all the women in Rhode Island, he had to pick the girlfriend of a maniac, sociopath. What bothers me is why he waited to kill her. He goes to the boat where they slept together, cracks Gennaro over the head, dumps his body overboard, and then he waits nearly three months to smash a television over Satowski's head. In his jealous rage, one would conclude, he would have killed her that night. That is the only thing about this case that I don't understand."

"Who knows what the hell goes on in the mind of a guy like Luther Banks," Donny said.

Sam turned left onto Suffolk Street, glanced at Donny in thought. "I'll be very relieved when Banks is in custody. Hopefully he won't leave any more bodies behind," he said, pulling up to a red light and stopping.

Donny folded his pad and put it in the inside pocket of his jacket. "Let's hope he confesses to both murders."

Sam didn't say anything, but thought it might not go so smoothly.

When Sam finished a good chunk of his paperwork, he decided to head over to Nicholas Gennaro's place. Donny asked him if he should come along, but Sam declined, stating he preferred to go alone. Donny was relieved by his answer and didn't lend dialog to that end.

Once again, Sam stood on the front porch waiting for the door to open. The neighborhood was deathly quiet except for a few singing birds and a wailing siren in the distance. The door opened and Maria Gennaro stood in the doorway with a puzzled look on her face.

"Detective, is everything alright?" She was anticipating bad news about her surviving son.

"Yes, may I come in, Mrs. Gennaro?"

"Of course," she opened the door and he entered. "May I get you something to drink?"

"No thank you. Is your husband home?"

"Yes, he's upstairs. I'll get him."

A few minutes later, Nicholas entered the living room where Sam was situated. Sam could tell by the look on his face, he wasn't exactly welcome.

"Please sit down. Maria gestured toward a lone antique chair with Lion's legs and brass studs.

The couple sat on the sofa directly across from Sam.

"Why have you come here?" Nicholas cut right to the point.

"I have some news about your son, Christopher, that I thought you would want to hear."

"Go on." He had Nicholas and Maria's full attention.

"We have reason to believe your son may have been killed by the jealous boyfriend of a girl he had been going out with."

Nicholas started to feel a bit lighter. "What are you talking about, what girl?" he asked.

"A few weeks ago, we found the body of a woman in a trailer park, she had been bludgeoned to death."

"I read about that in the paper. That happened in Walton," Nicholas said.

"That's right. Apparently, she was quite promiscuous and her boyfriend found out and paid her one last visit. Our forensic scientist found hair on your son's boat that belonged to the victim. It's a perfect match."

Maria cleared her throat. "Are you saying that my Christopher was dating the girl who was killed?"

"Yes, he was. We spoke with witnesses at the marina who saw them together. They actually had breakfast with your son and the victim. We think the killer may have found out about the two of them and went back to the boat to take his revenge."

"Wait a minute!" Nicholas stood up obviously alarmed. "That girl was just killed, not very long ago. Why would he wait so long after he killed my son to go after her?"

"That's the only question that isn't clear. He may have found out later on that she was seeing someone else and he finally snapped. We aren't sure."

Nicholas sat back down. "Who is he?" He crossed one leg over the other.

"His name is confidential at this time. I will say this; he is a real nasty guy - a Hells Angel."

"A Hells Angel!" Maria repeated. "The motorcycle gang?"

"Yes, he is also wanted for the Murder of a police officer in Alabama."

"Where is he now?" Nicholas asked.

"We don't know, exactly. He is a fugitive on the run. The last place we know of, is Alabama, where he killed the officer. That was a couple weeks ago."

Nicholas stood up and walked across the room. He picked up a framed picture of Christopher that was resting on the mantle place and briefly examined it. "So, what are you doing to catch him?" Nicholas asked.

"All local and state law enforcement officials are looking for him and the FBI is also on the case."

"Great, the FBI is on it too." Sam could sense his dissention for the bureau. He placed the picture back down where he found it.

"We will catch him, and when we do, hopefully he will confess to Christopher's murder."

"You have no other suspects right now?" Nicholas asked.

Sam stood up. "Right now, he's our main suspect, but we are always looking for more leads."

Nicholas stood up, and with sincere demeanor, he looked Sam right in the eye and shook his hand. "Thank you for coming here to tell us the news."

Maria put her arms around Sam and hugged him. Her eyes were welling up with water. "Thank You," she said before leading him to the door. Once outside, Sam stopped and stood looking at the house, wondering what they may be feeling *now*.

Inside, Nicholas embraced his wife, consoling her as she cried. An unimaginable burden had been lifted, and for the first time in months, they experienced some peace.

38

The farmhouse was situated on eleven acres, deep in the woods of a town with a population of four hundred and thirty three people. Hoptree, Alabama was a quiet farming community with a main access off highway 27, which made it a perfect hideout for the Alabama Chapter of the Hells Angels.

Luther sat on the front porch drinking a Budweiser and smoking a long, thin cigar. He wore a black cowboy hat with a single bullet hole through the front. It was a Mexican hat with a long, wide brim given to him by another member of the club, as a welcoming gesture, the day he arrived. He didn't like hats much, but the September sun was hot in Alabama.

The rocking chair he sat on could barely carry his weight and it made a slight crying noise as he slowly rocked back and forth. Many of the spindles that once held the porch railing firm, had been kicked out or pulled off and used as playful war clubs by the drunken bikers.

Less than half of the length of a football field away, sat a large red barn that was now a faded brown. Allman Brothers Band music was blasting through the seams of old pine that had endured too many parties. The roof was tattered with bullet holes, which made it less than comfortable when the rain came.

Stone came walking over with two beers and handed one to Luther. He stood five inches shorter and weighed sixty pounds less than Luther, but he was still a large man in the eyes of most people. He wore a Hells Angels leather vest that exposed his arms from his cannonball shoulders on down to his large hands. His arms were a chiseled cut of muscle and tattoo. Almost every morning, whether he was hung over or not, he would pump weights. His mustache was thick and curled up at the tips held together by wax, like a regulator in the old west. His long hair was tied into a ponytail that nearly touched the center of his back. His left eyeball was permanently scarred with a light red blemish from a fight he got into at a bar in Florida. His adversary jammed his index finger into Stone's eye nearly blinding him. It was the only fight Stone had ever lost. Once his vision was restored, he went back to the bar and waited outside for five hours for the guy to come out. When he finally did, Stone buried his seven-inch hunting knife into the guy's stomach, and with a twist and turn of the blade, he was gone, leaving the man dead in the parking lot.

Stone kicked his boot up and rested it on the second stair. "Do you like it here?

"Fuckin A." Luther took a swig of his bud.

"It's safe here. We keep a close eye on the drive coming in and the woods are thick with brush. I have it patrolled twenty-four-seven. It's amazing how a few lines of coke can motivate men," he laughed. "Why don't you come to the barn and do some partying. We'll be starting the barbecue in a short while."

"I'll come over in a bit. I'm just doing some thinking here."

"Alright then, see you in a while." Stone walked away wondering how long he would have to harbor Turk.

Since he arrived on the farm, Luther had befriended one of the members responsible for the gang's gun running operation. Extortion, drugs and prostitution was all good in Luther's eyes, but running guns was something he was naturally drawn to.

Marvin Erickson was a two-time loser, who had been arrested for possession of heroin with intent to distribute and various firearms violations eight months earlier. With a nest egg of cash and a slippery lawyer he was able to remain free while pending trial. He liked the fact that Luther was on the run for killing a cop. He hated cops. They were the nucleus for all his past troubles in life. Like most criminals, Marvin didn't take responsibility for his actions. His troubled past and time spent behind bars was directly related to the corrupt system and bureaucratic leaches of the world.

Luther was infatuated with the arsenal of weapons he kept locked up in the trunk of his Crown Victoria. The other Angels would occasionally harass him for driving the same type of car as the police. In his mind, it helped him to fit in with the law enforcement community, therefore, allowing him to squeeze out of situations on the road that might otherwise not be in his favor.

The two bikers drank whiskey, while Marvin displayed his guns one piece at a time, telling a story with each one. Luther sat watching and listening like a child at bedtime. The trunk was filled with everything from an AK47 assault rifle to a Walther PPKS .380 handgun. Luther didn't like or trust many people, but it was different with Marvin, for some reason they bonded.

***

Four special agents, along with three gang task force officers, sat in an over air conditioned room in the Biloxi field office. Michael Pepper was the field office agent in charge; he was chairing the meeting. Unlike most FBI agents, Pepper wasn't a lawyer, his background was in accounting, and he looked it. He was known in the bureau as a meticulous paper hound. Under his directive, everything had to be documented to the letter. It had been stated more than once, that he missed his real calling in life, by not becoming a line editor for a literary agency. The most dangerous assignment Pepper had undertaken was moving manila files into a new storage room, when he was assigned to the New York field office. The paper cuts were devastating.

Pepper, like many law enforcement officials who shined a seat with their asses their whole career, often seem to be the one with a chip on their shoulder.

He took off his glasses and pulled a handkerchief out from his back pocket and began to clean the lenses. He placed them back on his face and then opened a file that was stacked in a neat pile in front of him.

"Good morning gentlemen. Everyone knows why we are here. We have a renegade Hells Angel named Luther Banks, AKA Turk, AKA the Impaler. He is a very dangerous and mentally unstable individual. He has a history of violence that dates back to his adolescence. Gentlemen, Mr. Banks is wanted for the cold- blooded murder of an Alabama Deputy Sheriff and a woman in the State of Rhode Island." Pepper passed a five-by-seven photograph of Banks to the agent sitting next to him, and they began passing it around the conference table. "He's on the run and we have every reason to believe he may be here in Alabama. We have three gang task force officers here with us today." He gestured towards the three men across the table. "State police troopers Fence and Biggleman, and our own agent Kensington."

"We have reason to believe that he may be hiding out at a ranch in Hoptree where the main headquarters for the Alabama chapter is located. Now, we could go in there and browse around, but chances are we wouldn't find him. If we're able to find a judge to issue us a warrant, we could turn the ranch upside down and maybe get lucky, but that could get very ugly. This guy has no reason to come in peacefully. He knows he is facing a death sentence for a cop killing. That coupled with the chance that there may be upwards of thirty or forty additional gang members on the premises, we can't take the chance of taking casualties. It could very well turn into a war and we should avoid that at all costs. Banks is very high up in the order and many gang members will fight for him."

The other men sitting at the table glanced around at each other and they were all thinking the same thing. Pepper was full of shit. They would all prefer to just go in and take Banks out. They knew Pepper didn't want any bad press, and the paperwork would bury him.

"Trooper Fence was involved in an arrest earlier this year of a Hells Angels gang member. His name is Marvin Erickson." Once again Pepper passed a photograph around the table. "Erickson is a three time loser facing a life sentence. I spoke with the district attorney who is handling his case and he said it's a pretty cut and dry case. He was busted with guns and heroin and he knows he's in big trouble. The district attorney has agreed to make a deal with Erickson if he gives us Banks. He was reluctant to cooperate at first until the U.S. Attorney gave him a call on my behalf." Pepper couldn't help patting himself on the back. "We just learned before this meeting that Erickson's attorney contacted the U.S. Attorney's office and his client has agreed to play ball. He is going to wear a wire and try to get Banks to talk about the cop killing. He has also agreed to lure Banks off the compound so we can make the arrest without incident."

Fence's jaw began to tighten up. "And what are you offering Erickson for cooperating."

Pepper could tell by the look on Fence's face he wasn't going to like the answer. "If he follows through with setting Banks up and testifies in open court, he will be placed in the witness protection program."

"That's just fucking dandy." Fence said through a different shade of color. "I put a lot of time into this case. This guy is a major gun runner and you're going to put him right back on the street just because he rats out one of his biker buddies."

Pepper stood up. "Wait a minute, were talking about bagging a cop killer here. This is the way it's going to be, and it's been cleared by the U.S. Attorney's office." he rolled his shoulders back.

"I say we assemble twenty cops and go in and get him, and then bring Erickson to trial."

"Well, Trooper Fence, it's not your call, is it?"

He replied with a look of disgust. "I guess it isn't."

Pepper sat back down. "We are going to post five agents outside of the compound while he is wearing the wire in case something goes wrong. That was the deal we made for his protection. We have to make sure we aren't spotted." Pepper stood back up, collecting his photos and files. "We will meet again tomorrow morning at 10:00 am sharp to go through the game plan." He started toward the door and the other men stood to follow him. "Gentlemen, one more thing, everything we discussed here today does not leave this room. Don't even tell your wife about this. Am I making myself clear?" A faint yes and a couple nods of the head and they emptied the room.

***

Marvin Erickson's Ford pulled into the compound and came to a stop just short of the barn. He reached over and took out a half gallon of Jack Daniels that was tucked inside a paper bag. He removed the cap, and took a four gulp swig, and then sat back before taking one more. He could feel the alcohol calming his nerves, so he pounded down another and put the top back on. Inside the house, he found Luther alone watching television in the den. It was Wednesday evening and the farm was quiet, it would pick up again on Thursday.

"Hey Turk, what's going on?"

"Hey." Luther was watching an episode of Law and Order.

Marvin handed him the bottle of bourbon. "I have a new line of weapons. Want to check them out?"

Luther turned the bottle upside down for six-seconds bringing the liquid level down several inches. "Yeah." he got up farting a loud burst throughout the room.

After grabbing a six-pack from the refrigerator, they went out to Marvin's car and the story telling began.

"This is the Dirty Harry gun." Marvin took out a .44 Magnum Smith & Wesson. "Make my day," he said with a short, fake laugh.

"Luther took the gun from Marvin dropping the cylinder. He spun it and listened as it turned round and round. It was music to his ears, like a superbly played electric guitar, and then with a short whip of the wrist he snapped it back into place. "Dirty Harry was a pussy," Luther said with a half-smile.

Next to Luther, Marvin believed that to be true. "Yeah, he was," he quickly agreed.

They continued to guzzle the Jack and beer as Marvin took each piece out, holding a rag in one hand and the gun in the other. He could feel the wire taped to his chest. It occasionally tugged on his chest hair as he turned to the left and it was a reminder that he was putting his life on the line.

"I picked these guns up, today." He handed Luther a Glock nine-millimeter handgun. "I have a buyer I'm meeting tomorrow and I was wondering if you would come along?"

Luther didn't answer.

"It's cool; I have done business with these guys before. They are a couple of skin heads from Georgia."

"What's in it for me?" Luther handed the Glock back.

He took the piece, polishing it with his white rag. "I'll give you five-hundred."

Luther remained quiet. "And you can have any handgun in the bunch."

Luther reached into the trunk and took out a stainless steel colt .45 automatic handgun. "Okay, I'll take this one."

Both men were now getting pretty drunk and Marvin thought, if he had to do it, what better time than now? He knew the agents were monitoring the wire from the woods lining the compound and they could move in very fast, if necessary.

"So the word is you took out some bitch in Rhode Island. What did she do to piss you off?"

Luther stopped and looked at his new comrade with a stare that would scare Satan himself. "Why do you ask?" He took a slug from the bottle.

"No reason, I killed a girl once. Back in Tennessee, I carved her up with a fishing knife," he lied.

"Yeah, well I smashed a fucking TV over her head." He started laughing and Marvin reluctantly followed suit as the tape was rolling.

"Rumor has it you killed some guy on a boat up there too. They say she was having an affair with him behind your back. As far as I'm concerned, he deserved it."

"I didn't kill no fucking guy on a boat. Those bastards are trying to pin that on me? Fuck them."

Marvin was starting to feel warm and sweat was beading up on his forehead. He knew, if he gave any indication he was an informant, Luther would rip off his shirt exposing the wire and then he would rip out his heart. "And what about the cop? Man, I hate cops. What did you smash over his head, his car? Both men once again broke out in laughter.

"No, I just shot the pig through the eye."

"That's all?" Marvin started laughing again and Luther followed along.

They continued drinking for a couple hours until Luther passed out on the couch. Marvin drove home counting his blessings along the way. Morning would come fast and he had to be prepared for the set up.

The next day came fast for Marvin with only a couple hours of sleep and a hangover that left him with a pounding headache.

Luther watched through the window as his car pulled up and parked in front of the house. In Luther's left hand was a cold beer and in the other his new loaded Colt 45. He made sure Marvin gave him the piece before he retired for the night. Luther slept like a baby with his new gun in arms reach. He woke up and immediately pounded down two beers and a snickers bar. He had a bad feeling about the venture that they were about to undertake. He didn't like skinheads, and he didn't like the idea of leaving the compound so soon after wasting a cop, but he trusted Marvin, and wanted the gun and cash.

The trunk of Marvin's car was loaded with several guns as a decoration. He had taken four aspirins and his headache was subsiding. Luther got into the car and they were off. On the way to the meeting, Luther noticed that Marvin was a little shaky with trembling fingers and an awkward demeanor.

"Hey man, everything cool with you?" Luther asked while playing with his Colt.

"Yeah, I'm just really hung over from last night."

"I feel great." Luther boasted. "If one of those Kojak looking bastards tries anything funny, I'm going to get to try out my new friend here." His finger was on the trigger as he aimed the gun at the dashboard.

"These guys are cool, you won't need that. We have an agreement that we all stand by, no loaded guns brought to the meet." Marvin remembered the agent who suggested that he say exactly that to Luther.

"No guns at the meet? Fuck that. I don't like that idea at all," Luther roared.

"You'll have to trust me on this, Luther. I have met with these same guys ten times, and we have always kept our word, and everything has always gone smoothly."

"If you say it's cool, then I'll trust you." He reluctantly agreed.

The Crown Victoria pulled up near an abandoned cotton mill that was situated to their right. The building was old and beaten up and standing four stories high. To the left, Luther saw a pile of car tires that had been dumped and stacked next to a few old rusty abandoned cars. A huge array of wooden crates were scattered about and rotting to their demise.

A few minutes later, an SUV with tinted windows drove past them and turned around and parked facing them about thirty-five feet away.

"Skinheads driving a fucking Navigator? That's a first for me," Luther said in surprise.

"They have the money, why not?" Marvin's voice was shakier than before.

"You alright?" Luther was getting a bad feeling.

"Yeah, let's do this. Leave the piece."

Luther put the Colt on the seat and the two men got out of the car. As the Navigator's doors opened, Luther watched as the three men climbed out. He had known many skinheads inside the joint and out, and he knew what to expect, but these guys seemed out of the ordinary. They started to walk toward each other, breaking the gap. Marvin was standing to the left of Luther as they slowly walked side by side toward the SUV. As they got closer, Luther observed that only one of the three had his head shaved to the skin. The one on the left had a crew cut and the one on the far right had a full head of hair nearly touching his ears. They didn't look right to him. He didn't notice any tattoos, and their dress was a bit too conventional. As they approached, Luther noticed out of the corner of his eye something he didn't see when they arrived. There was something on the roof and it was moving. At that very moment, he knew there was a shooter stationed on the roof. Luther looked at Marvin and he could sense something was wrong. He recognized the look in Marvin's eyes because he had seen it a couple times in the past. It was the look of betrayal.

In a split second, Luther pulled out a knife with a six-inch razor sharp blade that he kept concealed in his rear waistband, behind his leather belt.

"You set me up!" Luther said prior to plunging the blade into the side of Marvin's neck. Before Marvin realized what had happened, his carotid artery was severed and his spinal cord was penetrated. The sharp cutting pain hit him instantly, and he knew immediately it was a death blow. As he fell to his knees holding his neck, the blood was spurting out like a punctured garden hose. He watched as a blurred vision of Luther ran toward the three men, screaming at the top of his lungs, like a Scottish warrior attacking the English. The first bullet hit Luther in the left shoulder, but that didn't stop him. Before the second bullet from the marksman on the roof struck him, he managed to bury his blade into the man with the bald head. Luther plunged his knife deep into the undercover trooper's right chest, and before he could do any more damage, he was hit in the chest with a bullet that pierced his lung. The force of the bullet knocked him to his knees. He tried to get up, but the other two cops were on him fast and kicking him until he stopped moving. As the cops rolled Luther onto his stomach and to handcuff him, he looked up and spoke through a blood-filled mouth. "I'll see you all in hell."

39

The tension surrounding the dinner table was hard to keep under wraps. It took quite a bit of convincing, but Nicholas finally caved in and agreed to have his son over for a Sunday dinner. Maria was relentless in her quest to have them all sit once again as a family. Nick accepted the invitation, declaring he was bringing his new wife along. From the very first glance, his father despised her and she could sense it. Maria, on the other hand, welcomed her with open arms. The tension began to ease as Nick handed out an envelope to each family member.

"Just a little gift from me and Tammy," Nick blurted out, feeling like Santa Claus. Tammy had fought with him earlier that morning after he told her of his intention to give each of his family members some cash. After she drilled him for half an hour, he finally gave in and agreed to cut each envelope back by ten thousand dollars.

"Twenty thousand dollars!" Marybeth nearly fell out of her chair. Ashley's reaction was a little less exciting, and she thanked him with apprehension. Maria opened her envelope and saw that she had gotten thirty grand. She smiled and gave her son a hug and kiss. Nicholas just kept eating with his envelope sitting in front of him on the table. He didn't reach for it.

"Pop, are you going to open it?" Nick asked.

"Later," he said without looking up. Nicholas thought he would take the money and use it to buy a tall monument to erect in front of Christopher's grave. He thought about buying one with an angel with its wings stretching from end to end. Maria would buy the new BMW she had always wanted, the silver three series with gray leather. Ashley was going to have a party and Marybeth didn't know what she would buy, but figured it would be something for her child.

The conversation was light and incremental. Nicholas didn't say more than five words, but Maria was happy with the progress. At least he's sitting at the same table as his son, she thought.

Tammy was watching the clock like it was a mountain of gold, and it was obvious to everyone except Nick. When desert was finished, Nick said they had to leave, because they had tickets to a concert. After hugging everyone goodbye, Nick approached his father. He stood facing the man who, unknown to him, was preparing to have him killed less than two weeks earlier. Nicholas was looking down and raised his head to look into his son's eyes. He didn't say a word, he just slightly nodded his head, and then he took a step forward and they embraced.

***

The two bullets that tore into Luther had not been enough to finish him. The first round that struck him passed right through his shoulder and exited out through his back. No vital organs had been compromised and even with a severe loss of blood, he was stable enough to go right into surgery and have the second bullet removed from his chest.

Once he was well enough, federal agents paid a visit to his hospital room and played the tape of him bragging to Marvin about how he killed Deputy Kensington and Sharon Satowski. They also brought it to his attention that he had killed a federal informant right in front of four witnesses. The trooper Luther stabbed was in stable condition and would survive, but that was an additional charge of assault and battery with a dangerous weapon with intent to murder.

With three murder charges against him, Luther called a lawyer, and within hours an attorney sat next to him in counsel. After arguing with his new attorney for an hour, Luther realized he was screwed. In the end, Luther agreed to confess to the two murders provided he would be extradited to Rhode Island to face the murder of Sharon Satkowski, instead of being tried in Alabama for a cop killing.

The feds agreed, realizing it would most likely be the case anyway, because it was the first murder committed, at least the first murder Luther had been charged with.

Luther never confessed to the murder of Chris Gennaro. He proudly testified about how he killed the other two people, but adamantly denied any involvement in the death of Gennaro. He was convicted and sentenced to life without parole. During his incarceration, he killed another inmate by jamming a pencil into his ear. Luther never showed any pity or remorse for any of his victims or their families. He had a heart made of stone due to a tormented childhood of abuse and neglect.

The legend of Luther was one that was talked about among the ranks of the Hells Angels for years to come. He had become a folk hero to outlaw bikers who had nothing more than a wish to one day earn a reputation and legacy similar to that of Luther Banks.

40

Driving by his house and seeing Benson's car in the driveway was beginning to eat away at Sam. He slowed down, as he drove passed the home he had built and was still paying for every month. This was the third time since the separation that he spotted the Judge's car in his driveway. It made him nauseous to think about what they might be doing together in his bed.

His tears had turned dry, and anger was taking over his emotional state of mind. Once clear of the house, he pushed his pedal to the floor, leaving behind the screaming sound rubber leaves on asphalt. He drove to a bar outside of town where nobody would recognize him and he drank until he became numb.

The next morning, Sam walked through the metal detector at family court and the alarm sounded off as he passed on through. Holding his badge up, he continued right past the court officer who gave him a nod of approval. He went to the clerk of courts office and asked the administrative assistant to see the case logbook for the day. He began to trace down the page with his index finger until he stopped at courtroom number three. Judge Benson was hearing a divorce case, and he thought the timing could not have been better.

Sam walked straight to courtroom number three and pushed open the door without losing stride.

"Judge Benson!" His voice was loud enough that he drew the attention of everyone in the room including Benson who sat behind the bench. "Don't you think it's hypocritical for you to sit on your bench and make decisions on a divorce case while you are fucking my wife?" The room went completely silent. "I checked and found out that you're married as well. Does your wife know you're cheating on her?" Sam's voice was getting louder and his face was turning red.

"Bailiff, remove this man immediately." Benson ordered.

The court officer moved toward Sam.

"What do you think these people would think about a judge who sleeps with another man's wife, and then helps her to get a restraining order and have him removed from his own house?"

Another court officer joined in and the two men took Sam by the arms and started moving him toward the door.

"You should be ashamed of yourself – you piece of shit." The sound of Sam's voice resonated throughout the courtroom, and soon after, the courthouse.

"One hour recess." Benson's gavel came crashing down and he got up and went into his chamber as Sam was ushered out of the courtroom. Most of the people in the room stood up and walked out, and others stayed, pondering what had just occurred.

Ben Seal, a reporter for the Providence Journal, sat taking notes. *What a story this is going to make.*

The next morning, the story was in the newspaper, covering a memorable part of the front page of the local section. There were photographs of Sam and Benson placed next to each other, as if they were boxers, facing off for the heavyweight championship of the world.

Sam sat at the kitchen table with Donny who was reading the story. "Sam, what the hell came over you to burst in his courtroom like that?"

"I was pissed off and completely lost it. Now everyone will know what a hypocrite, adulterer he is."

"Well, you're right about that part, but the heat is going to come down on you big time now."

"So be it. What are they going to do, fire me?"

"Yeah, that's a distinct possibility."

Sam looked at Donny in disbelief. "For what, speaking my mind? Telling the truth about a bad judge. I didn't commit any crimes."

"Politics goes a long way in this town. He's a judge, Sam."

"It's done," Sam said. "I don't want to discuss it anymore." He got up and went into the other room.

Twenty minutes later, Sam received a call on his cell. It was his boss Albert Burton, and he was furious. He ordered Sam to report to the DA's office immediately.

Two hours of sitting in the District Attorney's office really didn't accomplish anything, except it allowed several men time to vent and get the issue out in the open. When all was said and done, Sam walked away with a warning to stay away from Benson, and not to discuss the incident with the press or anyone else. He agreed, and went on his way content to still possess his gun and badge.

***

Judge Benson sat behind his desk at home. He was alone with a pen in hand and was writing the hardest letter he had ever written. The tears falling on the paper were causing the ink to smear, but he worked around it. After finishing, he sealed the letter in an envelope and penned his wife's name on the front. He thought about the press and how they had taken advantage of the opportunity to destroy a man's life - a judge. News had spread to every newspaper in the State and every news channel was covering the story. There was no end to it, he thought. It was a terrible nightmare, and he couldn't wake up.

A representative from the state attorney's office had come forth in the media stating they were investigating a conflict of interest and possible corruption allegations brought on by the restraining order. Being family court judges, this had put both Benson and Swenson in very peculiar predicaments within the justice system and the eyes of the public. The news of the incident had come out in a time where there was a lull in interesting local stories, so all media jumped on it like it was a free ride. When the media had a chance to nail a judge, they took full advantage of the opportunity, because it didn't come along very often. Many judges felt they had a blanket that protected them from prosecution; as if, they were above the law. This was the media's chance to show them differently.

Everywhere the judge went, people were looking at him with untrusting eyes and whispering under their breath. His photograph had been in the local paper 13 times and that didn't include newspapers in surrounding towns and the television coverage.

Benson's son had dropped out of school and came home to comfort his mother. She had moved out of the house and was living in a temporary apartment on the other side of town. Neither of them was speaking to Benson; his wife had filed for a legal separation and a divorce was imminent.

All contact with Susan was cut off and his family wouldn't take his calls. Benson's life was turned upside down. The words integrity, respect, loyalty and honesty were a bunch of letters he could no longer arrange in an order to make any sense. He felt totally helpless and all alone with his humiliation.

Benson went up to the attic and found his spot. He slipped a rope over the top of the rafter and slid the end through the small loop he had tied on the other end. He pulled it tight to the beam, not allowing for any slack. With the end of the rope he made another small loop and pushed the rope through creating a larger loop. He got a small sitting stool and placed it directly under the hanging rope. Standing on the stool, his knees were shaking as he placed the large loop over his head and pulled it tight around his neck. He made a sign of the cross with his right index finger, touching his forehead, stomach, and left and right shoulders. "God forgive me," were his last words. He took a deep breath and began to rock the stool that carried his weight. The stool finally fell onto its side and he dropped dangling on the end of the rope. His air was immediately cut off and he couldn't breathe. Benson decided to change his mind; he didn't want to die. He reached up pulling on the rope in an effort to untie himself. He couldn't get his fingers behind the rope; it was too tight. He struggled hard to get under the rope as his vision began to blur. He was suffocating and soon realized it was too late. There was no turning back now, there was no second chance. Everything went black and his arms fell to his side. The once prominent judge hung motionless in his attic.

The letter to his wife was leaning up against a picture he had on his desk of his family at a much happier time in their life. They were young and energetic with a bright future ahead of them. It was a time that would never be forgotten, but would be clouded by the memory of a cruel and devastating time in their lives – a time that would shape a generation to come and continue the curse that their father had so much wanted to change.

41

The news of Luther's confession reached Sam's office and he was waiting for the extradition paperwork to be completed so Luther could be transported back to Rhode Island. The testimony that Luther gave denying any involvement in the death of Chris Gennaro had left a very bad taste in Sam's mouth. He wanted to hear it from Luther himself.

Once Luther had finally been transported back to Rhode Island, Sam and Donny conducted an interview with him. The conclusion was that Luther was not involved in the Gennaro case. He had an air tight alibi that put him in Cape Cod that weekend. He had registered in a motel and had produced identification when he signed in. The night of Gennaro's murder, Luther was getting drunk at a bar. His story was confirmed by the bartender who almost called the police to have Luther removed. Luther Banks was a man not easily forgotten.

***

Nicholas was ringing up customers when Sam and Donny walked into his store. He looked up and acknowledged the two detectives with a nod of the head. Once he was done ringing up the last customer in line, he asked one of his employees to take the counter, while he went to his office to speak with the two men.

They were all seated, and an uncomfortable silence momentarily stopped time. Nicholas could sense that it was not going to be good news.

Sam rubbed his eyes; he appeared to be withdrawn and tired. "We have arrested Luther Banks, the Hells Angel, I told you about."

"That's good news." Nicholas sat motionless, waiting to hear more.

"There is no easy way to put this, so I'm going to just say it. Banks isn't responsible for the death of your son," Sam said.

"What? You told me he was."

"What I said to you was that it appeared as if he was responsible. He confessed to killing two people, but Christopher wasn't one of them."

"Maybe he's lying." Nicholas said, looking for reassurance.

"I'm afraid not. He has an airtight alibi that put him in Cape Cod at the time of your son's murder. I'm sorry." Sam and Donny could see the disappointment in Nicholas' face.

"If not him, than who? Who killed my boy?" He was pleading for an answer.

"We don't know," was the only answer Sam could offer.

Nicholas put his head down in disappointment and frustration. He motioned with the back of his hand for them to leave him alone. Without speaking, the two detectives left his office, closing the door behind them.

Sam and Donny sat eating a pasta and meatball dinner at a place that refused to take their money. It was nice to be appreciated by people in the community; they both agreed. They didn't want to take advantage, so they ate there once a month. Sam had forgotten to turn his cell phone on the vibration mode, and it rang out, causing people to frown at them.

"Sam Carra," he answered.

"Sam, it's me."

"I'm in the middle of something Susan, what is it?"

"Sam, I want to talk."

"Talk about what?"

"I was wrong, Sam. I'm sorry. I just want things to be the way they used to be with us." She hesitated. "I want to try again."

Sam got up and walked outside. "You want to try again?"

"Yes, Sam. I love you." Her voice was breaking up.

"You broke my heart, Susan. I was a good husband to you and you betrayed me. You put me through hell."

"I know Sam, I want to make it up to you. I will – I promise."

Sam thought about his young bride. How beautiful she was on their wedding day and how much he loved her. Then he thought about the torturous night at the motel, and the news of the dead judge. He let out a sigh and cleared his throat.

"It's too late Susan, I've moved on. The scars run too deep. You made the biggest mistake of your life and you'll have to live with it, just as I have."

"But Sam."

"Goodbye Susan." He hung up the phone and walked into the men's room where he washed his face. He felt bad and good at the same time - it was a confusing time. He combed his hair and straightened out his tie. He pushed open the door and started back toward his table, passing by an attractive blond-haired woman along the way. She smiled at him, as he walked passed. She had beautiful eyes, he thought, while smiling back at her.

42

The slip that Chris Gennaro's boat once occupied was empty and would be replaced by another in early spring. Nicholas paid to have it removed and eventually sold. The police were finished and it was no longer considered a crime scene. Nicholas thought there would have been closure by now, but his son's murder was still unsolved. The temporary relief he enjoyed when he thought the police had found Chris's killer was now gone, and the nagging pain was back and even stronger than before. All fingers were now pointing in one direction. There was only one suspect, and it was his eldest son. The Sunday dinners with Nick and Tammy had started and ended in a single day. Nicholas had once again refused to speak to his son. He went to his Chris' grave every week and sat looking up at the monument be had erected with the money Nick gave him. He could almost hear Chris' voice in the distance asking for revenge. Nicholas' pain was turning to anger with every passing day. He was drinking more than usual and his weight was decreasing from a loss of appetite. The whole family was beginning to worry about him, except Nick, he was partying and enjoying life harder than ever.

***

Dennis was in bed with two young girls that he brought home from a bar the night before. The sun was peeking through the window lighting up part of his bed. He didn't move, he just laid still looking at the girl's naked ass in the sunlight. It was so very round and soft. He began to get aroused thinking about what the two girls did with him in his bed just a few hours earlier. It's amazing what young girls will do for a little coke, he thought. The redhead was in her senior year of college and her friend with the black hair had dropped out. He figured them to be twenty-one, and didn't ask. He tried to remember their names, but the booze had made his mind fuzzy and out of focus. It started to come back to him, as he moved closer to the round ass next to him.

A ringing sound startled him and the girls began to stir. His cell phone on his dresser lit up ringing, destroying a beautiful moment. He wanted to get his gun from under the bed and shoot at it. He got up and flipped it open. "Yeah, this better be good." The two girls were now up and had moved into each other's arms and were spooning each other. Dennis didn't speak, he just stood listening and then he broke the silence. "Find him and call me once you do, so we can all meet." He hung up the phone and went back to bed.

After breakfast, Dennis had gotten another call, and he directed the two men to meet him at a batting cage in North Providence. When the two men arrived, Dennis was in a cage, cracking balls as they came at him seventy-miles an hour. Every ball that came at him, he made contact with, and many he knocked far into the outer net. The two men stood watching from outside of the fence. When the mechanical arm stopped, Dennis came out from behind the fence still holding onto the bat.

He approached the two men, stopped, and looked to his left and right. "You see I'm pretty accurate with this bat? I want straight answers or it will wind up on your fucking knees. Am I clear?"

"Yes." The shorter guy said, obviously scared to death. He wore a Yankees hat and spoke with a lisp.

"No problem, Dennis." Dan was the person who called him that morning. He was a runner for Dennis.

"Good, now tell me exactly what happened." He looked into the eyes of the kid wearing the Yankees hat; he could sense his fear and he savored it. He listened to the kid as he rambled on for five minutes.

"I was in the Post 677 getting drunk with a guy and he was talking about the Gennaro murder. He said he knew who did it."

"And how does he know that?" Dennis asked, tapping the bat against the palm of his hand.

"He said he saw the killer the night it happened." He went on to tell Dennis everything he had heard at the bar.

"Is that all?"

"Yes,"

"Are you sure?" Dennis was swinging the bat back and forth along the ground, like a pendulum – he hated the Yankees.

"Yes, that's all," he said in a quivering tone.

Dennis handed him the bat. "Let's go find your friend."

Franco, Dennis and the guy who was shooting off his mouth at the Post 677 sat in the back room of the Italian Club. Franco had gotten the entire story, and demanded he tell it twice just to be certain, before he called Nicholas and asked him to come to the club.

Nicholas entered the back room of the club not knowing exactly why his friend had summoned him there. He saw the three men sitting at the table and moved to greet Franco and Dennis with handshakes. "Who's this?" he asked gesturing toward the third guy who he thought was dressed like a bum.

"Take a seat Nicky." Franco suggested. Nicholas did as he asked. "This is Ricky Kane, and he has something to tell you. Go on Ricky; tell us once more what you saw."

"I help out at the Sunset Marina, cleaning up boats and stuff." His voice was shaky and his lower lip trembled as he spoke. "Last spring I had just finished a job at the Marina, and I was packing it in when I saw Nick Gennaro leaving the dock where his brother's boat was slipped." He looked at Nicholas and could feel the tension.

"Go on." Franco demanded.

"He was leaving the dock, looking around, and walking fast toward the parking lot. He seemed anxious – kind of nervous." Ricky hesitated. "Can I have some water?"

"No! Tell the fucking story," Nicholas yelled.

"Okay, the next day I saw the news on TV about the murder. They said he was killed the night before, the night I saw Nick."

"How do you know it was my Nick?" Nicholas asked with clenched fists.

"Because I know him, he kicked my ass once. It was him."

"I'll kick your ass, you son of a bitch!" Nicholas leaped forward grabbing Ricky by the throat and started choking him.

Franco grabbed onto Nicholas' arm and shoulder. "Nicky, take it easy!" Franco struggled to break his hands free from Ricky's throat. Ricky was gasping for air and making a wheezing sound. Dennis just sat watching with a smile, enjoying the show.

"Nicky, don't cut off the head of the messenger," Franco advised him.

"Why did you wait so long to tell us, you son of a bitch?" Nicholas pulled him to the floor and let go. Ricky was lying on his side attempting to catch his breath. "Why?"

"I was afraid," was all Ricky managed to say, and it wasn't spoken very clearly.

"Afraid of what?" Nicholas asked.

"Nick," he muttered.

Nicholas, appearing broken, was barely able to stand on his own two feet.

Franco looked at Dennis. "Get him out of here." Dennis picked Ricky up and ushered him out by the back of his collar.

Nicholas sat back down covering his face with his hands.

Franco stood behind him rubbing the back of his friend's shoulder. "Nick told the cops that he hadn't seen Chris since the night they bought the ticket," Franco said.

"I know," Nicholas said through his hands.

"Why would he lie about that?"

Nicholas lifted his head up and dropped his hands. "Because he did it," he said with a tear falling from his left eye.

"I'm sorry, Nicky."

Looking straight into Franco's eyes, he knew he meant it. "Thanks Franco." He got up and walked to the water cooler and took a long drink.

"What are you going to do?" Franco stood up and the two old friends stood five feet apart staring at each other in silence.

"I don't want to ever see him again. Will you take care of this for me?"

"Yes, I will."

"Please make it quick and painless." Nicholas walked out wondering if his agony would ever leave him.

43

A black 1991 Lincoln Continental sat idle with the engine running less than a hundred feet from the entrance to Nick's property. The car was in mint condition, and more importantly, it had a large trunk. It was perfect for the job, Dennis thought, when he first saw it pulling into the parking lot, earlier that day.

Dino, the owner of the car, sat behind the wheel. Dennis was in the front seat next to him and Mark sat in the back behind Dino.

"What time is it?" Mark asked.

Dino looked at his watch. "Three-thirty."

"I hope this guy isn't in for the night."

"Shut up, Mark." Dennis said as he flipped a page on the Daily News.

"Anyone mind if I smoke a cigar?" Dino looked at Dennis, he wasn't asking Mark.

"Just roll the window down and blow it outside." Dennis commanded.

Dino took out his cigar and placed it under his nose, breathing in to enjoy the smell. "Cuban's are the best." He took out his lighter and lit the Cohiba, and blew the heavy cloud of smoke out the window.

They had arrived in front of Nick's house after eating a big breakfast. Dennis didn't want to hear anyone complaining about being hungry, so he made sure they had their fill. About two hours after they arrived, they watched as Tammy drove off in her white BMW. Now, they were waiting for Nick to do the same. Dennis completely disregarded Mark's idea to go into the house, surprise him, and take him out. He figured there were too many things that could go wrong, and he had heard that Nick was pretty tough. He didn't rule out the possibility that Nick might have a gun or there might be another person in the house that could potentially be a witness. Dennis decided he had to be taken by surprise, on the street, where nobody would recognize them.

The plate on the Lincoln had been switched with a plate they had stolen after breakfast at the train station parking lot. They drove around until they found a black Lincoln and Dino quickly unscrewed the plate and they were in business.

"There he is." Dennis alerted them, and they all sat watching as his dark green SUV pulled out of the driveway and took a right, headed toward the main road. "Put out that cigar."

Dino threw the cigar out the window and put the car into gear. They followed at a safe distance until the SUV came to a stop alongside a package store in Tiverton. Dino pulled over along the curb and they observed Nick get out and enter the store.

"Perfect." Dennis became exhilarated when he saw Nick park alongside the store. "Pull over there next to his car. I'll get out here and wait for him to come out."

Dennis got out, checking the gun in his rear waistline. He stood waiting near the corner of the store. Dino pulled the Lincoln right up next to Nick's car and parked.

A few minutes later, Nick came walking out with a large brown bag in his arms. As he turned the corner, he was facing Dennis, and a nine millimeter, that was pushed into his ribs.

"Keep walking and be calm, or I'll splatter your fucking liver all over the wall."

Nick looked at Dennis and knew he wasn't kidding. "What do you want?"

Dennis escorted Nick to the Lincoln and pushed him in the back seat, where he met Mark, who was pointing a .357 magnum at him.

"Put the fucking bag on the floor." Mark barked.

Once he was back in the car, Dennis told Dino to drive.

"What the fuck do you guys want, money?" Nick asked.

"This isn't about money, Nick." Dennis turned around, also pointing his gun at him. "This is about your brother Chris."

"My brother, what about him?"

"You killed your own fucking brother for money. You're a scumbag."

Nick resented the accusation. "Fuck you." Mark shoved his pistol into Nick's ribs. "I didn't kill him." Nick said in a convincing tone.

"Then why did you lie about when you last saw him? You told the cops you last saw him the night you bought the lottery ticket. We found a witness who saw you at the marina the night he was killed. He said you looked very nervous and that you were in a real hurry. That was right about the time they determined your brother was killed. Now, you're running around with a pocket full of cash, having a big fucking party, and with the money from the winning ticket your brother bought.

"I lied because I knew they would think I did it. I wouldn't kill my brother, I loved him. I met him at the marina and he gave me the ticket to hold. Chris was always losing shit." Nick was talking fast and his eyes were shooting from Dennis to Mark and back.

"You're a fucking liar. Here is the deal, Nick. You are going to die today. If you admit what you did, I promise it will be quick and you won't feel a thing. If you continue to lie to me I'll make it slow and very painful. What it's going to be?" Dennis asked.

Nick's palms were sweating and he felt a lump in his throat. He tried to remain cool, but he was more scared than he had ever been. Looking at the men that abducted him, he knew they were serious.

"Who are you working for, my father?"

"Yes. You have broken that poor man's heart." Dennis said.

A worse feeling came over him and it started in the pit of his stomach. "I'm telling you I didn't do it."

Dennis rubbed the barrel of his gun against his forehead, as if he were caught up in thought or quelling an itch. "It's going to be a long night then."

Nick looked out the window. They were on the freeway heading under a short tunnel. Dennis turned his head facing the front. "Take the second exit," he ordered Dino.

Nick pinched the door lock pulling it up, and before Mark could react, he had the door open and was attempting to jump out. Mark reached over grabbing on to Nick's jacket, but Nick pulled away and pushed himself out of the vehicle. Dino slowed down as he saw what was happening, but the car was still traveling forty-five miles an hour. Dennis quickly looked back, watching as Nick began tumbling on the asphalt behind them.

Bang! Dennis watched as a car coming up from behind them hit Nick, sending him ten feet into the air.

"Holy shit! Pull over," Dennis yelled."

Dino pulled over to the side of the road and the three men looked on as a traffic jam ensued.

"Wait here." Dennis got out and walked toward the accident. As he got closer, he saw Nick lying in the street in a pool of blood. His right leg was contorted and twisted up behind his back. People were getting out of their cars to see what had happened. Dennis jogged back to the Lincoln and got in. "Let's get the hell out of here. He's dead." The Lincoln sped off, leaving Nick Gennaro behind, lying motionless in the street.

44

The life-support-system that provided Nick with oxygen, food, water, and body waste had finally been removed after being attached to him for three weeks. As he laid in his hospital bed, there was only one small bouquet of flowers with a card signed by his mother. He didn't feel much pain at all, except an annoying stiffness in his right shoulder and a sharp sting on his left side whenever he breathed in too deeply. From the waist down, he didn't feel anything at all; he was completely numb. His right arm was in a cast reaching his elbow; his lower extremity was encapsulated in a huge cast from his hips to his ankles.

Nick began to piece together what had occurred that left him in such a devastating state. He remembered being forced into the car at gunpoint, and then, what Dennis had told him about his pending doom. The last thing he recollected was opening the car door and jumping out. After that everything was a blank.

He thought about what Dennis had told him about his father being behind the abduction and attempted murder, the awful feeling in his stomach returned, and it traveled to his heart, where it stopped and took control. He began to cry like a little boy. The pain he felt now was worse than any physical pain he had ever endured. It was a nagging pain trapped deep inside of him.

The door to his room opened and a nurse came in to find him awake. She was a heavy-set woman in her mid-forties. Her hair was pinned up and she wore glasses that rested on the tip of her nose.

"Well, look who's up," she said in a cheerful tone.

Nick looked at her without talking. He discretely wiped away the tears with the back of his hand

"How do you feel?" she asked while checking his pulse.

"Like shit." *How do you think I feel?* "Where am I?"

"Providence hospital." She moved on to check his blood pressure.

"How long have I been here?"

"Three weeks." Once again, she babbled in a happy tone. Nick wanted to slap her.

"Three weeks! What's wrong with me?"

"The doctor will be here soon and he'll go over that with you. Are you in any pain?"

"No," he lied. He wanted a clear head to find out the extent of his injuries.

"Your mother brought you these beautiful flowers, yesterday. The ones she brought two weeks ago, I had to throw out."

"Has anyone else been here to see me?"

"Yes, your wife has been here, and the police."

"That's it?" He was wondering about his father.

"Oh, your friend was also here, Mr. Zollo. Are you hungry?"

"Thirsty," he answered without looking toward her.

"I'll get you some juice." She closed the door behind her as she left the room.

The doctor came in and picked up the chart on the foot of his bed. He flipped a page and then wrote something on it. "How are you? I'm Doctor Patel."

Nick looked at him and thought that he would prefer an American doctor. "What's wrong with me?"

"You had a very bad accident. You're lucky to be alive", he said in a robotic like, but convincing tone.

Nick's despair was turning to anger. "I know I had a fucking accident. What are my complications?"

The doctor stopped looking at the chart, and his facial expression changed. He pulled a chair up next to the bed. "You had a series of fractures, lacerations and abrasions. The most serious is the fracture to your spinal cord. The force of the automobile crushed your lumbar region causing paralysis. You also received a compound fracture to your leg, a dislocated right shoulder, and a torn posterior lip of the glenoid labrum.

"Can you just tell me in English?" Nick was agitated.

"You messed up your shoulder pretty bad and you broke your right arm, as well. You also fractured your right collarbone and you have three broken ribs on your left side." He hesitated before continuing. "Your left leg was broken and the skin on your right leg and buttocks were badly scrapped up. You also took around sixty stitches to your leg, arms and head. You received a concussion as well.

Nick was still, absorbing everything the Doctor had said. "Is that all?" he said in a condescending tone.

The doctor moved in closer. "Nicholas, you are paralyzed from the waist down. The trauma to your spine was tremendously devastating."

"Paralyzed! What do you mean paralyzed? I can't walk?"

"No, I'm afraid not. You are lucky to be alive." He said, again.

"Lucky, how do you figure I'm fucking lucky? Get out!"

The doctor placed his hand on Nick's forearm. "Nicholas… "

"I said get out, leave me alone." Nick turned his head away and the doctor got up leaving the room.

When Nick woke up, Tammy was sitting next to him in a chair. She had a star magazine and an ice coffee. "Hi Babe," she leaned over kissing his forehead. "How are you feeling?"

"Like shit." He tried to reach for a bottle of water that was on the bed stand. Tammy swiftly picked it up and held it for him; he took a long sip. "Push the button to sit me up." He pointed to the bed elevation button, and she did as he requested.

"Babe, what happened to you? The cops say witnesses at the scene saw you were pushed out of a moving car, and then you were struck by another car. Is that true?"

"I don't want to talk about it," he said defiantly.

"But, honey, I'm your wife and I have the right to know."

"I said I don't want to talk about it right now," he said in an agitated tone.

She tightened her fist. "Alright, has the doctor been here to see you?" She took a seat in the chair the doctor had just vacated.

"Yeah, some Indian bastard."

She had rehearsed this over and over in her head. "What did he say?"

"He said I'm never going to walk again, I'm paralyzed from the waist down." His eyes began to fill up.

"I know honey; I spoke with him last week. That's what I wanted to talk to you about. What are we going to do? We need to talk about how much money we have, and how much the medical bills are going to be."

Nick felt like he was in a straitjacket. "Can't that wait until later?"

"I called a lawyer the other day."

He turned his head to get a clearer look at her. "A lawyer, why?"

"Babe, we need to protect ourselves. Whoever pushed you out of that car has to pay the medical expenses. It could be in the hundreds of thousands, you know?"

"There won't be anyone paying the medical bills, except me."

"What are you talking about? We have to go after whoever did this to us."

"Whoever did this to us? I'm the one laying here paralyzed. How do you figure, us?"

"Because I'm your wife, and whatever happens to you, happens to me. These are my finances too."

"Your finances. The last time I checked, I won the lottery, not you. You brought nothing into this marriage except a pair of big tits."

"Fuck you, Nick. My lawyer said I'm going to get half of everything we have."

"You're already talking about taking half? You don't give a shit about me, do you? All you ever cared about was the money."

"What am I going to do, Nick. Spend the rest of my life wiping your ass and pushing you around in a wheelchair?"

Nick knew she had already left. "Get the fuck out of here. You're nothing more than a whore."

She quickly stood up pushing the chair to the side. "You'll be hearing from my lawyer."

"Get out!" The pain was setting in and it had now spread throughout his entire body, inside and out. The nurse passed Tammy as she stormed out of the room.

"Is everything alright Mister Gennaro?" She came over and pushed the button letting his bed down.

"No, everything is not alright." He stared at the flowers his mother sent. "I'm in pain, what do you have? I need something strong."

As the painkiller began to take hold, Sam and Donny entered the room. "Hello Nick," Sam said, pulling a chair up to the bed; Donny stood by the window watching.

"What do you guys want now?"

"Nick, we have witnesses that saw you pushed out of a moving car, before you were struck from a vehicle that was approaching from the rear. The car was a black Lincoln Continental and the plate attached to it came back as stolen. Do you want to tell us what happened?"

"No, I don't." Nick's words were less sharp than before.

"You may never walk again, and you don't want to get the people responsible for this?"

"I wasn't pushed, I jumped. You guys still haven't found my brother's murderer?"

Sam came back at him. "No, not yet." Donny and Sam made quick eye contact. It was a, 'who are you kidding?' glance.

"You guy's suck. You should both look for a different line of work." His words were dragging.

"Are you sure you don't want to tell us who was driving the Lincoln?" Donny asked.

"No." His last word was faint, and his eyelids became too heavy to hold up. He drifted off into a deep sleep and began dreaming.

Nick was sitting alone on his yacht as it sailed across the open ocean. There wasn't any land to be seen in any direction, and no other vessels. As far as his eyes could see, there was only the vast blue unforgiving sea. He looked down and saw water rising up to his knees. Frantically, he began looking for the leak, but couldn't find it. The water was quickly creeping up and had now covered his waistline. The boat was sinking. He swam to the radio and picked up the handset. "May Day, May Day!" He looked down and saw that the chord wasn't attached to the radio. He swam back to the deck and began yelling, "Help Me! Please help me!" The boat began to slip under. He was all alone with his fate.

Sam and Donny were sitting in the hospital cafeteria having a bite to eat. "Do you think he jumped?"

"If he did, it was to avoid certain death." Sam replied.

"I thought my family was fucked up," Donny said. "The brother kills his younger brother for money, and then the father attempts to kill the son, and in the process, turns him into a cripple."

"This is definitely a classic tragedy," Sam said.

"Yes, it is," Donny agreed.

"In the end, Nick Gennaro paid for his crime. Justice was served," Sam said.

Donny nodded in agreement and he took another bite from his sandwich.

45

The dog days of August had arrived and the temperature had remained in the mid-nineties or higher for the past nine days. Nearly everyone working in the DA's office was on edge and spent their days attempting to avoid the heat. Sam sat at his desk, working a fresh homicide that had occurred three days earlier. He was examining the coroner's report when his desk phone rang.

He snatched it up like a pro. "Sam Carra."

"Sam, it's Bob. I just got a call from the District Attorney in Hartford, Connecticut. You and Donny need to get up there right away. The DA's name is Harold Remington and he is expecting you this afternoon. Call me from your cell once you're on the road and I'll fill you in. I have a meeting right now and I have to go."

"Bob, I'm right in the middle of a case. Can it wait until later in the week?"

"Sam, trust me you'll want to go up there, today. I'll talk to you in an hour." The phone went dead.

The secretary in the Hartford District Attorney's office was an attractive woman that looked about thirty-five. Her hair was twisted into winding cocoon that looked like a hornets nest. She came over to greet Sam and Donny who had entered through the outer office.

"May I help you?" Her smile was less than ingénues.

"Yes, I'm Sergeant Carra, and this is Detective Burke from the Rhode Island State Police." Sam flashed his shield. She wasn't impressed.

"Yes, Mr. Remington is expecting you. Please follow me." She opened the security door and let them in. They trailed her to a large oak door that stood alone at the end of the hall. She stopped and turned her ear closer to the door, and after a short pause, she knocked twice.

"Come in." A male's voice resonated through the thick wood. She opened the door.

"The detectives from Rhode Island are here." She said to the man inside the room.

"Let them in." The voice on the other side sounded out. She motioned for them to enter and they complied.

The room was long and narrow with a large cherry desk positioned at the end in front of a window. Three men sat in dark- green leather chairs near the entrance to the room.

"Gentlemen come in, sit down." He stood extending his hand to Donny first and then Sam. "I'm Harold Remington. This is James Bickford, and he's represented by his attorney Scott Rane." They all shook hands and the detectives introduced themselves and took their seats.

Remington was a very tall, thin man, standing six feet, six inches. He was sharply dressed in a tailored gray suit draped over a white starched shirt. He wore black rimmed glasses for reading and he took them off as he spoke. The other two men appeared less tailored, and eager to get on with the meeting. The attorney wore a pinstriped suit and his client, a sport jacket that loosely hung off his shoulders.

"Gentlemen, I spoke with the District Attorney in Providence and asked that Detective Carra and Burke drive up here to hear what Mr. Bickford has to say. I'd like you to hold off on any questions until after you have taken his statement in its entirety." Sam nodded his head in agreement. "As we are all aware, you two have been leading the investigation into the murder of Christopher Gennaro. Mr. Bickford has information that will shed light as to who was responsible for this terrible crime.

Sam reached into his pocket and took out a pocket recorder and Donny retrieved his pad and pen. Both men fixed their eyes on James Bickford.

Bickford sat up straight in his leather chair, holding on to the ends of the armrests. "I know who killed Christopher Gennaro," Bickford said with a certain confidence.

The room went silent. *I know who did it too, his brother Nick, Sam thought.* "How do you know that?" Sam asked.

"Because, he was my cellmate in prison."

46

It was closing time and Nicholas had just locked up and was preparing to call it a day, when he heard a knock on the door. He peered out from behind the register to see who it was. He saw Sam and Donny standing with the sun behind them casting two long shadows across the storefront floor. He came around from behind the counter and turned the deadbolt, unlocking the door.

"I was just leaving." Nicholas' greeting was less than friendly.

"This is important, and it won't take long." Sam assured him.

The two men entered the store and followed Nicholas to the register where he had been pulling the daily receipts.

Sam stopped at the counter, staring into Nicholas' eyes. Both men stood looking at each other without speaking, like a Mexican standoff. Sam finally broke the silence. "We just left the District Attorney's office in Providence, where we took a full confession in the murder of your son Chris."

Nicholas' forehead became wrinkled and he had a curious frown that overtook his expression.

"Have you ever heard of a man named Spencer Thomas?"

Nicholas thought for a moment before responding. "No."

"Well, he knows you. Does the name, Walker Thomas, ring a bell?"

Nicholas' head started spinning and his legs began to weaken. He leaned forward resting his weight onto the counter. *He thought back, remembering the night he raised his meat cleaver bringing it down hard, slicing off Walker Thomas' hand. He remembered what he told Franco. "I don't want to ever see this piece of shit, again. He is to disappear."*

Sam watched as his face tensed up and he actually thought he could see Nicholas age right in front of him. "Apparently Spencer Thomas was doing ten years in prison for armed robbery. During his incarceration, he kept in close contact with his son, Walker, through weekly phone conversations and letters. He was released from prison a month before Chris was killed. In his confession, he stated that Walker had told him on a couple occasions that he was fearful of you. He said that Walker told him you threatened to kill him for hitting your daughter, whom he had been seeing. He said, that when his son vanished from the face of the earth, he knew you were responsible."

Nicholas couldn't believe what he was hearing. He wanted to scream at the top of his lungs and pull his hair out.

"Spencer Thomas confessed that after being released from prison he tracked down Chris and followed him on the night of the murder. He watched Chris and Nick talking together on the boat, and when Nick left the marina, he snuck up on Chris and beat him over the head with a hammer, and threw his body over board. How did he put it?" Sam looked at Donny.

Donny responded. "An eye for an eye."

Sam finished. "A son for a son."

Nicholas felt like he had been hit by a speeding train. He felt all life inside of him draining out, with a rush of pure agony replacing it. He was unable to speak, his knees gave out and he crumbled to the floor, sitting slumped against the wall, with a blank look on his face.

"I don't suppose you know anything about the disappearance of Walker Thomas?" Sam asked.

There was no response or emotion from Nicholas.

"Spencer Thomas' cellmate came forward and gave him up in order to make a deal with the DA. He was paroled a few months ago and was picked up last week up for violating his parole, so he turned over on Spencer, to avoid being sent back to the joint. We have a full confession and we have officially closed the investigation." Sam looked down at the broken man sitting on the floor. He knew there was nothing more he could do or say. "Take care of yourself, Nicholas."

Sam and Donny walked toward the door. Before walking out, Sam stopped and turned, taking one last look at Nicky the Butcher. He saw him through the glass case slumped on the floor, not moving. He looked lifeless, like worn out manikin. Sam spun the closed sign around so it faced the street and he closed the door behind him.

***

The apartment was a one bedroom disaster. An answering machine sat on the kitchen table and the message indicator was blinking on and off displaying twenty-four messages that had not yet been heard. Scattered all over the table were various medical bills, divorce papers from Tammy's lawyer, an astronomical tax bill from the IRS, a letter of foreclosure, and several other overdue bills that hadn't been opened.

Nick sat in his wheelchair looking out the window down onto the street. It was scorching hot outside and he watched as the neighborhood kids ran through water that was pouring out from an opened fire hydrant. He thought about his childhood and the hot summer days when he and Chris went fishing together. After fishing, they would run and jump into the lake and swim for hours, splashing and laughing together. The water was so cool and refreshing. It was the best time in his life.

He reached down and picked up his near empty bottle of Wild Turkey and took a long sip. He swallowed it down and took another, before placing it back down on the end table where his loaded .38 revolver rested. He turned slowly and continued to look out the window; he still wasn't drunk enough.

Made in the USA
Middletown, DE
07 September 2022

73333555R00135